HARLEQUIN® *Super*

THE
SULLIVAN
SISTERS

The Comeback Girl

Debra Salonen

By the author of
My Husband, My Babies
and *Without a Past*

$5.25 U.S. /$6.25 CAN.

"What if we got married?"

Donnie Grimaldo held his breath as he waited for Kristin's answer to his absurd proposal. She looked shell-shocked. Her mouth kept opening and closing as though she wanted to speak but couldn't.

"I'm sorry, Kris. You're right. It's a dumb idea."

She blinked rapidly. "You took me by surprise. I didn't know there were men like you left in this world. You'd actually sacrifice your freedom to provide a stable home for your son?" She took a deep breath. "Part of me wants to throw caution to the wind and say yes. But marriage is a big deal, Donnie. It's a legal state."

"It's only a big deal if we make it one," he told her, knowing as he spoke that his words weren't entirely true. He'd taken his first marriage very seriously, which was one of the reasons it had hurt so much when it ended. "This is a marriage of convenience, Kris. Think how good it would look to the courts if you were married to a well-established deputy sheriff. No judge would take your son away from you."

"But I came back to Gold Creek to make up for the past. Not to start a new lie."

He let out a sigh of frustration. "I understand. But for once, our history would actually work in our favor— the diehard romantics are probably expecting us to get back together. Only the two of us need to know that you'll be sleeping in my mother's quarters."

Not in my bed.

Dear Reader,

They say you can't go home again. Don't tell that to Kristin Sullivan. Her great-aunt is dying. Her sisters—Jenny and Andi—need her. But returning to Gold Creek isn't easy. It means owning up to her mistakes. It means risking what she treasures most—the love of her eleven-year-old son, Zach, when she introduces him to the father he's never met.

Kristin returns knowing she has bridges to rebuild— including the one with Donnie Grimaldo. Her first love. A cop. A father. A man set to leave Gold Creek for good— until fate intervenes and two friends decide to help each other out "for old time's sake." Which, of course, is a lie. They never stopped loving each other—but will they be brave enough to admit the truth?

Writing a trilogy is an incredibly intense process. It means committing a huge block of time to three connected stories filled with a multitude of characters who grow and evolve and are affected by outside forces beyond your ken. What works at the onset of the first book may no longer hold true by the time you reach the third. Each character adds new insights and dimensions to subjects you never planned to address. The setting—in this case, Gold Creek—becomes so real you find yourself looking for it on the map.

Ending this association is difficult. I already miss those Sullivan sisters and their men—Sam, Jonathan and Donnie. I miss the kids. The dogs. Even the busybodies at the Gold Creek Garden Club. Perhaps down the road a stretch, we'll drop back in to check up on everybody. In the meantime, please keep in touch. Write to me at P.O. Box 322, Cathey's Valley, CA 95306 or contact me through my Web site at www.debrasalonen.com. And if you get the chance, drop by the "Let's Talk Superromance" bulletin board at eHarlequin.com. So many authors, so much to chat about.

Debra

The *Comeback* Girl
Debra Salonen

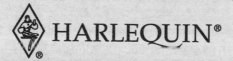

TORONTO • NEW YORK • LONDON
AMSTERDAM • PARIS • SYDNEY • HAMBURG
STOCKHOLM • ATHENS • TOKYO • MILAN • MADRID
PRAGUE • WARSAW • BUDAPEST • AUCKLAND

ISBN 0-373-71110-7

THE COMEBACK GIRL

Copyright © 2003 by Debra K. Salonen.

This edition published by arrangement with Harlequin Books S.A.

Visit us at www.eHarlequin.com

Printed in U.S.A.

To my mother, Daisy Bagby Robson, born in 1913.
Her pioneer spirit and unfailing love continue to inspire me.

CHAPTER ONE

August 21, 2002, Wednesday
Fresno, CA, Fresno/Yosemite International Airport

KRISTIN SULLIVAN HATED airports.

"Where is he?" she asked, scanning the phalanx of travelers headed toward the baggage area. No lanky preteen with white-blond hair in the crowd.

"He'll be here," her sister Andi said. "I spoke with Moira this morning. She said he boarded the plane in Chicago without a problem."

Kristin had debated the wisdom of sending her son to spend a month with her cousin in the Midwest, but Zach had begged to go. And it seemed a good idea not to have him around while she packed their belongings in Ashland, Oregon, and unpacked them in Gold Creek, California. He'd been adamantly opposed to the move.

"Let me keep him all summer," Moira had suggested. "He can go to camp in northern Minnesota with my boys. You know we love Zach to pieces, and you've got your hands full with the move and getting reacquainted with your family."

The move. After a decade-plus "on the lam"—as some people in town so snidely put it—Kristin Sullivan had returned home three weeks ago. To Gold Creek, an historic gold rush town in California's Central Sierras where she'd spent her first eighteen years.

"They probably stuck him in the last row," a second voice said.

Both of Kristin's sisters had insisted on accompanying her to the airport. Andi—Andrea Sullivan Newhall—sat on a low bench backed by greenery. Jenny Sullivan O'Neal—the oldest of the triplets—stood nearby, absently pushing a stroller containing her twins, Lara and Tucker, back and forth. The babies had fallen asleep on the hour-and-a-half ride from the mountains to this sprawling metropolis in the Central Valley.

Kristin squinted toward the security gate that led to the airplanes. A young man toting a backpack strolled toward them. He wasn't Zach.

"The plane stopped in L.A. What if he got off and didn't bother getting back on?" she asked, her nervousness escalating.

The relationship between Kris and her son had been strained for the four months prior to his departure. Ever since she'd broken the news to him about his father and her family, Zach had distanced himself from her. Normally a straight-A student—so bright he'd skipped a grade—Zach had let his schoolwork fall off to the point where he'd needed to spend six weeks in a summer tutorial in order to pass into seventh grade. This had necessitated post-poning their move from Oregon, which—her sisters agreed—was his intention.

Jenny knelt to wipe a river of drool from Tucker's chin. The twins would turn one year old next week and had several new teeth to prove it.

"There he is," Andi said, hopping to her feet. Although five months pregnant, Andi still ran several miles a day.

She pointed at the second wave of travelers moving toward them.

Kristin's heart did a double-take. "Oh my gosh. He's grown a foot." So tall, so handsome. So belligerent. Even from a distance she could tell that a month away from his mother hadn't improved her son's disposition.

He'd made his feelings clear from that day in March when she'd introduced him to her family. Since then, they'd been back a few times to participate in family get-togethers and to visit Ida Jane—Kristin's eighty-three-year-old great-aunt who had suffered a stroke. Ida Jane was the one person in the family Zach seemed to like.

By the time he reached them, Kris's heart was beating so fast she couldn't feel her extremities. She couldn't work up the spit to speak.

"Nice nose ring," Andi said, breaking the ice. "Got a bull to go with it?"

Zach acknowledged the teasing remark with a droll sneer, then he glanced briefly at the twins before looking at his mother.

"So. I'm here. Now what?"

Kristin wished she had an answer, but like so many times in her life, she'd leaped without looking ahead. She'd returned home to Gold Creek prepared to face the mistakes she'd made in the past, to try to heal some old wounds and to help care for Ida Jane, the only mother the triplets had ever known. She'd taken them in when they'd been orphaned immediately after their birth and had made them the primary focus of her life. Now Kris planned to be at Ida's side for as long as her aunt needed her. How Zach would adjust to the move remained to be seen.

DONNIE GRIMALDO reread the opening line of the official-looking letter. "'The associate administrator for civil aviation security is pleased to inform you that your application for employment with the Federal Aviation Administration's Federal Air Marshal Program has been approved.'"

It was official. He'd made the cut. He'd read somewhere that after September 11, more than one hundred thousand people had applied to the Federal Air Marshal Program. Obviously, he wasn't the only patriot looking for a way to contribute to his country.

"Donnie," a voice hollered across the open, mostly messy common room of the Gold Creek Sheriff's Department. "Where's the dang paper for the dang copier? When I find the person who moved it—"

Housed in a building that made a Quonset hut look stylish, the office supported six full-time deputies, the sheriff and three part-time dispatchers/clerks. Bethany Murdock, the person grumbling at him, was the department's student intern—a position Donnie had held a dozen or so years earlier, while in high school. Serious to the point of glum, Beth was the kind of person who would rearrange the world if someone gave her permission.

"I think we're out, Beth," Donnie said, rising. After tucking his letter under a stack of reports, he fished the key to the storage room from his pocket. "I meant to grab another ream on my way past this morning. Slipped my mind."

She advanced on him with a look that reminded him of his ex-wife. Sandy carried a grudge like most women carried a purse. Donnie tossed the key ring in the air—partly to test Beth's reflexes and partly to keep her from getting too close. She wore a fragrance he associated with Kristin Sullivan—his first love. Kris had returned to Gold Creek amid a flurry of gossip and speculation, and he'd been trying his best to avoid her. He didn't need his olfactory memories complicating the issue.

"Your mother called while you were on the phone with that state guy," Bethany said. "And your ex called, too. Jeesch. Where in my job description does it say answering service?" She caught the key ring with both hands.

At seventeen, Beth possessed a gawkiness he found mildly charming. It, too, reminded him of

Kristin, but Beth's attitude was more like that of Kristin's sister, Andi, who was married to Jonathan Newhall, publisher of the *Gold Creek Ledger*. Andi and Jenny, the third of the Sullivan triplets, were good friends of Donnie's. *Too bad Kris and I can't be—*

He didn't finish the thought. Why bother mending fences when he was leaving town?

"Did either of them leave a message?" he asked, ignoring the girl's grousing.

"Your mother said to call her if you had a minute. Sandy was more…um…" She fiddled with the keys.

Donnie gave her credit for trying to find a diplomatic way of saying his ex-wife was a witch. "Strident?" he supplied with a smile.

"If you say so." She shrugged. Her thin shoulders lifted the stiff uniform shirt that she wore with denim jeans in a sort of Don Knotts way. Beth was one of the few bright spots in his job. She was brash and testy at times, but eager to learn. She reminded Donnie of himself at that age—before the real world had intruded.

Donnie's idealism hadn't disappeared overnight. It had taken two elections—two terms under Sheriff Magnus Brown's so-called leadership—to grind it out of him.

He returned to his desk intending to give his mother a call, when a buzzer sounded, alerting him to the arrival of someone at the bulletproof glass entrance.

"I'll get the window. You get the paper," he told Bethany. "Those copies need to go out ASAP."

Donnie was still two steps away from the glass partition when he caught a glimpse of tousled blond curls and a sweetly compact body in a lime-green sundress. *Oh, Lord. Not today.*

He braced himself to greet his former high-school sweetheart. The winsome, slightly scatter-brained beauty who'd broken his heart.

Kristin Sullivan was standing with her back to the window as if preparing to flee. It wouldn't be the first time. That's what she did when things got hairy—she ran.

He pushed the microphone button so that he could be heard past the glass. "Kristin."

She jumped as if poked. When she spun around, her blue eyes were wide with surprise.

"Um…hi, Donnie," she said, stepping close to the small circular speaker. "I didn't expect *you* to come to the window. You're a captain now, right?"

In any other town he would have been a captain, but Sheriff Brown didn't share power easily. In Gold Creek's sheriff's department, the glass ceiling was made of iron. "We don't stand on ceremony around here. When everyone else is at lunch or out on calls, I still answer the phone and greet people. What can I do for you?"

She held up her hands. Small, white and lovely. He'd always loved to hold her hand.

"You need a pair of handcuffs?" he asked, try-ing to keep things light.

Her sunny grin was one that anybody in town would recognize. As a child, she'd been a favorite of the old men at the barbershop, who tolerantly emptied their pockets of change anytime she came by. Of course, they'd done the same thing for each of those Sullivan girls.

"Fingerprints," she said. "I was told I need to have them on file in order to complete my business license. Can you believe that? It's so twenty-first century."

He knew what she meant. Change might come slowly to Gold Creek, but it came. Especially lately. His old nemesis, Tyler Harrison, reportedly was buying up property all over town. And according to the grapevine, Ty had big plans in mind—perhaps even a strip mall.

Donnie wondered what Kristin thought of that development. After all, Ty was the father of her son.

"I believe Margie does those on Tuesdays and Thursdays," Donnie said, trying to picture the schedule he'd seen posted in the crime lab.

Kristin's face fell. "Oh. Okay. I'll come back next week."

If today had been Wednesday instead of Friday, he might not have opened his mouth, but he could tell she was disappointed at having to wait. "If you need it right away, I could probably help you. I used to handle all the bookings before Margie took it over."

"Really? I'd appreciate it, but I don't want to

put you out. If you're busy…'' She was sincere. One thing about Kristin Sullivan, she didn't fake her feelings. He'd only known her to lie once— about the reason she'd left town—and even that had been more a sin of omission than a flat-out lie.

''Step to the door. I'll buzz you in. You're not packing, are you?''

She blinked in confusion. ''*Packing?*''

''A gun.'' He smiled to show he was joking.

She tossed her head with a laugh. Her curls danced beneath the fluorescent lighting. ''Of course not. I thought you meant a picnic lunch, and I was immediately sorry I hadn't…not that you would…never mind.''

She rushed to the door, but Donnie took his time pushing the button. He could only see part of her face from this angle. The rosy shade of pink was a color he'd forever associate with the first time he'd kissed her. God, he'd loved her back then.

Kristin had loved him, too. But as a college freshman, Donnie had discovered a world filled with temptations. He'd done the honorable thing— broken up with her so they were both free to play the field. But he'd never expected Kristin to wind up with Tyler Harrison in the back seat of her great-aunt's Caddie.

Too bad she didn't… He let the thought go and pushed the button.

He took a deep breath then yanked open the door. Six inches shorter than his five-eleven and hardly an ounce over a hundred pounds, Kristin looked closer to Bethany's age than Donnie's. His birthday and the triplets' were exactly seven months apart, and he'd turned thirty last month.

"Welcome home, by the way," he said to break the ice. "I don't think I've seen you since you moved back—except at Jenny's wedding. And that was a little crazy."

To the family's dismay, Tyler Harrison had shown up at the Rocking M Ranch where Sam O'Neal and Jenny Sullivan O'Neal were holding their wedding reception. He'd demanded to talk to Kristin. Donnie and several of Sam's friends, including his lawyer, had managed to defuse the situation. Harrison had left without seeing Kristin.

"That freaked me out," Kris said. "I'd hoped to have more time to handle things diplomatically." She sighed. "But how diplomatic can you be when telling a man about a child you kept secret for nearly eleven years?" She threw up her hands in a manner that told him she didn't expect an answer.

"Have you and Ty talked since then?" he asked and immediately wished he hadn't. He didn't want to know about her troubles or any custody battle that might be brewing. He hadn't even met her kid yet, but word had it the boy had spent the summer with relatives back East.

She moved her shoulders slightly. "Our lawyers are talking. Apparently Ty has just got back from doing business in Japan. At least that's what his mother told Beulah Jensen who told Ida Jane who told me," she said with a rueful smile.

Donnie thought he heard nervousness in her voice. Not surprising. By all reports Tyler Harrison was now a man of wealth and power. Donnie didn't envy Kris in the least.

Good thing I'm leaving, he thought. He was a sucker for the underdog in any battle, and the last thing Kris needed was Donnie's interference in her life.

"Second door on the right," he said, nodding down the hall. It would have been all too easy to take her elbow and lead the way, but he'd learned a few things over the years and how to maintain emotional distance was one of them.

"Take a seat. As long as we're doing this, I might as well get our high-school protégée in here to learn the process." *And help defuse any tension,* he silently added.

She opened her mouth as if to ask him something but closed it and smiled. "Great."

Donnie hurried to the office area, where he found Bethany loading paper into the copy machine. "Have you done fingerprinting before?"

She finished aligning the paper and closed the plastic latch before looking at him. "Twice. Why? You got a criminal to book?"

He recognized the gleam in her eyes. Police work was ninety percent boring. The younger you were, the more you coveted the ten percent. Donnie couldn't fault her, though. Wasn't that a big part of why he was hell-bent on leaving? For the excitement?

"Nope. Sorry. Just a business license."

"We only do those on Tuesdays and Thursdays." Her tone reminded him of his ex-wife again. No one messed with Sandy's routine.

"It's either that or filing. Personally, I'd choose just about anything over the tombs—we lost a clerk back there once, you know," he teased. "The kid went in and never came out." Her reluctant smile made him wink. "And it *is* our job to serve the public."

She let out a weighty sigh. "Is she pretty?"

The question stopped him cold. "Who?"

"The fingerprint person."

"What makes you think it's a she?"

Bethany made a snuffling sound he recognized as a universal sound of teenagers. "You're a guy, and I guarantee if the person was a sixty-year-old man with loose dentures you'd be back at your desk."

Donnie chuckled. "I'll tell Mr. Groipe you said so."

Her eyes went big. Albert Groipe was the principal of Gold Creek High.

"She's pretty," Donnie said, letting her off the hook. "She's also an old friend. Promise you won't rat on me, okay? I don't want to be accused of showing favoritism to my cronies."

Her eyes narrowed with a suspicious look that reminded him of his son Lucas. *Strange. I used to be good with kids.*

KRISTIN PACED the confines of the small room as if it were a cell. She hadn't expected to see Donnie. Not that it was any big deal. They were adults, and she'd known they would run into each other from time to time. This was Gold Creek, after all. Population three thousand nine hundred and twenty. *Make that twenty-two.*

She used the few minutes that it took Donnie to find the student helper to piece together what she knew of Donnie's history since their inglorious breakup. The day after high-school graduation, she'd taken off for Ireland where she'd planned to get a job as a nanny. She hadn't seen Donnie at the ceremony, although she'd heard that he was present, accompanied by Sandy Grossman—the girl whose locker had been next to his all through high school. Kristin had always sensed Sandy's interest in Donnie, but he wasn't the flirtatious type. He was a one-woman man.

He'd certainly proven that the whole time they'd dated—from homecoming her freshman year until he'd broken up with her midway through her senior year. She'd understood his reasons for breaking up. College had presented a whole slew of temptations, and Donnie was honest about what he wanted in life—new places and new faces. Unfortunately, in her immature attempt to make him regret his decision...

Kris pushed the thought aside. Self-recrimination was a waste of time. If she wanted a guilt trip all she needed to do was talk to her son. A child who'd gone from little angel to demon spawn almost overnight.

"Kristin, this is Bethany Murdock," Donnie said, leading a small, skinny girl with wiry hair and poorly disguised acne into the room. "Her dad runs West Coast Auto Parts. Her mom's a photographer. Didn't she take the pictures at Jenny's wedding, Beth?"

The girl grunted. She looked five or six years older than Zach, but they apparently shared the same language. Kris's greeting was acknowledged with a nod.

"Get a print sheet, Beth, while I find the ink pad and some tissues."

Kris's heart rate went up a notch when he moved to her side, a wad of towelettes in hand. "I haven't done this for a while," he said, "but I think I can remember how. They say you never forget." His tone was pleasant, no innuendo implied.

She kept her arms at her sides to avoid touching him. Despite his genial manner, Kris felt an undercurrent of tension. Even though enough water had passed under their bridge to drown an elephant, their history remained painful, the issues unresolved.

She'd seen Donnie a few times over the years. At Josh's funeral. Her brother-in-law—Jenny's first husband—had succumbed to cancer just a few hours after the twins were born. And last spring Donnie had been instrumental in helping Andi's husband, Jonathan, clear his name after Jon was accused of murder. But this was her first sustained conversation with Donnie since she'd come home to live.

"So, tell me about yourself, Donnie. What's new?" she asked, anxious to keep some kind of conversation going. "I heard you and Sandy got married about a year or so after I left, right?"

His grunt sounded like a confirmation.

"Sorry to hear about the divorce. Ida told me Sandy married a movie star or something."

His friendly smile went flat. Bethany shot her a scathing look.

"He builds sets for a production company."

"Oh," Kris said, her nervousness growing. "You have a son, don't you? A couple of years younger than Zach."

"Lucas is nine. He turns ten next month."

"Then they're just a year apart. Zach will be eleven in November." Something in his eyes said he already knew that. Her face started to heat up.

"Do you and Sandy share joint custody?" She couldn't repress her curiosity. She'd be dealing with Zach's father all too soon.

"Theoretically," he said shortly.

Bethany made a growling sound and slipped between Donnie and Kris. Her bony shoulder made contact with the fleshy part of Kris's arm. "I can do this," Bethany said. "I've helped Margie before."

"Okay," Donnie said, apparently not noticing the girl's protective attitude. He gave Kris a friendly smile. She could use a friend. Too bad she didn't trust herself with men. She'd made a few mistakes over the years. From the marketing genius who'd lacked a conscience, to the ski instructor who'd lacked self-control. She was sick of riding the pendulum between loser and bruiser.

"So where are all the guys from your band?" she asked as Beth took her right hand and firmly made black impressions in the spaces allotted for each digit.

As a civilian deputy with the Search and Rescue program, Donnie had been in charge of his own little band of merry men, who'd moonlighted as Conundrum—a garage band that played all the local venues. "Rory, Jimbo and Bernie, right?" she asked, conjuring up an image for each name.

His low chuckle made the hair on the back of her hand rise. Bethany pressed down extra hard on Kris's remaining two fingers. *I'm not after your boss,* Kris almost said. The last thing in the world she needed right now was a relationship. She had to stay focused on her fledgling business, her son and her family.

"Jimbo's making long hauls to the East Coast. The rest are scattered. Not a lot of jobs in this area. You're pretty brave to set up your massage therapy office in Gold Creek."

"So I've been told. I'm hoping people will be open-minded enough to give me a try, but if not, I'll see what I can arrange with a couple of chiropractors in the bigger cities. I can commute, if necessary.''

''Is it true you're using the basement of the old bordello?''

''Yep. They laid the carpet on Monday. I love it. It's cozy and quiet. And it keeps my overhead down because I help out upstairs to offset my rent.''

The old bordello—once a house of ill repute, hence the name—now served as both a business and a home. Jonathan and Andi occupied the second floor, while Ida Jane lived in the family quarters on the main floor. The Old Bordello Antique Shop and Coffee Parlor—which Andi was now running—took up the front half of the building.

The historic structure was something of a white elephant and cost a fortune to heat each winter, but neither Kris nor her sisters could conceive of selling the place as long as Ida Jane was alive.

Bethany finished with Kristin's right hand and reached for the left. A crackling radio exchange erupted in the distance. ''That's Cory calling in,'' the girl blurted out as she dashed past Donnie.

''Cory?''

''Cory Brandell. Our latest hire. Quite the heartthrob,'' he said with just a touch of exasperation. Kristin could remember when Donnie had been the source of ladies' heads turning. Although there was no reason he couldn't still be, she thought. His dark-brown crew cut and hazel eyes reminded her of actor Matthew McConaughey.

''Let's finish this,'' he said, reaching for her left

hand. "I don't want to tie up your day any longer than necessary."

His tone was polite, businesslike. Nothing about his touch should have affected her as it did. A crazy tingle started at her wrist and bounced through her body like a fly caught in a lampshade. Donnie hesitated a second as if he felt it, too, but then he lowered his head and squinted at the paper as he aligned each finger in its little box. His thumb and index finger dwarfed her pale white digits. Her nails were closely trimmed and polish free.

"I was really surprised when I heard you were a massage therapist. Your hands are so small."

She sensed his unspoken curiosity about her choice of profession. "I use more than my hands," she said. "My technique utilizes my whole arm and body for leverage." She looked at him. "Some people still think of massage as something sexual. But it's a healing practice and it takes a lot of training to be a therapist."

"How'd you get into it?"

She was asked that a lot. "After I left Ireland, I moved to Wisconsin with my cousins, Moira and Kathleen. They were working and going to school and I'd give them neck rubs. Moira thought I was so good, she signed me up for a course at the junior college. I loved it."

She took the towelette he offered and wiped the black ink from her fingertips. "My teacher called me a natural. He said I could divine other people's pain through my fingers."

She felt a blush coming on and stepped back, pretending to search for a trash can. Donnie pointed to a gray plastic pail then led the way to the main room. "Did the people at County explain that you need to leave a check and a money order? One for us, one for the state."

Kristin dug in her shoulder bag for the sheaf of information she'd been toting around. It wasn't cheap to relocate a business, she'd discovered. Telephone lines, a new cellular company, a change of license plates and driver's license, new business cards and advertising. This was the last hurdle.

"Yes. I picked up the money order on Wednesday," she said, taking her checkbook from the zippered section of her purse. "Since Zach got home, I've—"

She didn't want to think about the frosty reception she'd gotten from her son. If it weren't for the warmth he'd shown Sarge, the bloodhound Jonathan and Andi had given Zach last March when he and Kris had come home for Jen's wedding, Kris would have sworn her cousin had sent home the wrong kid.

She set the money order on top of the application then took the pen Donnie offered and opened the blue plastic cover.

No checks. She'd used her last one at the DMV. "Perfect," she muttered. *Typical.* "I swear, Donnie, I'm never like this outside of this town. In Ashland, I was even asked to serve on the PTA. What is it about Gold Creek that brings out the worst in me?''

His chuckle was not unkind. He pulled out his wallet, but Kristin stopped him. "No. Don't even think about it. I'm not a needy waif panhandling for change."

"I know that. You're an old friend who will pay me back. Why delay this process because you're too proud to take a little help?"

"I don't need help. I'm capable." How long had she been trying to prove that? And now she'd messed up once more.

"I know you are," he said. "I saw the video of the twins' birth. You were a rock for Jenny."

His gentle reassurance calmed her anguish.

"Besides that, you've made it this far in the licensing process—which is no small feat, believe me. I've seen grown men weep at the bureaucratic hurdles the government throws up these days."

He removed two bills from his wallet. A twenty and a five. "This isn't a big deal, Kristin. I pay it for you, you send me a check. Simple."

"I'll run home, pick up some checks and be right back."

"Mail it. I'm living at my folks' old house on Granite Hollow."

"No, I want to get this cleared up right—" A sudden thought hit her. She'd promised to take the afternoon shift at the antique store and judging by the clock on the wall, she had ten minutes to get there. "I don't suppose you could swing by the bordello after work, could you? I told Andi I'd cover for her this afternoon.''

He hesitated just a second. ''Sure, if it makes you feel better. I've been meaning to stop by and say hello to Ida Jane, anyway.''

As he wrote out the receipt, he asked, ''Is your son ready for school?''

No. ''I hope so.'' Zach was registered, but Kris had no idea what to expect next week when classes began. He had never responded to a move this way before. At Jenny's suggestion, Kristin and Zach had visited a family therapist yesterday. The woman had concluded that Zach was ''perfectly *delightful*'' with normal fears, worries and concerns. Her advice: ''Keep the lines of communication open and spend more quality time with him.''

Maybe I could find us matching brick walls to bang our heads against, Kris thought.

Donnie passed the slip of paper across the chest-high counter. ''Thanks,'' she said.

She folded it and tucked it in her purse right beside her half-finished list of things to do. Between running errands, seeing to Ida Jane's needs and worrying about Zach, Kris felt frazzled. And she didn't have a single massage scheduled. If business picked up, who knew how she'd keep things organized?

She stifled a sigh. She'd been managing on her own for eleven years. She'd get through this, too.

''Kris, are you okay?''

She straightened her shoulders and tossed her

head. *Leave it to Donnie to pick up on her fears.* "Fine. Just thinking about all the things I have to get done today."

His eyes showed concern. Could he see how close she was to the edge? How little sleep she'd gotten the past few months, fretting that she'd screwed up the lives of everyone she loved? "Gotta run. I'll see you later this afternoon, then. I'll give you a discount coupon for a massage."

Not that she figured he'd ever use it. The memories between them—both the good and the bad— would probably get in the way of her therapeutic touch.

She bumped into three deputies on her way out the door—two strangers and Edgar Olson, who'd been the arresting officer the night of her disgrace. She faked a breezy hello, then dashed to her car.

If she'd been in Ashland, she would have handed each one of them her business card and talked about the benefits of massage for people who worked in stressful jobs like law enforcement. But something about Gold Creek robbed her of the confidence she'd fought so hard to acquire. And that scared her even more than the thought of facing Tyler Harrison—her son's father.

EVERYTHING ABOUT this sucky town sucks, Zach Sullivan decided as he looked out the window of the cheesy little house his aunt Jenny had given them to live in.

The rooms were small and the backyard was so

tiny he felt guilty making Sarge stay there. Yesterday he'd walked Sarge over to the bordello so the dog could play with Andi's sheepdog puppy, Harley. The bordello had a huge backyard.

Sarge was the only good part about this move, Zach thought. And Ida Jane wasn't too bad.

His mother's great-aunt was almost as old as the bordello. He liked her. He liked the building, too. He wasn't sure why. Maybe its history. He enjoyed listening to Ida Jane tell stories about the place.

Not that he'd ever admit that to his mother. No way. She'd lied to him for almost his entire life. He wasn't going to just forgive her for that.

Hell, no.

He shook his head. His blond bangs brushed against his eyelashes. His mom had never allowed him to grow his hair this long before, but he figured she was on such a heavy guilt trip he could probably murder somebody and she'd still forgive him.

She hadn't even given him any crap about his nose ring. Which was sort of disappointing. The damn thing hurt like hell to have put in. The least she could have done was faint or yell or something when she saw it.

Zach muttered the long string of epithets he and his cousins had spent weeks perfecting. Then he walked to the refrigerator and took out a Coke. Sarge, who'd been sleeping by the door, lifted his head.

Zach walked to where the old hound was lying

and sat down. He leaned back against the cabinet and closed his eyes.

School would start on Monday, and Sunday was the twins' first birthday party. A part of him had always dreamed of this kind of life—hanging out with family in a place where you felt kinda safe.

But if his mother thought he was going to let this stupid town and its stupid people—including his a-hole father—into his life, she was crazy.

He'd run away first. Maybe he'd stay with Moira and her family for a while in Chicago. He'd work the docks and save enough money to go back to Ireland where he was born. Zach had no memory of the place, but it had to be better than Gold Creek, California. Hadn't his mother left the first chance she got? Why should he stay?

If she made him meet his *father,* he'd do it. The guy was supposed to be rich. *I'll meet him, steal something valuable, then hock it for a ticket east.*

He stroked Sarge's long, silky ear and took a swallow of his soda. *Two tickets.* He wasn't going to leave Sarge behind. He'd missed the dog the whole time he was in Chicago.

The tightness in his chest eased a bit. A plan, Zach thought. It always helped to have a plan.

CHAPTER TWO

DONNIE CHECKED his watch before making the call. Since Sandy's life revolved around staying beautiful for her new husband, Boyd Baker, her mornings were devoted to a personal trainer. She seldom picked up the phone before two in the afternoon.

There were six rings before she answered. "The Baker residence."

Her tone was haughty and stiff. Donnie called it her English-butler voice. Sandy used it to discourage telemarketers—one of the jobs she'd held when she and Donnie were first married.

"It's me. Returning your call. What's up?"

Her hesitation made his nerves skitter with apprehension. Normally, she'd launch into some complaint about his lack of parenting skills or float a lengthy rationale about why she was going to arrive late to see their son. This felt different.

"I hate to sound overly dramatic, but are you sitting down?"

"Don't worry about me, Sandy. Just spit it out. I was leaving to run a few errands before I pick up Lucas. I know you said not to pack a lot of clothes, but he needs some new shoes and I—"

She made a huffing sound then snapped, "Things have changed, Donnie."

Not unusual. Happened all the time with her. Since her marriage to the wealthy set designer from L.A., her contribution to Lucas's *shared custody* had dropped dramatically. More often than not, a plane ticket showed up in her place. Donnie sometimes joked that Lucas had logged more frequent-flier miles than many executives could claim.

Unfortunately, air safety wasn't a joking matter. Another reason why Donnie had applied to become a Federal Air Marshal.

He knew that being an air marshal was a demanding job. Donnie wouldn't have even considered applying if Lucas hadn't been scheduled to move to Los Angeles to live with Sandy. This new custody agreement was a result of Sandy's determination to prove that Lucas was a prodigy on the guitar. The fancy school she'd picked out didn't start its new term until October first. And although Lucas had lobbied for a longer summer, Donnie thought it best to start him in school in Gold Creek to help facilitate the transition to a new curriculum. Lucas was a smart kid, but his grades didn't show it.

A chill passed through him. "What's going on, Sandy? Don't tell me you're backing out of our deal."

"Boyd just got the green light on the new Chris Columbus movie. I don't have all the details, but the location work is in South Africa. Boyd expects to be there for eight months. And I'm going."

The last was added as a definite. "South Africa?"

"Yes. I'm not sure where exactly—they're scouting locations this week, but the movie is a period piece and I have a feeling we're going to be someplace rather remote."

"For eight months? How long does it take to build a movie set?" He didn't hide his disgust. As far as he was concerned, Sandy had abdicated her parental duties the minute Boyd came into the picture.

"Boyd is very much in demand, and it's a tribute to the director's trust in him that he wants Boyd on-site the whole time they're filming," she said haughtily. "If they blow something up and they need a second take—oh, why do I bother trying to explain things to you? The bottom line is I'm not going to be able to take Lucas after all."

Normally Donnie accepted Sandy's self-involvement as a fact of life, but it really irked him when Lucas wound up shortchanged. He knew his son had not only been looking forward to the move, but he'd been bragging about it. Donnie had advised him not to burn any bridges, but lately, nothing Donnie said seemed to count for more than wasted breath.

"I'm sure they have schools in South Africa. Lucas will have one helluva learning experience," he said, then added pointedly, "You agreed to take him, Sandy, and I've made plans to be out of town for an extended period, so he'll have to go with you.''

Instead of flying off the handle, she sighed. ''I suggested that. But this is going to be a complicated job, and we'll be moving between sites. There's no way to provide a steady home life for a young boy. I'm afraid he'd fall further behind in his studies.''

Donnie's anger bubbled just below the surface. ''Oh, please,'' he said, keeping his voice low. ''Don't pretend this is about Lucas's well-being. You and I both know your only concern is making sure Boyd isn't screwing some wardrobe girl behind your back. That's what comes from a guilty conscience, Sandy.''

''You're being a jerk, Donnie. I can't help it, but this is the way things are,'' she said with finality. ''I have two weeks before we leave, and I'd like to pick Lucas up on Thursday and keep him a few days. It's Labor Day weekend. He won't miss much school, and I thought he and I could run to Redding to visit my mom.''

''But that Monday is his birthday,'' Donnie said inanely, unable to formulate any kind of rebuttal.

''I know. I thought we'd stop at the outlets and buy school clothes. Do you have a problem with that?''

''Would it make a difference if I did?'' His brain was scrambling to try to come up with a plan B. As long as his mother was willing to take over while he was away at training, he could still pull this off. Once he had his permanent assignment, he could move them both to wherever he was stationed.

"Well," Sandy said, her tone surprisingly mild, "it would be nice for Lucas's sake if we could be civil."

Rather than get into all old hurts, verbal fights and open hostility, he shook his head. "I've got to go. Fax me your itinerary, and I want a copy of your Africa plans, too. Americans are targets all over the world, you know." Because of his interest in becoming an air marshal, he'd been researching air-travel safety on a global basis.

"Boyd mentioned that, too, when I suggested taking Lucas with us. You should be thankful he cares enough to put his foot down."

If he hadn't been in the office, Donnie would have employed one of his son's favorite gestures— two fingers in a gagging motion. "I'll talk to you later. Goodbye."

After he replaced the receiver, Donnie scrubbed his face with both hands. His long day had just gotten longer. Bad enough he'd had his morning disrupted when Kristin popped in—an encounter that had left him feeling slightly off-kilter.

Ed Olson and Margie had commented on Donnie's absentmindedness. Ed, the officer who'd been first on the scene the night of Donnie's high-school altercation with Tyler Harrison, had muttered something about "old home week."

Margie, who'd apparently talked to Bethany, had

scolded Donnie for "entertaining lady friends in her booking room." Margie's tough bluster was actually a form of mothering.

"Who are you calling a lady?" he'd teased in return, but his heart hadn't been in it. Kristin had changed. Gone was her carefree attitude. She seemed more serious, focused.

"Kris was always my favorite triplet," Margie had added. It didn't surprise Donnie that Margie knew the Sullivan sisters—everyone did. "She was always so bright and pretty."

Pretty? That was one thing about her that hadn't changed. "Our Kris is fair, fey and sweet as a sugar cookie," her aunt once had said in Donnie's presence. The description had stuck with him, even though he'd had to look up the meaning of *fey*.

He picked up his car keys and left the office. His Toyota Forerunner sat at the far end of the lot behind the sheriff's office.

As he drove through town, Donnie thought about the night of the triplets' eighteenth birthday party. Late February. Chilly enough to keep two burn barrels busy in the backyard of the old bordello. Although he and Kris had formally broken up three months earlier, Donnie knew she wasn't seeing anyone, and he'd expected to find her there. Alone. Maybe missing him.

Donnie had enjoyed playing big man on campus for a while, but the glamour had worn off. And he'd found himself looking forward to seeing Kristin. He'd hoped they could make up. Get back together.

Only, she wasn't there. She'd gone off somewhere with Tyler Harrison. A guy Donnie couldn't stand.

Donnie had had a couple of run-ins with Harrison the previous July. To fulfill a community-service obligation after some prank he'd pulled on the last day of school, Tyler had been assigned to the Search and Rescue team Donnie led each summer. Tyler's belligerent attitude and smart mouth had left Donnie itching to teach him a lesson.

Fired up with beer, Donnie and a couple of his buddies had set out to find Kristin. And they did—in the back seat of her great-aunt's Cadillac. Half-naked. Flushed with passion or embarrassment. Donnie hadn't bothered to determine which. A blind rage had come over him—a fury so great he might have killed Tyler if his friends hadn't pulled him off. The incident had earned him a formal reprimand from the sheriff, three months in an anger-management course and the friendship and respect of the girl he loved.

He saw Kristin only twice in the weeks that followed. Once when he'd pleaded with her to support his version of the story—that Tyler had raped her—and second, at a meeting with the sheriff when she'd stated quite clearly that she and Ty had been engaged in consensual sex when Donnie attacked them.

At the time, he'd felt blindsided by her ''betrayal.'' It wasn't until he found out about Sandy's extramarital affair that Donnie had understood what a true breach of faith was all about.

He owed Kristin an apology. And he needed to get it off his chest before he left to begin his new life as an air marshal.

KRISTIN RESTED her elbow on the counter and plopped her free ear into her cupped palm. Her head ached and the conversation with her former landlord wasn't helping in the least.

"He put what where?" she croaked into the phone. "I'll kill him."

The last came out as an impotent threat—at least in her mind. But the uniformed man entering the antique store might take it differently, she thought.

"I'll take the cleanup costs out of Zach's allowance for the next twenty-five years, Mr. Baxter," she amended loudly as Donnie Grimaldo approached the desk. "I was sure I scrubbed every inch of his room, but it never occurred to me to look on the ceiling of his closet."

She listened to the retired air force pilot explain in detail about her son's fertile imagination. Apparently the graffiti included some explicit drawings of her landlord's anatomy and included a ditty about the man's ability to please his wife—and donkeys—in bed. Her face went from mildly burning to chili-pepper hot.

"I promise this will not go unpunished," she vowed. "You'll be receiving a letter of apology in the mail from Zach, and please feel free to keep my deposit. I'm sure it will take several coats of paint and maybe even therapy to remedy this.''

Kris kowtowed another few minutes before hanging up. Instead of facing Donnie, she dropped her head to the glass-topped sales counter.

''My son has been possessed by some freakishly obnoxious poltergeist,'' she mumbled.

''I hate to be the one to break it to you,'' Donnie said, amusement thick in his husky male voice, ''but it's called hormones. Welcome to the adolescent years.''

She looked up. *Damn. Still as handsome as he was this morning.*

Why couldn't he have a beer gut and receding hairline like most of the men she met? Donnie had been a hunk in high school—the homecoming jock everyone idolized—and he'd improved since then.

''We *used* to have such a good relationship.''

Donnie's sympathetic smile made her wish they were the kind of friends who hugged each other. A hug would have been nice. ''Zach has a lot on his plate right now,'' Donnie said. ''But, even without that, puberty makes kids think their parents are mindless morons.''

Could Zach's age be contributing to the problem? she wondered. Donnie was not only a man but also a father. Maybe that made him an expert. ''What can I do?''

He shook his head. ''I took Lucas to a counselor after Sandy and I split up. I'll never forget his parting advice. 'No matter how ugly things get, stick by his side. Someday he'll thank you for it.'''

"If he ever forgives me," she muttered, not intending to share the thought aloud. Embarrassed, she reached under the counter for her purse. "I have that check for you."

When she looked up, he was leaning on the counter, arms folded in front of him. Kristin fought the urge to run. It wasn't his fault he generated crazy feelings.

He straightened and took a step back. "Do you have any flyers or cards with your business number? I'd be happy to put them in the break room. I don't know a deputy on the force who wouldn't throw himself at your feet for a good massage."

Kris ripped the check along the perforated line. "How do you know I'm any good?"

Before he could reply, a shrill squeal of delight filled the air. "Bless my soul, it's Donnie Grimaldo. Aren't you a sight for sore eyes? Come here and give an old woman a hug."

Donnie's face changed. The lines bracketing his mouth formed shallow C-shapes and his hazel eyes lit up with joy. He strode purposefully to the doorway leading to the residence and swept Kristin's eighty-three-year-old great-aunt into a bear hug. "Miss Ida, I've missed seeing you at the office— no more bad checks coming in these days?"

Ida's lined cheeks blushed with pleasure, and Kris felt a funny catch in her chest. At times like this, she wanted to kick herself for letting so many years pass without visiting her great-aunt.

"Andi handles all that stuff now," Ida said, shaking her cane. "Took all the fun out of it when she subscribed to some kind of check-cashing service. What's the point of being in business if you can't nail a shirker now and then?"

The two chatted about inconsequential matters— the weather and mutual friends—for a couple of minutes, and then Ida said, "So, what's become of my car, young man?"

Kristin froze. Some days her aunt seemed to understand that Andi had totaled Ida Jane's old Caddie in an accident six months earlier. At other times, the older woman fretted about the fate of Rosemarie, Ida's name for the thirty-year-old, faded pink car.

Donnie glanced at Kristin before answering, then he said, "Miss Ida, cars like that are rare as hen's teeth, as my daddy used to say. I'm sorry to say there's a chance Rosemarie might be gone for good."

A prickle of moisture welled up behind Kristin's sinuses. How could she have forgotten how kind he was?

"Did you hear that, Jenny?" Ida exclaimed, looking at Kristin. "Rosemarie might be in some collector's showroom. We might never see her again."

Donnie raised his eyebrows at Ida's mistake, but Kristin didn't bother correcting her aunt about her name. Instead, she changed the subject, "When Andi gets back from her doctor's appointment, Auntie, maybe you and I could take Zach, Sarge and Harley to the park. Would you like that?"

"No, dear, I'm not feeling too peppy today. Why don't you take Donnie, instead? I'll fix a picnic. You two lovebirds deserve a little treat."

Kristin chanced a glance at Donnie, whose smile looked bemused, and maybe just a bit wistful. "I wish I could do that, Miss Ida, but I have to run along," he said. "I have to pick up my son."

"What son?" Ida Jane asked, her face contorting in the befuddled look Kristin and her sisters had come to know all too well.

Ida's doctors had attributed her declining mental acuity to residual effects of the stroke she'd suffered that spring as well as senile dementia. The diagnosis included the grim prediction that Ida would eventually need hospitalization, but the triplets had vowed to keep their beloved great-aunt at home.

"Auntie, would you watch the desk for a minute while I walk Donnie out?"

Andi had warned against leaving Ida Jane unsupervised, but Kristin tried to give their aunt as much independence as possible.

Donnie held the door for her; as she passed by, he asked softly, "How's she doing?"

Kris rushed past. He seemed taller, more substantial than she remembered. And his uniform made her nervous.

"She's doing pretty well physically after her stroke. But her mind isn't as sharp as it once was. But whose is?" she added with a lame chuckle.

Kris stepped to the railing and took a deep breath. A riot of mums, snapdragons and dahlias filled the flower beds below her. The hummingbird feeder above her head attracted ambitious dive-bombers that buzzed past like souped-up bees.

"Fortunately, we've found a doctor who specializes in geriatric care. He started her on blood thinners and an antidepressant, but we have to watch her like a hawk so she doesn't help herself to an afternoon toddy."

Donnie's low chuckle made her yearn for something she couldn't even identify. "The tables have turned, haven't they?" he said. "I remember when Ida worried about our partying."

The irony of his comment wasn't lost on her. Drinking was partly to blame for her present predicament. Maybe if she hadn't been hell-bent on getting drunk the night of the party, she wouldn't have wound up making love with Tyler. But then she wouldn't have Zach, and she couldn't imagine a world without her son.

Almost as if she'd conjured him up, a kid in sloppy jeans and a black T-shirt appeared at the end of the sidewalk—hound at his side. He moved with a graceless shuffle, head down. "There's Zach."

Sarge spotted Kris and let out a warbling bay. Zach looked up and froze. Even from a distance, Kristin could read his expression, which changed from curiosity to petulance. "Zach," she called, trying to sound upbeat for Donnie's sake. "Come and meet Donnie Grimaldo, an old friend from high school."

Zach gave Donnie a brief, castigating glance then cut across the lawn to avoid the porch altogether. Kristin wasn't surprised—he'd pretty much severed all but the most basic communication with her. But she was embarrassed by such a public display of rudeness. "Zach," she called.

Donnie surprised her by brushing her arm in a brief but supportive gesture. "It's okay."

Tears clustered in her eyes. "No, it's not," she snapped, stepping away so he wouldn't see her cry. "He's an obnoxious brat and he's punishing me for moving here. And for everything else, too."

She heard him take a step closer. "He's a kid with a chip on his shoulder. Give him space, but let him know you love him unconditionally. He'll come around."

Kristin wished she could believe that. She swiped away the tears with her fingers and turned. "I hope you're right. Sometimes it feels like I'm talking to a complete stranger, but I do love him. He's my life. I used to call us the dynamic duo. We did everything together, and we had a lot of fun. I hope he remembers that someday when he's not so angry."

Donnie put his hand on her shoulder and squeezed. "He will."

The connection went deeper than he'd intended,

she was sure. It spread like warm honey through her flesh, and she might have melted in a boneless heap if not for a sudden crashing sound from inside the store.

"Uh-oh," a small voice said. "Jenny, I've spilled the thingies."

"That's the second time she's called you Jenny," Donnie remarked.

"She gets confused. I'd better go. Thanks for helping me out this morning."

"No problem. I gotta run. Lucas is waiting for me to take him shopping," he said, hurrying down the steps. "Don't you hate it when you're late, and your son gets this look that tells you you're the worst parent in the world?"

Kristin wondered if this actually had happened or Donnie was just trying to be nice. "I know it well."

Donnie paused a moment. "I meant to get some business cards from you. Will you be home tonight? I usually go for a run after dinner. I could pick up a stack. Unless that's too late."

A run? It sounded like heaven. What she wanted most was to run toward the east and just keep going. "Sure. No problem. I'm staying at Jenny and Josh's old place, you know."

His chuckle curled around the wind chimes above her head and zinged her like a wet towel. "This is Gold Creek, Kris. Your new brother-in-law may have given "Glory's World" the ax, but there's still the grapevine."

He nodded goodbye and walked away.

Feeling a bit unsettled and a little blue, Kris went to investigate the source of the crash. A canister was lying on its side—paper clips spread in every direction. Ida Jane had started picking them up but had apparently got sidetracked. At times, her great-aunt's attention span rivaled Zach's at age four.

"Cool necklace you're making, Auntie," Kris said, noticing the chain of clips in Ida's lap.

She took a broom and dustpan from behind the counter and completed the cleanup. She contemplated salvaging the clips from the dusty mess, but gave up. As she dumped everything into the trash, she noticed a newspaper that had fallen behind some sacks. She pulled it free, intending to toss it away, too, but the headline caught her eye: Developer Plans Big for Gold Creek.

Kris hadn't had time to read the paper in weeks. On the way to the airport to pick up Zach, Jenny and Andi had been discussing a recent Chamber of Commerce meeting, but Kris had been too preoccupied to pay attention.

She drew up a stool beside her aunt and scanned the front page. To her surprise, two of the bylines were attributed to Gloria Harrison Hughes. Tyler's mother. Kris knew that Jonathan had made an effort to keep as many of the *Ledger's* original employees as wished to stay, but she'd been sure Gloria would leave out of loyalty to her brother, the previous owner.

For years, Gloria's column "Glory's World" had

chronicled local gossip, speculation, rumor and opinion with a free hand. Kristin and her sisters had, for the most part, basked in Glory's goodwill until the night Kris had wound up naked with Gloria's son. After that, the author's tone had changed.

Now the column was history, and Gloria had been assigned to cover local news—just as her son was making it.

"Auntie, listen to this." She read aloud from the article: "'Although Meridian, Inc. CEO Tyler Harrison was unavailable for comment, the company announced that it was exploring economic options in the Gold Creek area.'"

Ida gave her a look that said, So what?

Kris read a little farther, noting quotes from local residents. Those advocating change saw Meridian as the key to progress. No matter what the company planned, the result would be more jobs and increased property values. Those opposed wanted to keep Gold Creek virtually the same as it had always been.

"What do you think, Auntie?"

"Never trust a Harrison."

A shiver of unease made Kristin jump to her feet. Ty's father had embezzled money from the local bank to cover his bad investments then committed suicide when Tyler was about Zach's age.

"Maybe Ty wants to atone for his father's activities," she said, helping her aunt to stand.

Although Andi was one of those adamantly against anything that might destroy the character of

Gold Creek, Kristin was more concerned about Ty's timing. Why after eleven years without a word, was he now coming back to Gold Creek?

"Or could be he wants somebody to pay for what happened with his daddy," Ida Jane said.

Kristin didn't want to think about Ty. Any day now, she expected to hear from her attorney about a custody hearing. If Tyler Harrison was out for revenge, she knew whose name would be at the top of his list.

DONNIE FINISHED chopping a stalk of celery and added it to the salad he was making for dinner. Lucas was in his bedroom, no doubt playing the new video game he'd purchased with money Sandy had sent him. Donnie's mother was due home any minute from her exercise class. He'd encouraged her to sign up for Jazzercise after her checkup showed an alarmingly high cholesterol level.

They'd changed their diet, too, and Donnie had taken up running again. Unfortunately, Lucas resisted his father's invitation to join him. The boy was content to spend his free time playing video games or practicing guitar; the lack of exercise had contributed to a weight problem that had started when Donnie and Sandy first separated.

"Lucas, did you sweep out the garage?"

The mumbled answer could have been either a positive or a negative. Before Donnie could follow through, however, the kitchen door opened and a slim, attractive woman in baggy pink sweatpants and a loose T-shirt emblazoned with the words Dynamic Granny across the chest walked in. "Hello, dear, how was your day?" Maureen Grimaldo asked.

Usually, Donnie counted his blessings that his mother was willing to share a home with him and help raise Lucas, but Donnie couldn't help feeling guilty. Maureen Grimaldo was an active, vital fifty-four-year-old widow. She claimed she enjoyed a full life in Gold Creek, but Donnie felt she deserved more. And he planned to see she got it—once he completed his air marshal training.

He wasn't deluding himself about the demands this new job would make on his time, but with the additional income—and if Sandy would live up to her obligations—they'd be able to make it work.

"I got my approval notice today," he said softly. He'd shared his aspirations with his mother but very few others. Not even Lucas knew. Donnie hadn't wanted to broadcast his plans in case he was turned down.

Maureen dropped her gym bag and purse on a chair and rushed across the room. "Congratulations, honey," she exclaimed, hugging him. "I'm so proud of you."

He basked in her praise a minute then carried the salad bowl to the table. "How was your day? Did you hear from Aunt Roberta?" Maureen's sister hadn't been feeling well for several weeks and had been scheduled for tests today.

His mother poured herself a glass of water and

added a slice of lemon to it. "Actually, that's why I'm late. I stopped at the travel bureau on the way home. The news isn't good."

Donnie swallowed. *Travel?* "Sit down. Why don't you tell me about it before I call Lucas to the table."

Maureen kept it simple, as was her style. A cancerous mass near the kidney. Immediate surgery. A possible transplant in the future.

"A kidney transplant? You'd be the donor?"

She shrugged. "If I match. Roberta's the only one left on my side of the family, and she's such a wonderful person. I'll do whatever I can. But right now, I just want to be with her."

Donnie felt his dream slide a little farther out of reach.

"Isn't it fortunate that Sandy is taking Lucas this year," Maureen asked rhetorically.

Donnie nodded. Now wasn't the time to announce his ex-wife's change of plan. He loved his aunt, and he owed his mother far too much to make her feel badly about doing what she needed to do.

Two hours later, as his Nikes pounded the pavement and sweat dripped down the sides of his face, Donnie kept his mind purposefully blank. He should never have gotten his hopes up. If only Magnus wasn't such an odious boss. Donnie had been spinning his wheels—wasting his talent, some said—for nearly eight years. If Magnus Brown won a third term this November, Gold Creek would be in big trouble. At one time, Donnie had actually considered running for sheriff, but then had decided to apply to the FAM program instead.

There has to be a way to make this happen, he thought. *Maybe Sandy's mom could help out.*

Paulette "Poopsie" Grossman was in her mid-seventies, but she seemed older. It wasn't surprising, Donnie thought, considering the hard life she'd led. Currently, she lived in Redding with her eldest son, Elroy, who owned a ranching operation.

If Poopsie would move in... The idea suddenly struck him as so odious he stopped midstride and bent over to catch his breath. Poopsie was a whiny, cigarette-smoking junk-food addict. No way could he subject his son to that woman's company for any sustained length of time. Lucas had enough problems without adding Poopsie's influence.

Donnie just about to take off again when he looked around and realized he was only a block away from Kristin's house. He knew the place well since he and Sandy had socialized with Josh and Jenny when the couple first returned to Gold Creek after college.

The night had turned chilly. Donnie sprinted the remaining block and shot diagonally across Kristin's yard, vaulting over a mountain bike lying on its side beside a low hedge. A muted bark came from the backyard of the house.

Breathing hard, he rapped on the door. The exterior light snapped on. Donnie jogged in place to retain his body heat. There was a sound from behind the door but nothing happened. "Kris? It's Donnie. Do you have those cards for me?"

The door opened a crack, and the silhouette of a head became visible. "Hi," he said, again in a friendly tone. "Zach, right? We met this afternoon at the bordello. I'm Donnie Grimaldo. The cop."

The head moved a smidgen.

"Is your mom here?"

"She got a call."

His first thought—an emergency with Ida Jane— was tempered by the possibility Kristin might be giving a massage.

"Could I use your bathroom a sec?"

Zach made a rude noise. "Yeah, right. Like I'm gonna open the door to some a-hole I don't know. You think I'm nuts?"

Donnie stopped jogging. "No. I'd think that you were being smart if we were in the city or even in a town like Gold Creek if I were a complete stranger. But your mother tried to introduce us this afternoon. If you hadn't been so rude, we might have talked."

Although his face was shadowed, Donnie could see the boy's upper lip curl back in a sneer. "Well, too bad. 'Cause I ain't letting you in."

A pair of headlights pulled into the driveway, ending the stalemate. Donnie recognized Kristin's car. Her son slammed the door.

"Hi," she said. The light from the windows il- luminated her smile. "I forgot you said you might stop by. Have you been waiting long?"

He shook his head.

She opened the door with her key and motioned for him to follow. "Where's Zach? Didn't he answer the door?"

Donnie kept his distance. He was sweaty and she was perfectly lovely in her broken-in jeans and sloppy sweatshirt. And she smelled like...Kris. In high school, when other girls were testing fragrances, Kristin had chosen one and stuck with it.

He stepped away. "Mind if I use the facilities?" he asked, starting down the hallway.

"It's the second door—"

"I know," he cut in. "I've been here before."

Donnie used a washcloth and towel to freshen up. Before leaving the bathroom, he checked out the reading material in a basket near the toilet. A *Rolling Stone* magazine with Lenny Kravitz on the cover. A couple of copies of *Sports Illustrated* and a *Musician's Friend* catalog. The last had two dog-eared pages. Obviously Zach's choices.

So. He's interested in guitars. Just like Lucas, Donnie noted. *I wonder if he plays.*

"Hi, again," he said, looking around as he walked into the living room. "You've done a nice job in here." A rainbow-hued mobile in one corner was a bit New Age for his liking, but the dozen or so cream-colored pillar candles and profusion of plants made the area look peaceful and welcoming. There was no television, he noticed.

"Thanks. I call it feng shui on a budget," she

said, returning from hanging her son's jacket in the front-hall closet.

"Feng shui. I've heard of that. It's a kind of mushroom, right?"

She looked momentarily at a loss until she realized he was teasing. Her laugh spiraled around him in a cascade of color and light that sent him careening into the past. It made him yearn for a time—a feeling—that lived all too vividly in his memory. He'd loved her once, with a purity and sweetness that had known only hope and boundless possibilities.

But that had ended. They'd gone their separate ways and there was no changing that. He was poised for the future, and he wasn't going to blow it this time.

"Zach mentioned something about a call," Donnie said, feeling the need to make small talk.

"Ida Jane couldn't remember how to find *Jeopardy* on the new satellite dish Jonathan installed. Andi was asleep—wiped out from her doctor's appointment—and Jonathan was at a meeting, so Ida called me."

"Kristin to the rescue."

His tone must have come off less neutral than he'd intended because Kristin tilted her head in question. "Is something wrong?"

Yeah. Everything. "Nope. Everything's peachy."

Her lips flattened as if trying not to smile. "Me, too. If you overlook the guillotine hanging above my head."

For a moment, he was tempted to tell her about his dilemma.

But before he could open his mouth, Zach walked out of the kitchen to Donnie's right. Suddenly grateful that he hadn't spilled his guts, Donnie looked at Kris and said, "Do you have those cards and flyers?"

Kris walked directly to a small, antique desk with curved legs and a matching chair upholstered in dusky-gold silk. The upper part of the desk sported a row of cubbyholes along the back. The desk had been in the triplets' study room at the bordello.

Donnie remembered the room well. It was where he and Kris had made love for the first time. Each a virgin. Each nervous, needy and certain their love would last forever.

"Did you used to date my mom?" a youthful voice asked. The tone held enough hostility that at first Donnie was afraid the boy had read his mind.

"Yes," Donnie answered.

He heard the boy's implied question as well. To ask it would have left Zach vulnerable. Exposed.

"I was a year ahead of your mother in school. She was a cheerleader, and I played football. We went steady for a couple of years. Right, Kris?"

She nodded, but looked too surprised to speak.

"Then I went off to college, and your mother discovered I wasn't the only fish in the sea." He tried to keep his tone light, but the look on Zach's handsome, troubled face made him feel like a jerk. The boy deserved the truth, but Donnie wasn't sure how much Kristin had told him or wanted him to know.

"You broke up, and she got together with my...dad?"

Donnie wasn't sure why Zach had chosen to include him in this discussion. He looked to Kris for guidance.

"Are you sure it's not you? That you didn't knock her up and for some reason she's not telling you?"

The question hit Donnie hard. *If only...*

"Zachariah Sullivan," Kristin said sharply. "That's enough. I explained what happened and who your father is."

"Yeah, but you obviously slept around. You could be wrong," her son returned nastily.

Before either adult could react, the boy shot from the room. His bedroom door slammed resoundingly.

Kristin looked stunned.

Donnie reacted without thinking. He walked to her and pulled her into his arms. A heartbeat later she burst into tears. He felt her link her arms behind him. Donnie lowered his chin and breathed in the smell of her frothy curls. So sweet, so...

He opened his eyes, marshaling his thoughts. He knew better than to go down that road. He could comfort an old friend without losing his head.

Kristin seemed to regain her composure at the same moment. She stepped back and dug in her pocket for a tissue. "Thanks," she mumbled. "That was nice of you. And generous. He's been acting out a lot, but that's the first time he's attacked a stranger.''

"It comes with the territory. I'm a cop.''

She cocked her head thoughtfully. ''Well, you're a really good cop.''

For some reason, her praise was comforting. It didn't take away his disappointment at the thought of having to turn down the FAM program, but it helped. "I guess I'm okay for a local yokel.''

She must have heard more in his tone than he'd intended. ''What's that mean?''

Donnie sighed. ''Nothing. Sorry.''

He turned to leave, but she stopped him. ''Talk to me, Donnie. I cried on your shoulder, now it's your turn.''

"I'm fine. The politics of the job get to me every now and then. You know how it is in small towns. The good old boy network is alive and well.''

She made a rueful sound and picked up a small gray box that had gotten pushed behind a stack of magazines. ''I guess I assumed that would have changed by now, but don't tell me you're having second thoughts about your career. I don't believe it. You always wanted to be a deputy.''

"I used to love my job, but it's been a while since I felt that I'm making a difference here.''

She opened the box and took out a couple dozen business cards. ''So, why not put in for a transfer? I bet the California Highway Patrol would jump at the chance to have an officer with your experience. Or the FBI.''

She made things sound so simple. Without intending to, he confided to her, ''Actually, I've been accepted into the Federal Air Marshal Program. I applied last fall.''

''Donnie,'' she exclaimed, her face alight with joy. ''That's fantastic. Congratulations.'' She gave him a quick hug then blushed as if regretting her impulsive act. She turned back to the desk to find a rubber band to wrap around the cards.

His response—equally inappropriate—died the moment he recalled Sandy's news. ''The only problem is, I can't accept the offer.''

''Why not?''

He snickered softly. ''Because my ex-wife is going to Africa, and my mom has to help take care of her sister in Texas. Which means I'm not going anywhere soon.'' He couldn't prevent the bitterness from seeping into his tone.

''Oh, Donnie, I'm so sorry.''

He looked away. He didn't want her sympathy. There was still a chance he could pull this off if he could find a perfect housekeeper who could take over completely while he was away. A housekeeper Lucas would be happy to stay with. For the first time since his divorce, Donnie was sorry he didn't have a wife.

CHAPTER THREE

KRIS STOOD in the doorway of her spare bedroom trying to imagine what it would look like with a young boy living there. Probably just as messy as Zach's room, she thought with a smile. Ever since last week when Donnie had mentioned his dilemma, she'd been tossing around the idea of volunteering to take in Lucas while Donnie attended his training.

Regretfully, her reasons were not completely altruistic. First, she needed the money she'd have to charge him, and second, her image could stand the polishing that would come if Donnie accepted her offer.

Her bank account was just about empty. The move had been expensive, and while she'd given three massages last week, she knew from experience that it took months to establish a steady following.

In the meantime, the money kept flowing out— food, health insurance, car payments. But financial woes aside, she needed every possible advantage when she and Tyler went to court. She'd talked to her attorney on Wednesday right after he got a call from Tyler's lawyer. Things were finally starting to happen.

"Mr. Harrison has been ill," James Rohr, her attorney, told her. "He apparently contracted some kind of food poisoning while in Japan, then needed to be hospitalized upon his return to the States. A bleeding ulcer, I believe."

"I'm sorry about that. Did learning about Zach's existence contribute to it?"

"I certainly hope not, but we should be prepared to counter that charge if it comes up. I'll hire a detective to look into Mr. Harrison's medical history. If we can prove this was a preexisting condition, we can argue—"

She'd been forced to interrupt. "I'm not sure I can afford to hire a detective, Mr. Rohr. I know the smart thing would be to do everything to ensure that Tyler can't take Zach away from me, but he won't be able to do that unless he proves I'm an unfit mother, right?"

"Mr. Harrison's attorney has a reputation for being extremely tenacious, Kristin. You have several weak spots. You often take evening appointments, correct? Zach is unsupervised presumably for hours at a time. Plus, your history of moving frequently will work against you. And the fact you kept Zach's existence a secret is problematic. I'm afraid they may try to paint a picture of you as irresponsible."

You're a flighty airhead, Andi had shrieked at Kristin the night of the party. *You never think before you act. How can anyone ever trust you again?*

Kristin had spent the past decade trying to prove that she'd changed, but she hadn't been entirely successful. Even if every move had been a step up, her record could be construed as capricious. And the blotches on her credit report would look bad. They were the result of her poor choice of friends, rather than faulty bookkeeping. A business partner who used their joint credit card for personal use, a roommate who'd run up the phone bill then skipped town.

Maybe if I could show that someone as rock solid as Donnie Grimaldo trusted me to care for his kid...

"I'm taking Sarge for a walk," Zach said, catching her daydreaming.

Kristin spun around to find her son standing in the hallway—Sarge at his side. She was so shocked that he'd voluntarily approached her and actually spoken to her, she couldn't reply.

"Don't forget about your massage," he said before turning away.

Old habits.

Ida Jane used to tell people that Kristin was the triplet who was born without an inner clock. While her sisters were always punctual, Kristin was late for everything. Zach had been acting as her unofficial appointment secretary ever since he'd learned to tell time.

"Thank you for reminding me. The lady from the sheriff's office is sending over one of the deputies. She said he hurt his back yesterday and was refusing treatment. I guess I'd better head to the shop." She hesitated then asked, "Do you and Sarge want to be my escorts?"

Zach reached down to stroke the dog's head. *Thank goodness Jonathan suggested giving Sarge to Zach.* After Sarge's previous owner, Lars Gunderson, was murdered, Jonathan and Andi brought the old hound home. The timing had coincided with Kristin's introduction of her son to the family. The dog and the boy had seemed destined to meet.

"Sarge likes to chase rabbits in that empty field by the fairgrounds," Zach said, turning away.

At least it wasn't a flat-out no. She followed him outside. She wanted so badly to hug him, her fingers twitched.

"Zach," she called out when they reached the sidewalk. The boy and the dog paused. "I love you."

The tips of his ears got red, as they always did when he blushed. He shrugged as if her words were a bulky coat that didn't fit well. A grunt was his only verbal reply. She took that as an *I love you, too, Mom.*

She was still smiling when she reached the bordello. The traffic noise grew louder. A steady stream of travelers would be headed to the mountains for Labor Day. Gold Creek stores would get a ton of business. Andi was more than ready for that.

Kris loved autumn, although the California version felt an awful lot like summer. She was glad she'd dressed in baggy cotton capri pants and a tank top. Her sandals made a slapping sound against the sidewalk.

Kristin missed Oregon—her little house in Ashland, her friends and loyal clients. But it was good to be back in Gold Creek. Moira had been urging Kris for years to reconnect with her sisters and great-aunt.

"You've let your little mistake grow into this great horned beast that threatens to devour you," Moira had said two summers ago when she'd brought her kids to Oregon for a visit. "You will never allow yourself to fall in love and have a normal life until you make peace with the past."

"I am at peace," Kristin had argued. "Zach and I are—"

Moira had stopped her. "You and Zach are a small dysfunctional family. He needs to know his father, and you need to tell Tyler you're sorry for cheating him out of his son's first years of life."

Only Moira could get away with those blunt comments. She'd been Kristin's labor coach when Kristin had been eighteen, unmarried and scared out of her wits. Moira's family—Kristin's father's family—had offered her a home in Ireland when she'd been desperate to leave Gold Creek. The three months after her debacle with Donnie and Ty had been the hardest of her life. She'd felt sick to her stomach most of the time—alienated from her sisters and the town that had helped raise her.

It was no wonder she'd been too miserable to

attribute her malaise to morning sickness. Moira's mother—who had given birth to nine—had noticed right off. But rather than send Kristin home, her aunt had given Kris the help she needed to deliver the baby. Then Kristin had earned her keep by caring for her uncle's dying mother until Moira and her sister Kathleen were ready to move to Michigan, where they had lined up jobs.

Kristin had moved with them to Grand Rapids. She'd stayed home with her infant son and taken care of their tiny apartment, doing all the cooking and laundry while her cousins worked and went to school. With the help of a cooperative day-care center on campus, Kris was able to take some college-level courses, as well. She'd studied massage, and she'd slowly developed a client base that had allowed her to take courses in shiatsu, myofascial release and Reiki, a form of energy healing.

Then there'd been a crazy nomadic period where she'd inched her way westward. She'd been working at a ski resort in Utah when the man she was dating suggested they move to Oregon. While the relationship didn't pan out, she'd fallen in love with the Rogue River Valley.

But Gold Creek was in her blood. Her soul. And she *was* glad to be home. Despite the challenges facing her.

When she rounded the fence at the corner of the bordello's property line, she spotted a white four-wheel-drive Toyota Forerunner in the parking lot in front of the entrance to her shop. She trotted the last few yards then came to a dead stop.

"Donnie?"

The man leaning against the front fender straightened stiffly. "Hi."

She'd been expecting a deputy, but not this particular one. A full range of emotions raced through her mind. Was she ready to treat Donnie Grimaldo? Did she have a choice? *It's business,* she reminded herself. "Are you hurt? The woman who called said you'd hurt your back and were in a lot of pain."

He shook his head. "I just tweaked something. Margie saw it as a chance to play matchmaker. I called your house, but no one answered."

Was he being truthful? Even from a few feet away, she could see the lines of tension on his forehead. She kept walking till she reached the car.

"Well, I'm sure Margie meant well."

"She can't help herself. It comes with being the mother hen of the department."

Kristin liked the gentle humor she heard in his tone. "Well, it's probably a good thing that you don't need my services. I'm not sure either of us would be able to relax." The look he gave her made her regret her candor.

Their awkward silence was broken when the door to the bordello opened and Andi stepped outside— a big smile on her face. Kristin didn't think she'd ever seen her sister look happier and more radiant.

The triplets were fraternal, not identical, and although they shared a certain family resemblance,

Andi favored their father's side of the family with her bright russet-colored hair and compact build.

"Hi, Donnie," Andi called, curiosity evident in her tone. "Are you here to see the back quack?"

Donnie shook his head. "Not professionally." He looked at Kris and added, "But if you have time, I'd like to talk."

"I'd reconsider if I were you, Don. She's so good I'm thinking about having a bumper sticker made up that says, Any day you can have a massage is a *great* day."

Andi's support meant a lot to Kris. Her acceptance had been another factor behind Kris's move. If Andi could forgive her, then there was hope that the rest of those she'd hurt might also.

"Let's go inside. I'll show you around." Kristin unlocked the door and pushed it open, then made an ushering motion. Donnie seemed to hesitate.

Andi, who was wearing a sleeveless, Hawaiian-print smock dress, leaned over the railing and called, "Don't worry, Donnie. She won't bite. It's against the massage therapist's code of honor."

Kristin waved her sister away and pulled Donnie inside. The ambient lighting from two small lamps on either side of the waiting-room couch cast a warm, comforting glow. "This is the reception area. I hope to have an appointment secretary some day. Poor Zach gets tired of keeping me on track." She moved past him to turn on the light inside the smaller room where her table was set up. "This is the treatment room."

He gave the place a cursory glance, then asked, "Can we talk?"

"Are you sure you don't want a massage instead?" she asked lightly.

He shook his head but a slight smile softened the severity of the motion. "Just let me say my piece. Please."

He took the lone chair, a funky Turkish sling that Ida had given her as a welcome gift. "I need to get this out in the air. You know, the stuff from our past," he said. "We haven't talked about what happened and—"

"You deserve an apology. I know. I've been—"

He leaned forward to rest his elbows on his knees. "No. If anybody owes anyone an apology, it's me. I was jealous. And I had no right to be."

Kristin's throat felt too tight to swallow. She forced herself to take a deep breath. "I...I don't know what to say, Donnie. It never crossed my mind that you shared any of the blame for what happened. You didn't make me go off with Ty. That was my choice, and I have to live with the results."

He shook his head. "Kids parked all the time back then. You and I used to make out in Ida's car whenever we could get our hands on the keys."

She leaped to her feet. "Listen, can we agree that we both behaved badly, and call it even?" She shoved her hands in her pockets and shrugged. "The whole thing got blown out of proportion because we were Gold Creek's idea of the perfect couple. You know—the proverbial Prince Charming and Cinderella who were destined to live happily ever after.'' She tried to laugh, but the sound got caught in her throat. ''So what if we blew it? It's ancient history. Let's forget about it and get on with our lives, okay?''

He didn't answer right away, so she walked into the adjacent room and turned off the light she'd left on. ''Now, how 'bout we go upstairs and I fix you a smoothie—for old times' sake?''

THE WORDS WERE completely innocuous—no innuendo implied—but Donnie couldn't prevent the less-than-innocent image that sprang to mind. ''Uh. No. Kris, I don't think so. I just stopped by to humor Margie and get the other stuff off my chest. Lucas is home alone. Mom's at some garden club thing.''

Kristin's smile was tolerant and slightly embarrassed. ''Sure, I understand. I'm a single parent, too.''

She moved toward the door, then paused and said, ''I'm glad your back is okay, but you really should take it easy for a few days.'' She gave him a serious look. ''Back pain is usually punishment for not paying attention. You do know the correct way to lift and bend, don't you?''

Donnie nodded. He'd been angry over something Magnus had said. Distracted and in a hurry, he'd tried to move an uncooperative drunk out of the

back of his patrol car without waiting for help from
a second officer. The man had flailed wildly, knocking Donnie to one knee, a motion that had sent his
back into instant agony.

"I've had a lot on my mind."

"Do you want to talk about it?"

What good would talk do? Maureen and Sandy
were leaving. Which meant Donnie had to stay.
And Lucas, after hearing about his mother's change
of plans, had turned surly and distant. Not that Donnie blamed him. Disappointment was hard to deal
with at any age.

Kristin stroked his hand—a touch as soft and
sweet as a child's kiss. "Never mind. It's not my
business."

Donnie sensed her withdrawal, and she hadn't
even left the room. What was it about first love that
didn't let go of your heart? he wondered.

Something she'd said earlier struck him. "Did
people really think of us as the perfect couple?" he
asked.

His question obviously surprised her. Ducking
her head shyly, she walked to the desk and made
some kind of notation. "My sisters did, but I think
they liked the idea of your taking care of me. I'm
pretty sure they thought I was a screwup. And you
could definitely do no wrong."

He snorted softly. "Guess I fooled them—and
everyone else." He'd played the role expected of
him, from man of the house after his father died, to
class president and standout quarterback. He'd fol-

lowed all the rules, but Donnie knew that beneath that all-American exterior beat the heart of a rebel. Which might explain why he'd always hated Tyler Harrison. Whose long hair, motorcycle and James Dean attitude had seemed to mock the fundamental tenets of Donnie's life.

College had afforded him a chance to test his wings, and he'd distanced himself from Kristin, with her girl-next-door sweetness, afraid she might hold him back. But when he'd found her with Ty, something had snapped. Instead of a prince, Donnie had turned into a frog. A rabid frog.

Shaking the absurd image from his head, Donnie changed the topic.

"How's your business doing?" he asked.

"It could be better, but I'm counting on some word-of-mouth advertising. You know gossip is the lifeblood of Gold Creek."

He smiled. "True, but have you forgotten what a conservative town this is?"

"I was hoping that progress and the Internet would have softened the citizens up. A little, at least. Are you telling me enlightenment hasn't reached Gold Creek yet?"

Donnie laughed. "We've had two elections since you last lived here, and Magnus Brown won landslide victories in both. I swear each year we get less progressive. At this rate, we'll be pushing our patrol cars Fred Flintstone–style in a couple of years."

She cocked her head. "Why don't you run for office? You're the golden boy."

"I actually did consider it, but then 9/11 happened. The world changed, and I wanted to do more."

"I think you'll make a terrific marshal," she said. Her smile made his heart beat faster.

He tried not to notice the way the fabric of her shin-length pants hugged her hips when she leaned down to straighten the papers on her desk.

Kristin glanced up and caught him looking. He turned his head and faked a yawn. "I'd better get going."

"Pain from your back keeping you awake?" she asked. "Or is it your child-care situation?"

"The latter," he replied.

She took a deep breath. "Do you have a minute? I'd like to talk to you about that. Maybe I can help. And you can help me."

She sat on the sofa and studied him. He could tell by the serious look on her face she wasn't looking forward to broaching the subject.

"Obviously, we'll have to figure out the specifics, but it occurred to me that we might be the answer to each other's problems," she said, twisting her hands nervously. "You need someone to look after Lucas while you're in training, and I need to present the best, most stable appearance possible when Tyler takes me to court."

Before he could respond, she added, "I have a spare bedroom. Lucas could stay with me while you're gone."

Move Lucas out of the only home he'd ever

known while both his parents ran off to pursue their own agendas? That was an option Donnie was reluctant to consider.

"I'm in the process of looking for someone to move into my house," he said. "A house-sitter—and someone who would take care of Lucas." "Find a housekeeper slash nanny" had been Sandy's suggestion when he'd tried again to get her to stick to their original plan.

"Would you consider the job?" he asked.

"My moving into your house will have the whole town talking," Kris said softly. "It won't help me look stable and responsible."

An idea struck him. It raced through his mind with the same titillating charge he felt when he discovered the missing link in a crime he was trying to solve.

No. Ridiculous. Talk about jumping from the frying pan into the fire.

She needs stability, the illusion of permanence. I could give her that—who's more entrenched than me?

And who better than a loving mother with nearly eleven years' experience to care for his son? He opened his mouth then closed it so hard his teeth clicked. *Don't be an idiot, Grimaldo. Keep your mouth shut. Don't say a word...*

"What if we got married?"

CHAPTER FOUR

DONNIE HELD HIS BREATH as he waited for Kristin's answer to his absurd proposal.

She looked shell-shocked. "What did you say?"

Donnie felt a rush of anticipation. "I said we could get married."

"That's what I thought, but you can't be serious."

His brain shifted into high speed. "Why not? It wouldn't be your traditional happily-ever-after thing, because we'd go into it smart. Each with specific goals and realistic expectations. A year or two ought to get us past this crisis point."

Kris's mouth kept opening and closing as though she wanted to speak but couldn't. Her eyes were big, and she appeared on the verge of tears.

Donnie could have kicked himself. He reached out to touch her arm. "I'm sorry, Kris. You're right. It's a dumb idea."

She blinked rapidly. "You just took me by surprise." Her voice was thready, and she cleared her throat before adding, "I didn't know there were men like you left in this world. You'd actually sacrifice your freedom to provide a stable home for your son?''

''I wish that were true, Kris. I'd really like to be the hero here. But, truthfully, this is all about me. My dreams. My goals. It's pure selfishness.''

''Don't be so hard on yourself. We're all selfish at times. Look at me. I dragged my son from town to town. That's not exactly something I'm proud of, you know.''

''The fact that you've moved around quite a bit doesn't make you a bad mother. I've seen you with Zach. You're patient and kind, and he knows you love him no matter what kind of jerk he's being at the moment.''

Before she could say anything else, he added, ''Lucas would be lucky to have you in his life, Kris.''

She cocked her head so earnestly his heart twisted in his chest. ''You really think I'm a good parent?''

He nodded. ''Of course. You were the first person I thought of asking to be my housekeeper, but I knew that wouldn't be fair to you. I couldn't afford to pay you what you'd deserve, and you're right—people would gossip. But if we got married, you and Zach would be on my insurance. And my house is paid for, so you wouldn't have any rent. And you could use my car.'' He felt embarrassed listing the mundane, practical advantages. They were hardly reasons for marriage. *Forget love, what about the car payment?*

Kristin took a deep breath, which caused her bosom to press against the thin material of her tank top. Donnie looked away. This was business; he wasn't going to let hormones play a factor.

"I don't know, Donnie. A part of me wants to throw caution to the wind and say yes, but I have a reputation for making impulsive decisions. I've spent the past ten years trying to overcome that image. What would people think if we suddenly got married?"

"The ones who know our history—which, in this town, is just about everybody—would probably think we were back in love."

"But we're not."

Love. Donnie had no intention of going down that road again. Twice was enough. "My dad used to say that a scalded cat fears even cold water," Donnie said. "So this will be purely a business arrangement. We could sign some kind of prenuptial agreement that states we take away exactly what we brought into the marriage—no more, no less. Although I'd throw in half the proceeds from the sale of the house into the settlement."

"You're selling your house?"

"Air marshals are based in large cities because they're on call a lot of the time. That's why I agreed to let Lucas move to Los Angeles and live with his mother this fall. I'd hoped to move there, too, after my training."

"But now?"

He shrugged. "Obviously, I can't count on

Sandy's help. So, what I'd like to do is keep Lucas in school here while I'm in training, and then sell the house once I have a permanent station.

"Or, if I'm based on the West Coast, I could commute until he starts high school and make a move then."

"What about your mother? Won't she want to return once your aunt is better?"

He sighed. "We had a long talk last night. She was honest with me—and with herself—for the first time. She loves Lucas and she's glad that she was here for me when I needed her, but she'd like to travel more. Maybe even date again. I told her it was about time, and we both think she'd be happier in Texas."

He looked down. He didn't want her to see how much it embarrassed him to have to admit this. "She already raised her family, Kris. Lucas is my responsibility, not hers."

"Do you have any idea where you'd be stationed?" she asked a minute later.

He shook his head. "No, but San Francisco is only five hours away. If I could get SFO or Oakland, I'd have it made. Then," he continued, "if you and Lucas and Zach got along, we might be able to put off moving until both boys are done with school. Assuming you wanted to hang around that long."

Kristin looked up sharply. "I'm through moving, Donnie. This is it. I hope to buy a house, put down roots."

"I'll sell you my house, Kris. By the time I'm stationed, your business will be established and you won't have any trouble qualifying for a loan."

Both were silent for a few minutes, then Kristin said, "I don't know what to say. Marriage is a big deal, Donnie. It's legal."

"It's only a big deal if we make it one," he told her, knowing even as he spoke that wasn't entirely true. He'd taken his first marriage very seriously, which was one reason it had hurt so damn much when it ended. "This is a marriage of convenience, Kris. Yes, it's another move on your record, but marriage to a well-established deputy sheriff would look good to the court.

"And, for once, our history works in our favor— the diehard romantics were probably expecting us to get back together all along. Nobody but the two of us has to know that you're sleeping in my mother's quarters, not my bed."

Something in her face changed, he couldn't tell what.

"Unfortunately, that's a problem, Donnie."

He didn't understand. He'd assumed she'd be thrilled to know that he didn't want a physical relationship with her. "Pardon?"

"I came back to Gold Creek to unburden myself—not to start a new lie."

Her honesty humbled him, but he'd learned the hollowness of living life to please other people. He decided to be blunt. "Here's the deal, Kris. You're a beautiful woman. It would be damn easy to move you into my house…and into my bed. But that wouldn't be fair to you. I tried marriage once and was flat-out miserable.''

He let out a sigh of frustration. ''I can give you my home, my car, my name—even my child, but not me. So, if you choose to do this, you need to know there's no happily-ever-after. I just don't have that in me.''

Kris's blue eyes were serious and reflective, an expression he couldn't recall seeing. There was something else—a look that told him she, too, didn't harbor any illusions about love.

''It's up to you whether we keep this between us or tell the world, Kris. All that matters to me is that my son is being cared for in a safe and loving environment.''

She was silent for a minute. Then she held out her hand as if to shake on their agreement. ''I'll agree to marry you on one condition—our sons have to approve.''

ZACH DIDN'T RECOGNIZE the car pulling into the driveway behind him, but it didn't take a rocket scientist to figure out who was driving it. That cop. The one who used to date his mom. Her old friend from high school. Was he going to be her new boyfriend? Probably. Maybe he was the real reason they'd moved to Gold Creek. Zach was beginning to believe his father was just make-believe, since he hadn't seen the man or heard from him.

Sarge left Zach's side and trotted across the grass

to check out the vehicle. His hackles were raised until the driver's-side door opened and a man stepped out. "Hey, Sarge. How ya doing, buddy?"

The old dog jumped up, his big paws landing squarely on the guy's chest.

"Down," his mother said sharply. She pushed Sarge away.

Zach rushed to his dog's defense. "He's only being friendly. Isn't that what you want? For us to be more friendly?"

He dropped to one knee and hauled the animal against him. The bloodhound slobbered across Zach's arm then licked his face. Sarge was Zach's only companion, mostly by choice. Zach simply hadn't bothered to try and make new friends.

His first week at Gold Creek Middle School had been pretty much what he'd expected. He just hadn't decided yet whether or not he was going to make the effort to fit in. Part of his decision would depend on what happened with his father—the jerk-wad who hadn't even bothered to show up.

"Sorry," the cop said. "Your mom thinks my back is messed up. I've told her it's fine, but she doesn't believe me."

Zach eyed the two. Something was going down. He'd seen his mom hundreds of time with clients, and she never looked this way. Sorta embarrassed and edgy.

He stood up and started toward the house, Sarge at his side.

"Zach, honey, I need to talk to you."

Oh, great, here it comes. Zach knew whatever it was, he wasn't going to like it, so he pretended not to hear her. He unlocked the door and stepped inside.

"Zach."

"I got homework," he said, shrugging off her hand.

"Sweetie, please. This is important."

"Not to me. Can't be to me—'cause you don't care about what's important to *me*."

She made a sad sound that squeezed his gut. He didn't like hurting her, but sometimes he couldn't help himself.

"Actually, this is something that concerns you," the cop said. "But you need to stop feeling sorry for yourself long enough to listen."

Zach swung around in shock. Nobody talked to him like that. Nobody had the right. Before he could decide what to do, his mother stepped between them. "Inside! Right this minute."

Zach knew that tone. She didn't use it often, but it meant he wouldn't get a moment's peace unless he did as she asked. He turned on his heel and strolled into the living room. This wasn't his home. It was just the place he was living *now*. His home was in Oregon.

His mother directed the cop to a chair by the fireplace then she took Zach's hand and led him to the sofa. She sat down beside him but let go of his hand. Thank God. Just what he needed—to look like some kind of mama's boy in front of his mother's ex-boyfriend.

"What?" he asked. Even to his ears, the word sounded like a snarl.

He kept his eyes on his shoes, but he felt the adults look at each other. Something told him this was serious.

He looked up and caught them—the cop scowling, his mom shaking her head. "Just freakin' tell me," he shouted.

"Donnie needs our help. He needs someone to watch after his son. Lucas is a year younger—"

The cop interrupted. "He's in fifth grade."

Like I give a sh—

"I...we..."

"I asked your mother to marry me, Zach. And she's given me a provisional yes, depending on what you and Lucas think of the idea."

Zach heard a funny ringing in his ears that made the words coming from the man's lips sound funny. He thought he caught something about marriage. "Marry my mother?" he said, trying to make sense of it. No way. That couldn't be what he'd heard.

He looked at her. She was pretty. She wasn't real old, like some of the moms he knew, but...

"No." He jumped to his feet without intending to. "You can't."

"Sit down, Zach. Let us explain," she said, reaching out for his hand.

"No. Forget it. If you marry this guy, I'll ask the judge to let me live with my dad. And if he doesn't want me, I'll move to Chicago and live with Moira." *Because if you marry this guy, you won't be around when my real dad comes. We'll never have a chance to be a family.*

He saw the shock and hurt and fear on his mother's face. As he turned to leave, he glanced at the cop. There was a hint of a smile on his lips, as if he'd known exactly what Zach was going to say. As if he *knew* what Zach was thinking. But that couldn't be, because Zach had never told anyone about his secret wish.

He started away, but the cop said in a soft, even voice, "Zach, this would be temporary. If your father comes back and wants her, I won't stand in his way."

His mother made a gasping sound, as if she'd just choked on a cherry pit. "Oh, sweetheart, is that what you're thinking? That Tyler and I..." Her eyes were sad and she blinked hard. "Oh, Zach, no. I'm sorry, but no. That's never going to happen. Your father and I weren't meant to be together like that."

"How do you know?" Zach cried, wishing he could stop himself. "You'd marry this guy, but you won't even give my dad a chance?"

His voice sounded high and squeaky. Sarge lifted his head and looked at him with concern.

"It's not the same, Zach."

The cop sat forward, his elbows on his knees. "Zach, your mother and I are proposing a business arrangement. I could hire her to be my housekeeper and look after Lucas, but there are benefits to marriage. For one, you would both be covered by my health insurance, and secondly, she would have my name and support when she goes to court to discuss your custody. I won't actually be living with you much of the time because I've taken a job that requires me to travel a lot. You and your mother would move into my house and she'd watch after Lucas."

"We'd have to move?"

"Yes. I have a big house at the edge of town. Sarge would feel right at home. My mother lives with us now, but she has to go to Texas to take care of my aunt."

"Zach, we've known from the start Jenny's house was only temporary," his mother said. "If someone buys it, we'd have to look for another place to live, anyway."

She looked down and said in a soft voice, "In all honesty, this isn't just us doing a big favor for Donnie. He'd be helping me, too. Like he said, we wouldn't have to pay rent and we'd have medical insurance."

Zach frowned. He knew they didn't have much money. He always hated it when his mom looked sad because she couldn't buy him the things he wanted. He suddenly regretted having said he'd go to live with his father.

"What about…you know. My dad? What would he think?"

"I don't know, Zach," his mother said. Her tone

was tired—the way she used to sound when she was working so hard in Ashland. Some nights she'd fall asleep with her clothes on. "Ty and I haven't talked. But I'll call my lawyer in the morning and see if we can set up a meeting."

The cop cleared his throat. "Just so you understand, this was my idea, not your mom's. She said the final decision would be yours and Lucas's. He's with his mother at the moment, but I'll talk to him as soon as I can. If you're both against the idea, we'll drop it."

Zach's impulse was to say, "Fine. Drop it." But he didn't. "Can I go to my room?"

His mother closed her eyes and nodded. She sank back on the couch. If the cop weren't here, Zach might have hugged her, but he couldn't look like a baby in front of the man his mother was planning to marry. Zach needed to think about this. Why couldn't his mother be like other moms? Why couldn't their lives be normal?

KRIS BRACED for a door slam, but it didn't happen. She opened her eyes and found Donnie on one knee in front of her. His dark eyes were narrowed with concern.

"That went well, don't you think?" she quipped.

His lips turned up slightly. "I think you're very brave, and you handled that with style and grace."

She rolled her eyes. "Very funny. I just told my son I was prepared to lie to the world in order to get a decent health care plan."

The smile disappeared. "That's not it at all. You offered to help, and I took it to the next level. You want to hang this on someone's shoulders, put the blame where it belongs."

She sat up straight. "Here's the deal. I won't say anything about the plan to anyone until we've worked out the details, but if we decide to do this, I won't lie to my family. I've lied to them for nearly half my life. I won't do it again. If you and I can talk our sons into supporting this decision, I will need to tell my sisters and Ida Jane the real reason we're doing this."

He nodded. "My mother has to know, too."

Sooner or later the truth about their marriage would become common knowledge—this was Gold Creek, after all, but gossip wasn't admissible in court. Was it?

Donnie reached out and took her hand. "I can see your brain churning. Let it go for now. If it doesn't work out, there's always plan B."

"What's that?"

He grinned. "I have no idea."

Something tight loosened in her chest and she could smile again. Donnie had always had that effect on her.

He helped her to her feet. "I'd better go. You look like a stiff breeze could knock you over."

She followed him to the door. He was right. She *was* exhausted. But for some reason, she was loath to let him go.

He didn't turn back, just strode purposefully to his vehicle. "Sweet dreams," he called out.

Hah. She'd be lucky to sleep. Period.

She locked the door, turned off the lights and slowly trudged toward her room. A crack of light visible beneath Zach's door snapped off as she approached. The snub hurt, but she had never let her son go to bed without a kiss and she wasn't about to start.

She opened the door and squinted into the gloom. A thumping—Sarge's tail against the floor—was her only greeting. The hallway light helped her navigate to the bed. Her son was under his covers, his back to her.

Kris stopped to pet Sarge then leaned over and brushed back a lock of hair to kiss Zach's cheek. He smelled of toothpaste, and soap.

"I love you, Zachie." She whispered the nickname she'd called him when he was a toddler. He was supposed to answer, "I love you, too, Mama."

He didn't say a word.

Kristin's eyes filled with tears. Maybe she was completely wrong to be considering Donnie's proposal. Her only allegiance was to her son. Not to an old friend she'd once loved. Maybe she didn't even know what love was—except when it came to her son. And if her actions were going to affect Zach's feelings for her, perhaps she should rethink everything.

Zach moved suddenly, flipping to his back. "Do

you promise you'll at least talk to my father before you do this...thing?''

Kristin nodded. She'd been waiting for Tyler to approach her, but now she was going to have to make the first move. "I don't know exactly where Ty is, but I know someone who should be able to tell us—your grandmother."

Zach's mouth dropped open. "Who?"

"Your father's mother lives in town. I told you that. I haven't contacted her because...well, to be honest, I'm nervous of her. She's disliked me and my sisters for a long time, and I'm not a very brave person, Zach. You know that. A brave person doesn't run away and hide. A brave person deals with her mistakes and takes responsibility for them.''

She saw him flinch. "Not you, love. You were a gift, not a mistake. My mistake was not being honest from the start. One little lie compounded into this huge deception, and now I have to pay for that. My only regret is that you're suffering, too.''

He didn't say anything.

She stroked his hair. "Tomorrow, I'm taking you to meet your grandmother. Perhaps she can tell us how to contact your father. If not, I'll go through my attorney. But I promise I will talk to him, face-to-face, if possible, before I make any decision about marrying Donnie.'' She tilted his chin upward and waited until his gaze met hers. "Okay?''

He nodded then pulled back and turned over.

It wasn't "I love you, too, Mama," but it was a start.

DONNIE TOOK A SIP of coffee. His stomach was a mess thanks to a sleepless night. After leaving Kris, he'd returned to an empty house. His mother was at a going-away party with her Gold Creek Garden Club friends; Lucas had spent the night with Sandy.

Donnie had used the silence of the empty house to reflect on the wisdom of his proposal. He'd asked himself whether or not he was being incredibly selfish.

He thought about Lucas. The boy hadn't been happy for months. Donnie blamed himself for a lot of that. He'd been so busy at work and with his own dreams and plans that he hadn't given Lucas the attention the child craved. And now he was actually considering leaving Lucas with Kristin and taking off. So the answer to the question about whether or not he was being selfish had to be *yes*. Now the question was, what was he going to do about it?

His mother's suitcases were sitting by the door awaiting Sandy's arrival. His ex had volunteered to give Maureen a lift to the Sacramento airport since it was on her way to Redding.

"All packed?" he asked when his mother dashed into the room—the fifth time in five minutes. "Are you sure you don't need my help?"

She looked a little scattered but excited, too. Donnie detected a glow in her eyes that had been missing for a long time. "No, I'm fine. Just a few last-minute things. I'm taking the bare minimum with me, but I don't want to forget anything important.

"You'll ship the rest to me next week, right?" She'd insisted on boxing up all her belongings to make room for the nanny-slash-housekeeper. The big stuff was in his garage.

"A live-in nanny's going to need her own space," Maureen had insisted when they first discussed the possibility of his hiring someone. "My quarters are perfect—separate bath, microwave, minifridge, private entrance, carport. Whoever you hire ought to love it."

Donnie had been picturing someone like the Robin Williams character, Mrs. Doubtfire, at the time. Now he tried to imagine what it would be like having Kristin living twenty feet away.

"Oh," Maureen said, snapping her fingers, "my extra pair of glasses. I'd better have them with me." She spun on one heel and disappeared down the hallway.

Donnie took another sip of coffee. *Should I tell her about Kristin or not?* Last night, as he'd contemplated the magnitude of his proposal, he'd felt like an idiot. He'd talked to Kristin twice in ten years, then out popped a marriage proposal. It was ridiculous. *He* was ridiculous. He'd caught a glimpse of something good—two friends helping each other out—and he'd plunged in.

"When does your ad come out in the paper?"

Maureen asked when she returned. She pulled out a stool at the counter where Donnie was sitting, but didn't sit down.

Donnie reached for the coffeepot and freshened the cup in front of him. Something told him not to tell Maureen anything yet. Why burden her with his problems? She had enough on her mind.

"Wednesday," he said. *Unless I cancel it.* "Sandy's taking Lucas shopping on their way back from Redding. I thought I'd paint your room this weekend."

"And shampoo the carpet," she added sternly. "And put up the new blinds I bought on sale last month. You still haven't hung them."

Donnie faked a petulant sigh. "Nag, nag, nag." He gave her a hug to prove he was teasing.

She briefly rested her head against his shoulder then said, "I know I sound like a broken record, but you need a wife. Then I wouldn't be the one having to remind you of what needs doing."

He let her go and turned slightly. It was the perfect opening. Maybe he should test out his proposal on her. "Actually, Mom, I've—"

Before he could complete the thought, the front door opened and his son shuffled in, a lumpy backpack slung over one shoulder.

"Good morning, Lucas. Is your mother outside?"

The boy nodded. "I forgot my Yu-Gi-Oh! cards," he mumbled, walking to the side-by-side refrigerator. He pulled out a quart of chocolate milk and swished the carton twice then popped off the plastic cap and guzzled the liquid. The pink lid bounced on the floor like a top before rolling to a stop near the stove. When he was done, Lucas set the empty container on the counter and turned to walk away.

Donnie and his mother exchanged a look. "Son," Donnie said, his tone controlled. "Please put that into the garbage."

The boy turned slowly. He let out a long sigh then picked up the container and dropped it in the trash compactor. Donnie nodded toward the lid. Lucas shook his mop of unnaturally black locks before stooping to pick up the object. He shoved it in his pocket and left the room.

Maureen sipped her coffee then said, "I hope the housekeeper you hire is up to the challenge."

Donnie knew exactly what his mother meant. While he didn't doubt Maureen's devotion to her grandson for a minute, Donnie knew Lucas was a difficult child, and he wasn't sure anyone—even a mother as patient and loving as Kristin—could handle him.

As if reading the doubt that attacked him, Maureen put a hand on his shoulder. "You're a good father, Donnie. I don't know any single father who could have done better."

A horn sounded.

"Better hustle, Lucas," Donnie called out.

He put his arm around his mother's shoulders and hugged her against him.

Maureen tilted her head and looked at him. Her ever-sharp antenna must have picked up something, because she said, "Ida Jane told me you visited the antique shop. I assume you went to see Kristin."

Donnie kissed her cheek. "I never could keep much from you. I did see Kristin. We're adults, Mom. She's a devoted mother and a good businesswoman. There's even a chance she might help me out with Lucas."

His mother stiffened. "Like be your housekeeper?"

"We're still working out the details."

Her lips compressed and a line of worry crossed her forehead, but Donnie didn't give her time to fret. "It's all just speculation at the moment. I wasn't going to tell you until it was settled. Put it out of your mind. My ad comes out Wednesday, and I'll get this figured out. You are going to fly away and let me worry about what happens here, right?"

It took a few seconds for her to smile again, but she did. She hugged him fiercely then whispered, "If I survive the drive to the airport with Sandy, the rest—even Bobbie's transplant—ought to be a piece of cake."

He was still chuckling when the door opened and his ex-wife breezed in without knocking. "Hellooo," she called in a contrived English accent. "Lucas, sweetie—"

For some reason, the customary prick of anguish, stemming, Donnie figured, from his deep-seated sense of failure, failed to materialize. Usually being around Sandy left him feeling melancholy and aching for what could have been.

Instead of fretting about the past, he smiled at his ex-wife. "Good morning, Sandy. Coffee?"

She waved a glittery hand in dismissal. "No thanks. I'd love to stay and chat, but you never know about traffic and we don't want Maureen to miss her plane."

Donnie carried his mother's luggage to the car, being careful to lift and bend properly. He grappled Lucas into an awkward hug before the boy could climb into the back seat. Although Maureen had volunteered to sit in the back, Sandy had vetoed the suggestion, saying, "Lucas will have his nose buried in some game by the time we hit the highway. I want someone to talk to."

It was on the tip of Donnie's tongue to point out that their son would benefit from Sandy making an effort to talk to him, but he caught his mother's warning look. She was right. He couldn't change Sandy, any more than he could change the past.

After one last tearful hug from his mother, Donnie watched as Sandy reversed. Her window slithered down and she stopped to tell him, "I'll bring Lucas home Monday night. You have my cell if you need to reach us."

Donnie plastered a smile on his lips and waved. He had some serious soul-searching to do. Then he had to make a decision about what would be best for his son.

CHAPTER FIVE

"I DON'T KNOW what kind of car Gloria drives, so I can't tell if she's here or not," Kristin told Zach Saturday morning as they pulled into a parking place in front of the *Gold Creek Ledger*.

Their excursion had been delayed because Lillian Carswell, retired librarian and one of Ida Jane's closest friends, had arrived late for her massage. The dear woman's profuse apology had tacked another ten minutes on the clock, but Kristin still gave her a full hour as scheduled.

"You have the hands of an angel," Lillian told her as she paid her bill. "I've passed out your cards to all my friends, but they're foolish tightwads. I can't get it through their heads that forty dollars' worth of prevention could avoid thousands of dollars in doctor bills."

Kristin wished all her clients were so appreciative of her work. Most exclaimed about how good they felt once the massage was over, but only a committed few scheduled follow-up visits. So, Kris went out of her way to keep good clients—like Lillian—happy. Even if it meant ignoring Zach, who'd spent the whole time lurking on the bordello's porch like a gargoyle.

Kristin hadn't heard from Donnie. And in the light of day, she felt a little foolish about accepting his proposal. People shouldn't get married for such lame excuses as financial security and health insurance. She planned to tell him that once she tracked down her son's grandmother and talked to Tyler.

Perhaps she was overreacting. Her assumption that Tyler Harrison posed a threat to her custody of Zach was based on fear and guilt. Kris knew how she'd react if their situations were reversed. But why assume the worst? Maybe Ty had grown up and wouldn't be vindictive.

"Do you want to wait here or come with me?" she asked her son, who was slumped in the passenger seat as if afraid to be seen with her.

"Wait."

The monosyllabic kid had returned.

Kristin got out of the car and walked toward the bungalow that housed her brother-in-law's newspaper. Jonathan Newhall had bought the *Gold Creek Ledger,* lock, stock and building, shortly after the murder charges against him were dropped. The poor man had ended up at Sam's ranch suffering from amnesia, then three months later had found himself charged with the murder of the old miner, Lars Gunderson, who'd befriended him and who'd turned out to be his uncle. Kris's sister Andi had never given up believing in Jonathan. Now the two were expecting a baby in December.

Kristin had almost reached the recently revamped entrance when the door opened and Jonathan stepped out. He blinked against the midday brightness and pulled up short. "Kristin," he exclaimed. "What's up? Need a new ad?"

She hadn't planned on discussing her true objective with anyone. She stumbled around for an excuse before deciding she had nothing to hide by admitting the truth. "Um, no, not yet. Gotta make some money before I can spend it, you know." She tried to peer past him, but a set of gingham curtains blocked the view. "Actually, I was looking for Gloria."

Jonathan peered over her shoulder toward the car. A keenly intelligent man, he obviously made his own deduction. "She doesn't work weekends. You might catch her at home, but I heard her mention attending the state fair." He pulled a cell phone from his pocket. "You could call first."

Kristin swallowed. "Okay."

He punched in a two-digit code then handed her the tiny, lightweight object. "I'll go say hello to my nephew while you talk," he said, walking away.

Kristin's gaze followed him. Jonathan was a handsome man, fit and smart. He loved Andi with the devotion of a newlywed, yet their relationship—the part Kristin saw—was filled with good-natured teasing on both sides and a fundamental respect Kris envied. Kris was thrilled that Andi had found her soul mate. *Why can't I be as lucky as my sisters?*

"Hello?" a woman's voice said.

Kristin pictured the person at the other end of the line. Late sixties. Petite, with elegantly coiffed silver-blond hair. Always immaculately dressed in suits, hose and heels. Kristin didn't believe she'd ever seen Gloria out of uniform, so to speak. "Hello, Gloria, this is Kristin Sullivan."

There was a long pause before the woman answered. "I'm surprised to hear from you. What do you want?"

"I thought you might like to meet your grandson. We're at the *Ledger,* but obviously you're not here today."

Well, duh, as Zach would say.

The second pause was even longer than the first. "You've been back for several weeks. Why now?" Gloria asked. *Was that a tremor in her voice?*

"I've been waiting to get something resolved through the courts," Kris said, which was partly true. "But, it's taking so long I decided it was silly for you and Zach to live in the same town and not know each other."

Gloria made a funny sound, but when she spoke, her tone was all business. "I need to check with Tyler first. At what number may I reach you?"

So formal. Kristin looked at her son, who'd gotten out of the car and was chatting with Jonathan. Zach gravitated toward men like flowers to the sun. He needed a father or a father figure in his life.

Enough of this foolishness, she decided. "You can't. My cell phone is dead," she lied. "How 'bout we just drive out? If your son decides you can't meet your grandson, then we'll leave. See you in about fifteen.'' She pressed the End button and marched to her car.

''Thanks,'' she said, handing Jonathan his phone.

''That went well, I take it,'' he said, grinning.

''As well as can be expected. That woman has always been a—'' Kris stopped herself when she saw her son look at her. ''Never mind,'' she said. ''I'm just glad you've taken over the paper, Jon.''

She saw the look Zach and Jonathan exchanged and closed her eyes, regretting her comment. Jonathan patted her shoulder. ''Don't feel badly, Kris. I've had at least twenty people tell me the same thing. Gloria used to scare the pants off people— then write about their indecent exposure.'' His infectious chuckle made Kristin laugh, too.

''She really had it in for the Sullivan girls,'' Kris said once Zach was out of earshot. ''Not that I blame her for hating me, I guess. But my sisters shouldn't have been made to suffer for my crime.''

Jonathan lowered his voice. ''You shouldn't blame yourself either. Crimes of passion are the most defensible. We all have our moments.''

She smiled her gratitude and got in the car. Jonathan was a very nice man; her sister was lucky. *Donnie is a nice man, too. And just as handsome as Jonathan.*

She pushed the thought from her mind. ''Are you okay, honey?'' she asked Zach.

He didn't speak until they turned onto Stockton

Hill Road. Then, keeping his face toward the window, he asked, ''Why isn't her last name Harrison?''

Kristin turned onto the street leading to an enclave of homes sitting on five- and ten-acre parcels. ''Your grandmother was a widow when she married Mr. Hughes. He's dead now, too. Jenny said he had a heart attack a few years ago. Tyler's father, Arthur Harrison, was the son of the local banker. The Harrisons were very well off by Gold Creek standards. They had the first swimming pool in town.

''But Ty's father made some bad investments and wound up losing the bank—and a lot of other people's money. He…uh, died when Ty was about your age. Maybe a little older.''

Kristin felt ashamed that the details of Tyler's father's suicide were fuzzy. She'd probably been focused on making the cheerleading squad or worrying about whether or not Donnie Grimaldo liked her.

''That sucks,'' Zach said, looking out the window as the car slowed to maneuver around a curve.

''I think it was very hard on your father. I didn't know him well, but I seem to recall he had a lot of friends before that happened. Then he just sort of disappeared into the background. I remember him wearing black all the time. And he stopped participating in school functions. He worked at the grocery store part-time and bought himself a Yamaha motorcycle when he turned sixteen.''

Catching a glimmer of interest in her son's eye,

she scolded, "Don't even think about it. No way, José."

His lips twitched, but he didn't smile. "What happened then?"

"Gloria's brother owned the newspaper, and she went to work for him. That guy was a real weirdo. I don't think anybody liked him, and the paper was a joke. But it was the only game in town so people bought it. She started writing a gossip column called 'Glory's World,' and people read it to find out what everybody else was doing."

"Did she write about what happened with you and my dad?"

"Here we are," she said, ducking the question.

Zach looked at her. "If you and my dad had gotten married, would you be divorced by now?"

Kris swallowed. "Probably. We barely knew each other, sweetheart. We were drawn together for reasons that seemed important at the time." She looked at him and smiled. "But I don't know what we'd still have in common, except you."

He didn't say anything. She glanced out the corner of her eye and saw him staring straight ahead. A shiver of premonition passed through her.

She followed his gaze. There, beside Gloria, stood a tall, dark-haired man that could only be Tyler Harrison.

ZACH GRABBED the steering wheel when his mother's hands fell limp at her sides. She'd gone white when she spotted the man standing on the porch. So Zach didn't have to work too hard to figure out who he was.

My dad.

Tall, thin, dark hair. He couldn't see the resemblance his aunts had made such a big deal about. Maybe the guy's eyes were like his. And the nose.

So what? He didn't look rich. Or powerful. In fact, he looked kinda sickly.

"Well, let's go meet your father," his mother said, regaining control. She parked the car then reached across the seat to squeeze Zach's hand.

He knew he had to move, but he was scared. Real scared. What if the guy didn't like him?

When his mother first told Zach the news that his father was alive and didn't know he had a son, he'd been furious with her. But now Zach was going to protect her, even if he was still mad at her. Especially for dragging him to Gold Creek. She might have screwed things up for them, but she was still his mom.

When she opened her car door, Zach opened his. They approached the house—a two-story box with white columns like some mansion from an old movie. Everything in the garden looked neat and tidy.

Sarge would hate it here, Zach thought, looking around.

"Kristin," the man said. His voice was strong. Like he was used to bossing people around.

"Hello, Tyler. This is a surprise, but I'm glad you're here. It's time you met Zach."

His mother's fingers dug into his arm, but Zach didn't flinch. He lifted his gaze and immediately became engaged in some kind of staring contest with the man who was his father.

"Actually, Kristin," the man replied, never breaking eye contact with Zach, "the time for that was eleven years ago."

Zach didn't like the man's attitude. He bristled defensively.

His mother jostled his arm, so he'd look at her. "Zachie, I love you so much, but you don't have to fight my battles," she said softly.

Then she looked at the man on the porch. "Is this how you want it, Tyler? A battle? Isn't it possible we both made mistakes?" she asked. "Can't we let the past go and move on?"

The man whispered something to his mother, who looked at Zach briefly, then disappeared inside. Zach felt his mother brace her shoulders as Tyler walked toward them.

"No, Kristin, we aren't going to let bygones be bygones. We're going to court. My lawyer has advised me to sue for full custody. According to him, there's not a court in this land that won't take one look at the evidence and declare you an unfit mother."

Zach jumped forward, his arm out like they taught him in football. "You're wrong. She's a good mother."

To Zach's surprise, Kristin slipped past him and faced Zach's father. "You're both right. I am a good mother. I've always tried my best, and Zach knows how much I love him—even though the past few months have been tough.

"But you're right, too, Tyler. I was selfish. And scared that you'd try to take him away from me."

Tyler seemed surprised by her candor, but his eyes narrowed suspiciously and he asked, "Does that mean you're abdicating your parental rights? You're giving him to me?"

The thought made Zach shiver. He wished now that he'd brought Sarge along. What if this guy took him away? What if—

"No, Tyler, I'm not giving up anything. I'm offering to share our son with you. Late, yes? But it's not too late. He's the most incredible child you'll ever know. And if you fight me for him, you might win in court, but you'll lose a whole lot more."

Zach could tell her words affected his father. Zach was so proud of her he almost smiled, but when she turned to look at him, he saw her tears, and it made him sad.

She hugged him so hard his ribs hurt, then she stepped away. She made a sniffling sound as she dug in her purse for something. A second later she passed him her cell phone. "Do what you have to do, Tyler. I brought Zach here this afternoon to meet your mother. He can call me at the bordello when he's ready to come home."

She took Zach's chin between her thumb and fingers and made him look into her eyes. The tears were there, but she looked determined, too. She wanted to do the right thing. She was brave. He could be brave, too. For her sake.

DONNIE PROPPED one booted foot on the bottom rung of the wire fence and rested his elbows on the painted one-inch pipe that made up the horizontal railing. About twenty feet beyond, in the middle of the arena a cowboy worked a spirited young gelding, putting the animal through its paces.

The late-afternoon sun soaked into Donnie's shoulders, melting some of his tension. When he couldn't find Kristin, he'd come to the Rocking M. No Kris, but maybe Sam would have an answer for Donnie's dilemma.

"I'm worried about you, my friend," Sam said. "Something's troubling you. How can I help?"

"How much beer you got?" Donnie joked. They both knew Donnie had given up drinking years ago. A quick temper was only aggravated by alcohol, and Donnie had learned a long time ago that he wasn't a *happy* drunk.

Sam's chuckle was just the therapy Donnie needed. "How 'bout a fresh-squeezed lemonade? Greta just made a batch."

Once Sam had disappeared into the two-story cedar log home opposite the arena, Donnie weighed the benefit of spilling his guts to his friend. He didn't doubt Sam's discretion, but Donnie was hesitant to mention the proposal until he'd talked to Kristin.

If the whole thing blew up in his face, the fewer people who knew about it the better.

The twenty-something cowboy in the arena—apparently sensing an audience—looked over his shoulder. He acknowledged Donnie's presence with a cocky grin and tip of the hat. Donnie felt a small jolt of envy. He'd almost forgotten what it was like to work at a job you loved.

"Donnie," a woman's voice called.

He turned to greet Jenny O'Neal. It still amazed him how different the Sullivan triplets were from each other in looks. Jenny was the tallest and carried herself with willowy grace. Her long hair fluttered in the wind. Dressed in denim jeans, a neatly pressed blouse and sneakers, she held hands with two toddlers—one in boots, diapers and a T-shirt asking, What's a Guy Gotta Do To Get a Horse Around Here?; the other in patent-leather shoes and a ruffled pinafore.

Donnie gave Jenny a peck on the cheek before squatting to greet the children. "Hi, guys, how are you today?"

A rush of one-year-old babble washed over him, making him smile. Lara offered him the rag doll she carried, then snatched it back before burying her face against her mother's leg. Tucker dropped to the ground butt first.

"How's it going?" Jenny kept her eyes on her son. "Did Maureen get off?"

"Yes. Early. Sandy dropped her at the airport."

Jenny's look of mock horror made him laugh.

"So, what are you doing out here? Does it have to do with my sister?"

Was she a mind reader?

"Andi said Kristin gave you a massage after work yesterday."

Gold Creek—where gossip flies at the speed of sound.

Donnie shifted slightly. "No. We just talked." His response sounded innocent enough to his ears, but Jenny suddenly blinked, eyes wide. "Oh my God. You and Kris? Again?"

He tried to protest, but a movement near the ground caught her attention, and she suddenly swooped down and snatched up her son. "Tucker, what did you just put in your mouth? Show Mommy. Open up, sweetheart."

The little boy's mouth was ringed with dirt. He opened wide and a beetle scrambled off his tongue and dropped to the ground. Jenny let out a horrified squeal. "Water," she shouted.

"Will lemonade do?" an amused voice said from behind them.

Jenny swiped a plastic tumbler from the tray her husband carried. "Bugs. Yech. We don't eat bugs, Tucker. You know that." The child resisted her efforts to clean his mouth and tongue, finally wailing in distress.

Donnie took a slug of the tart drink Sam offered then returned the glass to the tray, which Sam had set on the tailgate of a nearby truck. "Let Uncle Donnie hold him."

The child was heavier than he looked and twice as squirmy, but he calmed down after Donnie set him on his shoulders. Tucker's gleeful cry made his sister look up and demand similar treatment.

"Now see what you've started," Sam said, picking up his daughter.

Although most people believed Sam had adopted the twins and married Josh's widow to keep the family intact, Josh had told Donnie the truth. Sam was the twin's biological father. He'd donated sperm when Josh discovered he was infertile. Donnie had kept the information to himself. These four were a family, period. That was all the world needed to know.

In a way, that was how he viewed his proposal to Kristin. What they did was *their* business, right? But he knew it wasn't that simple.

A birdlike twitter made Jenny reach for the cell phone sticking out of her hip pocket. "I brought this along in case Ida Jane needed me. I hope everything's okay," she said before pushing the talk button.

"Hello?"

She nodded and smiled, letting her husband know it wasn't anything serious. "Hi, Kris. What's new?"

Donnie automatically took a step closer to eavesdrop on Jenny's conversation.

"Right now? Let me ask." She covered the phone and looked at her husband. "Kris is calling a family meeting. She says it's important. Can you come with me?''

Sam looked at Donnie, who said, "Don't worry about me."

"Tell her we'll be right there. Did she say what it's about?" Sam asked.

Jenny shook her head. "No, but I'm thinking Tyler. Do you want details?"

Yes.

"No. We'll find out soon enough."

Jenny conveyed Sam's words then listened for a minute. Her eyebrow shot up, and she looked at Donnie. "Actually, he's right here." Both friends eyed him intently. "No, I'm not kidding. I'm looking at him as I speak. He has Tucker on his shoulders."

Donnie looked up and Tucker grabbed his nose. One finger hooked a nostril, making Donnie yelp.

"Okay, I'll tell him. Gotta go before the poor man loses his nose. See you soon."

Donnie bent over so Tucker's mother could grab him. "Tell me what?" He straightened with care, heeding Kristin's advice to avoid back strain.

"To come with us. She wants you there, too." She stared hard at him. "Donnie, you're blushing. What's all this about?"

Jenny obviously expected an explanation. He lifted his shoulders and said, "Well, it might have something to do with the fact that I asked her to marry me."

"You what?" Sam sputtered, choking on his lemonade.

"You're kidding," Jenny exclaimed. A second later she was hugging him—squishing Tucker between them. "It's about time."

"THANK HEAVENS for cell phones," Kristin told Ida Jane after hanging up on Jonathan.

"Why are they all coming again, dear?" Ida Jane asked, watching as Kris set out plates and silverware. "Is it Thanksgiving already?"

Kristin had picked up a bucket of take-out chicken and a couple of side dishes, because feeding people helped her feel in control of a situation. Her cousins always knew when Kris had had a bad day because they'd come home to a complete meal.

"Nope. Just a late-afternoon picnic. Without the ants and meat bees."

Ida fussed with the arrangement of marigolds Kris had plucked from the flower bed. "I remember a picnic at Lake Tullock, and the bees were so bad one of you girls got bitten on the tongue. Andi, I think. I took a couple of wieners from the package and set them out on a rock a few feet away so the bees would leave us alone. Remember that?"

"Vaguely. Was that the time we water-skied with some friend of yours? I can picture his boat, but I can't remember his name."

"Horace Shelton," Ida said with confidence. At times her distant memory was so clear, it shocked her nieces. "He was sweet on me for the longest time."

Kristin smiled. She slowed her frantic pace and looked at her great-aunt. "How come you didn't marry him, Auntie? He was a nice man as I recall. Was it because of us?"

"In a way," Ida Jane said. "He *was* a nice man, just not the right man." Kristin had heard the story of Ida Jane's true love—a man who'd fallen in love with her sister, Suzy, then been killed in the war.

Kristin took Ida's thin, withered hand. "But it couldn't have been easy raising us alone. If you'd married Horace…"

Ida squeezed Kristin's hand. "He was a friend, dear. I didn't love him. Love is the only reason to get married."

Her aunt's words—innocent as they were—nearly made Kris groan aloud. What could she possibly have been thinking when she'd agreed to marry Donnie?

Ida looked around. "Who's coming, again?"

Kristin kissed her aunt's forehead then repeated the list. Andi was less patient with Ida's memory problems, but Kristin had been through this effect of aging with her uncle's mother so she knew what to expect.

A few minutes later, the first of Kristin's guests arrived—Jonathan.

"Hi," he said, setting his briefcase on a stool in the adjoining mudroom. "Where's Andi?"

"Upstairs lying down. She had a rough day.

Computer problems. I told her she could skip this if she wanted, but she said she'd be here no matter what.''

Jonathan snatched a bun from the basket and headed toward the door. "I'll check on her, then be right back. For some reason, I feel like I'm to blame. If I hadn't lent you—"

Kristin grinned ruefully. "Letting me use your cell phone doesn't obligate you, Jon. I would have gone to Gloria's anyway."

"Gloria?" Ida Jane asked. "Is she coming? I can't stand that woman. She's had it in for this family ever since Art Harrison made eyes at Suzy one Christmas."

Kristin almost dropped the bowl of coleslaw she'd been carrying to the table. "I beg your pardon? Gloria's hubby had the hots for Grandma Suzy?"

Ida waved away the suggestion. "My sister attracted men like the color red draws hummingbirds. Art and Suzy were *socializing* one Christmas Eve. Nothing happened, but Gloria got her knickers in a knot."

Kristin shook her head. Gold Creek was a labyrinth of old intrigues and secret agendas. She lowered the flame beneath the kettle of beans then returned to sit down with Ida Jane. "Ida, can you remember what happened to Mr. Harrison? His suicide?"

"He invested big in a housing development near the lake—and used other people's money to do it.

The lots didn't sell, and the bank investigators were coming for him. He probably would have gone to jail. The boy found him, I believe."

Kristin shuddered. There was so much she didn't know about her son's father, and now they were poised for battle. She'd gone to his mother's with an olive branch only to have it snapped in two by a man who looked every bit as powerful and unforgiving as she'd feared he might be.

The back door opened again and three people entered. Kristin's gaze never made it past the first in line. Donnie. His broad shoulders beckoned like a haven, but she walked to the stove instead. *This is my problem and I can handle it. I'm not going to fall apart.*

Jenny's chatter and Sam's deep voice blended into the background when Donnie appeared at her side and asked softly, "Are you okay?"

"A little freaked-out, but I'll survive. I saw Tyler. And now that I know where I stand, I need to make plans."

He nodded. "I kinda figured that was the case. What can I do?"

She handed him a pot holder. "Please take the beans to the table. I'll call Andi and Jonathan."

"We're here," her sister said from the doorway.

Jonathan guided his wife to a chair then went to the refrigerator and filled two glasses of milk. "Milk, anyone?"

"Water for us," Jenny replied from the sink.

"Something stronger, Kris?" Donnie asked. "Iced tea?"

"Yes, please. The pitcher's on the table."

She piled the chicken, which she'd kept warming in the oven, on a platter and carried it to the table. Donnie pulled out a chair beside him. Kris felt her family watching as she sat down.

She cleared her throat. "Thanks for coming on such short notice. Jen, who's watching the twins?"

"Sam's mom is visiting for a few days," Jenny said, folding a napkin in her lap. "Diane's turned into quite the loving grandmother."

The word made Kristin shudder as she pictured Gloria's chilly greeting. *Nothing grandmotherly about that woman.*

"Besides," Jenny added as she passed the rolls, "this sounds like adult talk. I notice your son isn't here."

Kristin's throat closed and she said softly, "That's because he's with his father."

Her sisters gave identical gasps of surprise. The men exchanged looks. Donnie shifted his chair a little closer to hers.

"It's about time, right? Eleven years. I took Zach to meet his grandmother, and Tyler was there. What could I do—run and hide? Been there, done that."

Andi waved her fork. "Okay. We've engaged the enemy. Now, we need strategy, people."

Kristin smiled. Andi had served in the U.S. Marines and she reverted to the old lingo every once in a while.

Jenny spoke before Kristin could reply. "Do we know for sure that Ty is the enemy? What did he say, Kris? Is there going to be a court battle or will he work out some kind of shared custody with you?"

Kristin took a sip from her glass. "No, Jen, I don't think he's amenable to compromise. He made it quite clear that he will do whatever it takes to be named Zach's custodial parent."

Sam sighed. "Is that what Zach wants? A judge will be the one to decide, and there's no judge around here who would take a child away from his mother without a legitimate reason. What Kristin did was wrong, but she was eighteen. We've all made mistakes at that age."

Something in his tone and the look he gave his wife made Kristin wonder if there was more to the story, but Andi diverted her attention. "I don't know why we're acting like a bunch of cowering sissies. So she raised Zach alone. She did a damn good job, and she had no reason to believe Ty was anything more than a hoodlum."

"And mental instability runs in the family," Ida added.

Kris's attorney had mentioned the possibility of raising this defense as well, given Arthur Harrison's suicide. "And we all remember what a temper Ty had," Jenny said. "Look what happened with Donnie."

All eyes turned to the man beside her. Donnie touched his napkin to his lips, even though Kris hadn't seen him eat a bite. "That wasn't the finest hour for either of us. But I don't think there's anything on his record."

Jonathan said, "I realize I'm coming into this saga late, but didn't Harrison leave town before graduation? And he never made any attempt to reach Kris."

Donnie looked at her, an apology in his eyes. "A moot point, I'm afraid. By not letting him know about Zach, Kristin violated Tyler's rights. If he finds a sympathetic judge—"

"Which is why I need your advice," Kristin interrupted, looking at each member of her family. "Last night, Donnie and I discussed an option that could be beneficial to us both. But it's a bit extreme, and I'm open to other suggestions."

Donnie touched her sleeve. "Kris, can we talk in private?"

His proximity made butterflies dance around the few bites she'd managed to swallow. It really would make things simpler if she wasn't so darn attracted to him.

"Now?"

He nodded.

"Come on, you guys," Andi said testily. "I get my fill of little secret conclaves at the Chamber of Commerce. Just tell us what's going on."

Donnie pushed his plate aside and set his elbows on the table. When he moved, Kris caught the scent of outdoors. His cheeks were tinged with color, his hair wind-combed. He reminded her of the boy she'd loved with all her heart.

He linked his fingers and hunched forward slightly. "Last winter I applied for a job as a Federal Air Marshal. I didn't tell anyone—except Sam, who was one of my character references—because I honestly didn't think I stood a chance. But I just found out that I've been accepted."

Jonathan let out an appreciative sound. "Good for you, man. Congratulations."

"Thank you. Unfortunately, I'm not going to be able to accept it."

"What?" Kristin asked. She couldn't believe what she was hearing.

"When I applied for the job, Lucas was going to be living with Sandy in Los Angeles. Her plans changed, and now he's staying with me. Last night, when Kristin and I talked, I thought there was a chance I could still pull this off if I found someone I trust to live in my home and care for my son." He looked around the table. "Obviously that person is Kris. We discussed the possibility of her moving in with me." Kris heard Andi's little noise of surprise. "But because of her situation with Tyler's possible custody suit, I decided it would be better for her reputation if we got married."

Jenny and Sam said nothing, which led Kristin to conclude that Donnie must have already broken the news to them, but Andi leaped to her feet. "Are you nuts? That's a horrible reason to get married.

No offense, Donnie, but I'd shoot you if you'd have asked me.''

Before Kris could respond, Donnie cleared his throat and said, ''It's a moot point, Andi, because it's not going to happen.''

Kris sat back, stunned. ''What do you mean? You're unproposing now?''

''I'm sorry, Kris. I tried to reach you. I ran by the bordello, and when I didn't see your car there, I drove to the ranch.''

''They've been sweet on each other since they were kids,'' Ida Jane said, obviously not noticing the tension surrounding her.

Jenny who was sitting beside their aunt patted her shoulder and said, ''Ida, dear, that was history. They're just friends, now.''

Kris felt her sisters' stares, but she was focused on Donnie. ''You should have told me. If you didn't want to marry me—''

He made an off-hand gesture. ''I was so greedy. I wanted it all. But last night, after I left you, I sat in Lucas's room and tried to picture this through his eyes. His mother is in Africa. He's lost his chance to attend a fancy school in L.A. And his father not only abandons him for a job flying around in airplanes, but leaves him home with a stepmother he doesn't know.''

Andi grunted. ''When you put it that way, it sounds like a Grimm's fairy-tale.''

''Granted Lucas would have the finest care available—a loving mother with eleven years' experience, but he'd still feel abandoned. I know. My dad died when I was Lucas's age, and I felt the same way.''

Kristin's momentary disappointment fled. She could recall long talks with Donnie on this very subject. How strange, she thought, that it had taken him so long to spot the similarity in his and Lucas's situation.

''I'm sorry, Kris. I should have done more thinking before I opened my mouth. As much as it kills me to say this, I can't leave.''

Kristin felt a powerful emotion take hold of her. Compassion, regret, respect. She couldn't define it, but it made her want to throw herself into his arms and never let go.

''Why'd you apply for that job in the first place?'' Andi asked. ''I thought you liked it here.''

''I did. I do. Although working under a man like Magnus…'' He didn't say more, but Kris saw the look he exchanged with Sam.

Jonathan sat forward, his expression serious. ''So, if I understand this correctly, Donnie, you asked Kristin to marry you and be your housekeeper while you went off to be an air marshal. And, Kris, you agreed to this because…help me out here, I'm a little foggy on your motivation.''

''Partly to strengthen my position when I go to court. Partly to prove that I'm here to stay. I know you all think this is just another temporary stop, but you're wrong. I went away because I didn't feel as though I belonged here anymore, but Gold Creek is home. Donnie offered to let me buy his house once he got settled in his job.''

Andi snickered. ''A house is nice, but the whole thing sounds a little too cold to me. Did this gig include sex?''

''Andrea,'' Jenny scolded.

Sam coughed. ''I'd like to say something. I know this is strictly between the two of you, but I've been privy to some of what Donnie has been experiencing at the sheriff's office. Our current sheriff's dealings are self-serving at the least and damaging to the town. When Josh was alive, we approached Donnie about running for the office.'' He sighed. ''Obviously, a lot has changed since then, but, now, I think it's clear what has to happen.''

Kristin checked each person's face to see if she was the only one who didn't know what he was talking about. Donnie wouldn't meet her gaze. When she could stand it no longer, she asked, ''What?''

''Donnie needs to marry you and run for office.''

CHAPTER SIX

BY THE TIME Donnie walked Kristin to her door, it was almost eight. They'd spent the entire evening at the bordello discussing the pros and cons of his bid for sheriff. Jonathan and Andi were ready to sign on as campaign managers, Jenny and Sam had left a check to open a ''war chest.'' No one seemed to have any doubt that Donnie and Kris would ''get with the program,'' as Andi put it.

Donnie was tired—both physically and emotionally—but he'd followed Kristin in his car so they could talk alone. ''When do you expect Zach home?'' he asked as she unlocked the door.

''I don't know. I was hoping he would call. You don't think Ty would...''

Donnie touched her arm. ''Don't worry. Tyler's too high-profile to try to abduct Zach.''

''It happens. You hear about parental kidnappings all the time.'' Her voice broke.

''Tyler's got too much at stake. He won't go into hiding.''

They were close enough that he heard her exhalation. He knew she believed him. Trusted him. ''According to the newspaper articles,'' he added,

"Tyler has a lot of money tied up in Gold Creek at the moment. I can't picture him just leaving."

She opened the door and started inside. "Do you want anything to drink?" she asked, walking to the kitchen.

"No, thanks. I'm fine."

She returned a second later, a glass of water in hand. "I read in the *Ledger* that Tyler's company is planning to build a shopping mall. That will surely kill the downtown merchants. Do you know anything about it?"

Donnie had been hearing rumors for months. In fact, even before Josh died there'd been the hint that developers had their sights set on Gold Creek. "There's been talk that Meridian, Ty's company, is working with Cal-Trans," he said, using the colloquial name for the California Highway Department.

"To do what?"

He wasn't anxious to say. "It's probably rumor," he said, sitting down on the couch. "Even Andi hasn't been able to pin down any specifics, and you know how tenacious your sister can be."

She followed him, kneeling on the cushion adjacent to him. "Tell me what you know. I hate feeling out of the loop. And Andi's right. If we're going to fight, we need to understand how the enemy thinks."

Donnie looked around. They were alone. On a couch. He remembered a time when they'd have been in each other's arms with only one thing on their minds, given an opportunity like this.

"Donnie."

He smiled apologetically. "Sorry. Woolgathering. I honestly don't know much. But I did overhear some county planners who were in the office the other day talking about the number of traffic accidents that have taken place over the years at the intersection of Main Street and the highway.

"I got the impression that with those kinds of numbers, Cal-Trans might be able to procure funds to assist in rerouting through-traffic around town. Like they've done in Sonora."

She sat back sharply. "Gold Creek isn't as quaint and tourist-attractive as Sonora. A bypass would kill the downtown businesses. The Old Bordello Antique Shop and Coffee Parlor gets at least half its income from drop-in traffic."

Donnie made an offhand gesture. "I wouldn't get too excited about it. The plan has been on the books for years and never been implemented. I remember seeing a mock-up of the proposed bypass at the sheriff's office back when we were in high school."

"Tyler worked with you one summer, didn't he?" she asked. "The judge ordered him to because he'd ridden his motorcycle through the hallway at school and crashed into the big display case by the principal's office, remember?"

Donnie remembered that event all too clearly. He'd been the one who'd gotten stuck baby-sitting the stupid jerk that entire summer when the judge placed him on Donnie's Search and Rescue team. "You're right. He did."

"Maybe that's where he got the idea for what he wanted to do."

"The bypass hasn't been introduced at any of the city council meetings that I've attended. And Andi would tell you if anything's been said at the Chamber of Commerce."

Kristin didn't look particularly mollified. Impulsively, he reached out to give her a hug. She stiffened for a second then relaxed. "I've been wanting to do this all night," he said. "You looked sorta shell-shocked from all the political talk."

She moved away too soon for his liking, but he let her go. She stood up and paced to the picture window. Turning to face him, she said, "Donnie, my *family* may have approved of this harebrained scheme to get you elected, but I haven't. When I agreed to marry you the other night, things were different. You were leaving town. Now, you're staying in Gold Creek and running for office.

"The more I think about it, the less I like it. Andi's crazy if she thinks the past won't get dredged up. Neither of us wants that—not just for my sake or yours, but for Zach's. And Lucas's."

She was right, of course. Political skirmishes could be brutal. Every aspect of a person's life is subject to public scrutiny.

"And there's no way we could fake a marriage. That would mean asking the boys to pretend we're a family even though the two of us aren't...well, together.''

The talk at the table had shifted from marriage to campaign strategy so fast, Donnie hadn't had time to think about how Kristin would fit into the plan. Her sisters had simply acted as though this marriage was a given.

''Then we just have to be together,'' he said simply.

She dropped her arms, mouth open. ''What?''

He rose but didn't approach her. His heart was racing. ''Marry me for real, not pretend.'' Even though this proposal made less sense than his previous one, he meant it.

Despite the shadows, he could see the tears forming in her eyes. She swallowed, then lifted her head defiantly. ''That isn't funny.''

''Am I laughing?''

''But you can't...''

''Love you? Why not, Kristin? The truth is I never stopped loving you.''

She shook her head as if she didn't believe him. He couldn't blame her. He'd let his hurt feelings and foolish pride ruin everything between them.

He started toward her. ''Listen, there's been a lot of talk tonight. Go to bed now. Sleep. Maybe tomorrow things will look different.

''If you want to consider my proposal—*tonight's* proposal—'' he added with a smile ''—there's something you should know.''

He paused until she made eye contact. ''The minute I throw my hat into the ring I'll be out of a job. I plan to e-mail my regrets to the FAM program in the morning. So, you could land up married to an unemployed bum.''

She almost smiled, but the sound of a car distracted her. Kristin pulled open the drapes. Donnie could see past her. A single figure emerged out of the full-size luxury sedan in the driveway. Gloria's car.

Kristin flew to the entry. Donnie kept his distance, but he didn't leave. He was curious. Meeting his father for the first time must have been a highly emotional experience for Zach.

''Hi, sweetheart. Was that Tyler who brought you home?'' Kristin asked when her son entered. Her arms started to lift, as if to hug him, then dropped to her sides.

''His mother. He fell asleep about an hour ago. Right in the middle of *Harry Potter*.'' Zach moved slowly, as if exhausted. He didn't even seem to notice Donnie.

''She said I could finish watching the movie before she drove me home,'' Zach added softly.

Donnie could sense that Kristin had a million questions for her son, so he started to leave. ''I'll call you tomorrow, Kris.''

''Did you really break his nose?'' Zach asked before Donnie had taken two steps.

He recognized the tone. Belligerent yet respectful. In a boy's world, power and force were synonymous. ''It was a stupid fight, Zach. We were both teenagers and we should have known better. Fighting never solves anything.''

Zach started to turn away but Donnie added, ''I may have won the fight—I was a football player and much heavier than your dad—but I lost everything that was important to me. Your mother's l...friendship, the respect of the man I was working for, and my football scholarship. Fortunately, a judge made me take a course in anger management. Now I know what anger really is and how to control it.''

Zach stopped. He didn't turn around, but Donnie heard his question clearly, ''What is it?''

''Brain chaos. You have so many things happening at once, your brain can't process them, and you react in ways you would never choose if you could think clearly.''

Zach didn't say anything more, passing by his mother without a word.

Donnie thought he saw her smile, but she turned away to follow her son down the hall. Donnie closed the door behind him. No answer to his proposal, but that was just as well. He doubted her answer would have been the one he wanted to hear.

KRIS WASN'T SURE how to talk to Zach about his day. She stopped to wait for him, knowing he'd come through the kitchen after retrieving Sarge from the backyard. Zach took his responsibility seriously.

"Did he miss you?" she asked when the two came in.

"How could he? He didn't know about me."

She flinched. "I meant Sarge, not Tyler."

Zach took a soft drink from the refrigerator and opened it without checking with her, then walked into the living room where Kris was standing and plopped down sideways on the recliner; Sarge followed.

"Can you tell me about it? What's he like?"

He shrugged. "Okay, I guess. Doesn't talk a lot. He looked sorta sick some of the time and had to take a bunch of pills. He told me about his business and a little about his life, but mostly we just sat there."

Kristin was glad Tyler hadn't given Zach the fifth degree about his childhood.

"His mother had a lot to say, though. She hardly ever shut up." Kris bit down on a smile. "She had stacks of photo albums and told me all about her life and how she married my...uh, grandfather. She had lots to say about his family."

"You could ask Ida Jane if you want a second version of all that." They looked at each other, and the tender look in his eyes made her smile. *He likes Ida Jane.* "If you catch her on a good day."

"Is she senile? That what Mrs. Hughes said."

Mrs. Hughes, not Grandma. "On her good days she's sharper than some people half her age. I wouldn't call her senile."

He took another drink then asked, "What does my birth certificate say?"

"About your father?"

He nodded.

Kristin's heart fluttered oddly. "It names Tyler Harrison as your father. Address unknown."

He stroked Sarge's ear. "So you didn't lie about me. You just didn't tell anyone. His mother called you a liar."

The tightness across her chest eased a tiny bit. "My family in Ireland knew the truth. They were with me when you were born. For a while I considered staying there, but I missed America too much.

"When Moira and Kathleen moved to Wisconsin, I went along. I wanted you to have the same kinds of experiences I'd had growing up. And I wanted to be closer to my family, in case Ida…" She blinked away her tears. For years she'd been able to block these feelings, telling herself she was better off alone so Zach wouldn't be judged for her mistakes.

"How come you never brought me here before? Were you ashamed of me?"

A pain stabbed below her ribs. "You know that wasn't the reason, Zach. I was ashamed of myself, of my deception. There were so many times I picked up the phone to call home to brag about you—like when you won the spelling bee in third grade. I knew you were a genius." That brought a slight smile, but it faded when she added, "When I realized I couldn't tell anyone, I cried for hours."

Zach didn't look particularly sympathetic. She didn't blame him, and she doubted she could ever make him—or anyone—understand how slowly and insidiously the lie had taken over her life. "Have you ever seen a cartoon where some guy paints himself into a corner and can't move?"

His nod may have been a yes or a shrug. "That was me. The dufus in the corner. I didn't know I was going to have a baby when I left for Ireland.

"When I found out you were on the way—" she smiled at him "—I wanted to call home. But Ida Jane was on a buying trip to the midwest; Andi was working at a pack station in Toulumne where there wasn't a phone, and Jenny and Josh were hiking the Pacific Crest Trail."

She'd been entirely alone for the first time in her life.

"I know it probably sounds foolish, but when you're eighteen you don't have a very clear view of the big picture. At the time, I saw this as my chance to prove to the world that I wasn't a flake. I was determined to take care of myself and my baby without any help from my family and the town of Gold Creek."

He didn't say anything, so she went on. "My aunt and uncle helped, of course, but I worked harder than I'd ever worked in my life while I lived in Ireland. I cooked and cleaned and cared for Uncle Sean's mother. I remember being so tired at night I didn't even have the strength to be sad.''

Kris pictured one damp and chilly night when she was so exhausted she thought she might pass out. As she'd crawled into bed beside Moira—in a room they shared with four cousins, ages ten to twenty—Kristin had been ready to give up and go home, but then a fluttering sensation moved beneath her belly.

She'd felt a sudden, palpable spurt of selfishness and she'd known she wasn't ready to share her baby with her family, her town and certainly not the mean-spirited witch who wrote the gossip column. And, beneath it all, was a reluctance to tell Donnie. Because that would mean facing the fact that her silly, romantic dreams were gone for good.

''After you were born, it was surprisingly easy to keep you a secret. I just didn't communicate much with Ida and my sisters. I had my cousins and I made new friends. I accepted the estrangement from Jenny and Andi as part of my punishment for lying, but it turned out you were the one being punished for my mistakes. I wouldn't blame you if you never spoke to me again.''

He sighed heavily and got up. ''I'm going to bed.''

''Do you…did you…does Tyler want to see you tomorrow? It's Sunday. I told Andi I'd help out at the store, but…''

''He's going to call in the morning. I have to work on my writing assignment part of the day.''

"Okay. G'night," she called as dog and boy trudged down the hallway. Kristin didn't move for a good ten minutes. She had to force herself to go to bed, but once there, she turned on the television and sank under the covers, letting the blue-gray light fill the darkness. She put the volume on mute and set the timer, in case she actually fell asleep.

She was still awake when it snapped off four hours later. A guilty conscience made for a lousy bed partner.

DONNIE SURPRISED HIMSELF by waking up early enough the next morning to attend the first service at the little nondenominational church he'd joined after the divorce. He and Sandy had been active church members of the Gold Creek Presbyterian Church throughout their marriage, but he'd needed a change after they split up. As he'd told his mother, "She got custody of our faith."

The minister—a plump woman with a jovial apple-cheek smile and kind heart—preached about the importance of acceptance. The songs and psalms gave him a certain sense of peace, even though his life was upside-down.

When he returned home, the house seemed very empty, so he turned up the radio in the garage and dug through years of accumulated possessions. By the end of the day, the garage sparkled. Even his workbench was neat and tidy.

He'd checked in with Kristin twice by phone. She was handling the antique store for Andi, who'd taken Ida Jane to visit friends. Kris told him Tyler had invited Zach to have pizza with him in a nearby town.

Donnie could imagine how unnerving it was for her to deal with Zach's feelings about his father. He'd offered to take her out to dinner, but she'd declined, pleading a headache. He promised to call after he'd talked to Lucas.

To his surprise, the large red SUV pulled into the driveway—a day ahead of schedule. The rear passenger door opened, and Lucas jumped out, dragging his backpack. Three or four shopping bags followed.

Donnie hurried to help. "Hello, son. That was a fast trip. Welcome home."

Lucas's grunt didn't exactly encourage conversation. "How was your visit?"

Lucas slammed the door and bent over to pick up two bags. He used the bulkiness of his backpack to ward off any attempt Donnie might have made to hug him. "Grandma coughs a lot and has to cart around a tank of oxygen. Uncle Elroy has a new wife who complains all the time, and her bratty kids got on my nerves."

The passenger-side window hissed down, and Sandy backed up enough so she was parallel to Donnie and Lucas. "I love you, honey. Sorry we had to cut the trip short. I promise to make it up to you next time."

Lucas grunted some kind of acknowledgment.

"I left a message on your machine," Sandy told

Donnie, as if this change of plan was somehow his fault. "I have to run. I tried Boyd on the cell and couldn't find him. I'm afraid he might have fallen off a ladder."

Donnie wisely kept his opinion to himself and stepped out of the way as she pulled around to leave. He picked up two outlet-store bags filled with brand-name jeans, shirts and a couple of sweat-shirts.

It bothered him that Sandy thought she could buy their son's affection. But if designer labels improved his son's self-image, Donnie couldn't really object. Lucas had struggled with his weight since first grade when Donnie and Sandy separated. His sedentary lifestyle didn't help, but Donnie's attempts to interest his son in sports had backfired.

"I'm not you, okay?" Lucas had cried when Donnie suggested PeeWee Football. "I'm not a star athlete like you. Just leave me alone."

Donnie carried the bags inside. "Lucas, how about a fried-egg sandwich for dinner? I've been too busy to cook."

"Had burgers in Modesto," Lucas told him. He pulled a plastic box out of his backpack. "See what Mom bought me for my birthday?"

A much-coveted, hard-to-find video game.

"I'm sure you're anxious to play it, but could we talk first?"

Lucas sighed. "What?"

Donnie took a carton of eggs from the refriger-ator. "Well, I'd like to hear about your trip, for starters. But if you'd rather not talk about it, then we need to discuss the immediate future. What's going to hap—''

Lucas made a grumbling sound and collapsed onto one of the three stools at the counter. "If this is about the dumb nanny, forget it. I won't stay with a baby-sitter. I'll be ten tomorrow. That's too old for a nanny."

Donnie could feel his son's temper escalating. Like his father, Lucas had a short fuse. "This would be a good time to take a deep breath, son. Your voice is rising. We can't have any kind of productive dialogue if we're yelling at each other."

"No nanny," Lucas snapped.

"Good. Because I don't plan to hire one."

That earned a startled look that quickly changed to suspicion. "What then?"

Donnie's pulse quickened. "First of all, I'm not going anywhere. I turned down the job. Now I'm thinking of running for sheriff." When Lucas didn't react, Donnie added, "And I might get married."

Lucas's mouth dropped open. "Who? Mom?" A furious blush told Donnie his son regretted the mistake.

"That would be a little difficult since she has a husband," Donnie said as gently as possible. "Actually, Kristin is an old friend of mine who just moved back to town. We dated in high school. She has a son a year older than you. She hasn't said yes, by the way. They want to come over tomorrow to meet you."

Lucas said nothing, so Donnie continued. "Her name is Kristin Sullivan. Her great-aunt owns the antique store. Her son's name is Zach. He's in seventh grade."

Lucas's eyes narrowed. "You're marrying some woman just to get out of paying for a house-keeper?"

Donnie almost smiled. "No, son. If she says yes, it will be because we care about each other," he began. But the truth was he didn't know how to explain to a ten-year-old why he and Kris were getting married. He wasn't sure *he* knew the real reason himself.

Lucas's expression turned to one of cynicism. "Whatever. Can I go now?" Lucas grabbed his video game and stormed out of the room.

THREE HOURS LATER, while munching on an apple, Donnie called Kristin.

"I've talked to Lucas," he told her without preamble after her initial hello. It was ten-thirty, but she didn't sound as though she'd been on the verge of sleep.

"Oh?" Her tone sounded braced for bad news. "So what did he say?"

"Pretty much what I expected him to say. *Whatever*," he said, mimicking his son's huffy sigh. "Don't you just hate that word?"

Kristin's laughter warmed him. "It's right there at the top of the list," she said. "Along with several others I prefer to spell rather than speak aloud. What else did he say?''

Donnie sighed, then added, ''I cornered him in his bedroom a few minutes ago. He said he doesn't care what I do as long as you promise to leave him alone and don't try to mother him.''

''He's just a little boy, Donnie. I think we need to give him time.''

''I agree in theory, but Jonathan called a few minutes ago. Apparently the filing date has passed. If I want to run, it will have to be a write-in campaign. Do you know how risky that is?''

She didn't answer.

''Kris, I have to decide soon.''

''Donnie, do you honestly think I'd help your chances?''

''Yes. People in this town love a wedding. And my marrying one of the Sullivan triplets will definitely gain me points.'' He could hear her breathing. ''Kris,'' he said softly. ''We both know politics isn't the only thing driving this proposal. I want to marry you for a lot of reasons.''

She was quiet for a long time. Donnie really didn't want to have this conversation over the phone. ''The other night when I proposed, it might have been for the wrong reason, but, Kris, it felt right. I could run for office as a single man—and I will if you turn me down. But why don't we do what you suggested—lay our cards on the table with the boys? Bring Zach over here tomorrow. It's a holiday and Lucas's birthday. Let's all four discuss this face-to-face.''

''I'd like to meet Lucas, but I'm not agreeing to anything until we've all had a chance to talk.''

They ironed out the details of their meeting then Donnie said good-night. He hung up the phone and picked up the stack of FAM paperwork he'd accumulated. He couldn't help feeling a little regret. He would have liked to give this a try. Too often in the past he'd taken the easy route. Was he doing it again? It didn't *feel* easy.

The phone rang before he could step away from the desk. Assuming it was Kristin, he said, ''Change your mind?''

''Donavon?''

''Mom. How's Aunt Roberta?''

''Not good. They've got her on a dozen different medications. I'm so glad I can be here with her.''

Donnie made a note to send flowers. ''Me, too.''

''What's been decided on your end? Have you talked to anyone yet—no, wait, the ad won't even be out till later in the week, will it? I've lost all track of time.''

Donnie took a breath and let it out. ''Actually, Mom, I have news. I'm not taking the air marshal job. And I've asked Kristin Sullivan to marry me.''

His mother didn't answer for a good minute. ''Kristin? But, Donnie, what about your dreams?''

''Mom, Lucas needs me here. Besides, Kristin has always been my real dream. You know that.''

''Marriage is a big step, Donnie. Are you sure?''

He'd been practicing this speech in his head all day. "Kris and I have known each other since we were kids, Mom. We're soul mates." As he spoke the words, Donnie knew they were true. "And there's more, Mom. I'm going to run for sheriff."

A long sigh filtered through the phone line. "I know you'll make a wonderful sheriff, son, but single men get elected, too. If you're marrying Kristin just to win an election…"

Donnie tried to answer with bluster, but she cut him off. "Forget I said that. I'll keep my nose out of it since I can't be there to help, but, Donnie, you know you can call me if the…engagement doesn't work out."

He expelled a sigh. "Thanks, Mom."

"Tell my grandson I love him and miss him and I wish him a very happy birthday."

"You got it. I love you, Mom."

"I love you, too, Donnie. You're a remarkable man. Kristin is a lucky woman."

He chuckled. "I'll tell her you said so."

"That's probably not a good idea. Mothers are notoriously prejudiced when it comes to their sons. Actually, I saw Kristin the day before I left. She's still very pretty. But I can't help remembering…"

"Things are different this time," he told her. "Ty Harrison is back, and it sounds like he might use Kristin's reputation for not putting down roots anywhere to obtain custody of Zach."

"So by marrying one of the town's leading citizens, she has integrity and stability on her side."

Donnie made a face. "I don't know about the leading-citizen thing, but Kris loves her son and will do anything for him. I'm hoping she and Lucas will hit it off."

"What does Sandy think of the idea?"

"I'll let you know after I tell her."

They ended the conversation because a nurse interrupted to administer something to his aunt. He wished his mother a good night then hung up.

One hurdle out of the way. Sandy would be next. She deserved to be informed about this since this plan affected their son's welfare, but she wasn't entitled to be a part of the decision-making process.

He rose thoughtfully and turned off the lights. In the corner, propped against the fireplace stood the old Ibanez guitar he'd found in the storage closet. His son had received a shiny new bass for Christmas. This electric guitar was the one Donnie had bought after his first paying gig. With new strings and a little TLC, it might just help Donnie connect with Zach.

ZACH HELD the business card under the high-intensity light of his desk lamp. His father—*his* father—had given it to him earlier, while the woman who was his grandmother had gone to the store. For some reason, Zach couldn't make himself call Gloria *grandmother*. Maybe because she was so different from Ida Jane, who felt like a *gramma*.

Ida was as huggable as a teddy bear. Gloria was stiff and nervous. Her energy seemed to wear down his father, who wasn't anything like Zach had imagined. In his dreams, his father was powerful and vital.

Zach flipped the card over and looked at the hand-written telephone numbers. He'd refused to arrange a future meeting until he'd spoken with his mother. Would acting too friendly with his father make her sad? Even though he was angry with her, Zach hadn't seriously considered living with his father. His mother needed him. She lost track of time; she wore her wristwatch upside down.

He didn't know what would happen if she married the cop. And his kid. What would that be like?

Zach remembered begging his mother for a little brother one Christmas. He'd gotten a Nintendo, instead.

He got into bed and turned off the light. If his mom was serious about marrying this cop, Zach would just have to lay down a few rules with the kid. Zach didn't need a brother anymore. And after eleven years without a father, Zach finally had one. So he definitely didn't need a stepfather.

CHAPTER SEVEN

"THIS IS Zach's favorite cookie," Kris told her great-aunt as she removed a pan of sumptuous-smelling cookies from the old but reliable oven. Kris had come to the bordello to bake. It was easier than trying to find utensils in her still-unpacked boxes.

"Where is the boy this morning?" Ida Jane asked.

Always an early riser, Ida was already awake when Kris arrived at the bordello. The sun was now shining brightly, and the kitchen smelled of warm chocolate and coffee.

"Outside with the dogs. I was going to let him sleep in, but he was up before me."

Kris handed her aunt a still-warm cookie. "Taste."

Ida looked particularly dramatic this morning dressed in a purple velour robe; the sunlight filtering through her silvery hair resembled a crown. She took a bite then closed her eyes and made appreciative sounds as she chewed.

"Mmm. It *is* good. Ralph Bascomb at the bakery used to brag about his secret recipe. Wasn't this good, though. He died a couple of years ago, you know.''

More like twenty. Kristin kept the thought to herself.

Ida munched in silence while Kris scraped the last bit of dough from the bowl and added two final globs to the pan.

She leaned over to put the sheet in the oven. The heat wafted over her and she felt a sudden sense of déjà vu.

''Auntie, do you remember when we used to do the dishes together? I'd stand on a chair to wash while you dried? You told me that someday I would be big enough to reach the upper cupboards, but I didn't believe you. I thought I was going to stay little forever.''

Ida Jane turned her head to stare out the window.

''Kristin was my helper,'' Ida said a moment later. Her eyes filled with tears, and she started to cry. ''My poor Kristin. She ran away from home, and it was all my fault.''

Baffled by her aunt's words, Kristin snagged a cotton flour-sack towel off the counter and raced to Ida Jane's side. ''Auntie, what are you talking about? You were never to blame for my going away. I went to Ireland to be a nanny, remember?''

Ida Jane didn't seem to hear. Her thin shoulders shook as she muttered nonsensically. ''Poor little girl. Too sensitive. Like her mother. Needed more love. I was too busy to pay attention, and she ran away.''

Kristin looped her arm around the older woman's quivering shoulders and offered soothing words of support. "I'm right here, Auntie. I went away, but I came back. And I'm never leaving again. I'm home for good."

Kristin felt a current of cooler air funnel across her bare ankles and looked toward the doorway. Andi stood frozen, hair a mess, seersucker pajamas wrinkled. "What's going on?" she mouthed.

Kristin motioned her to enter then spoke to the elderly woman. "Auntie, everything's going to be just fine. You've got your whole family together again. Here's Andi in her pj's. She came for milk and cookies. Right, Andi?"

Ida Jane looked up, sniffling. A tentative smile made her lips turn up. "She always showed up when I baked. Nose like a bloodhound."

Andi snorted delicately. "I beg your pardon. That was Jenny. I hardly ever eat sweets."

Kristin threw the towel at her. "Liar."

Andi grinned unabashedly. "What are you doing here so early, sis?" she asked, opening the refrigerator and taking out a carton of milk.

"Most of my kitchenware is still in boxes, so I brought my mess over here. You don't mind, do you?"

Andi laughed. "Yeah, right, like I'd turn down fresh-baked goods. My husband was twitching in his sleep, and I figure the minute his nose deciphers this aroma, he'll swoop down like a vulture on fresh roadkill."

Kristin made a face. "*There's* a lovely image to help whet the appetite." She checked the cookies in the oven then faced her sister, who was perched on her usual spot on the counter. "I forgot to ask, how's the bordello's historical designation coming? Are you getting anywhere with it?"

"Yup. I'm getting nowhere fast." Andi ran a hand through her hair. "Even with Sam's stepfather's help—Gordon's been doing a bunch of online research for me—there are gaping holes in our documentation."

"Like what?"

"Well, according to a couple of the history books, the original house was moved to this parcel from another location. But no one's quite sure where that was. Or when the move took place.

"Plus, a fire destroyed part of the upstairs at some point, which necessitated remodeling. Then this part of the house—" she made an encompassing motion "—was added as late as 1908 or 1918. I can't make out the writing."

She sighed. "No wonder Ida didn't register the place before this. It's practically a full-time job, and she was too busy raising us and keeping her business going."

A sudden bang made all three women start. They looked toward the doorway where a half-awake man—stubble-faced and bleary eyed—stumbled into the room. Barefoot, in a white undershirt and baggy gray sweatpants, he moved like a zombie toward the pile of cookies.

Andi let out a loud sigh. "See what I have to put up with in the morning? Neanderthal man." Her tone was a mixture of amusement and love. "Quick, give that man coffee."

Kristin filled a cup and passed it to her brother-in-law who already had crumbs bracketing his lips. "Mmm, good cookies," he mumbled.

"Thanks. Have a seat."

Jonathan kissed his wife then gave Ida a hug before sitting down in the chair across from her. "This is a pleasant surprise. I love the smell of cookies in the morning."

Andi toasted with her glass. "Me, too. When are you going to learn how to bake?"

Jonathan blinked. "Me?"

Kristin and Ida Jane looked at each other and laughed. Kristin felt a pang of regret at having missed moments like this for too long. She really was very glad to be home. No matter what happened with Donnie and Tyler.

Jonathan opened the *San Francisco Chronicle* and said, "There's an article about pan-Pacific trade. Didn't you say Tyler just got back from Japan, Kristin?"

"That's what Jim Rohr told me."

"Hmm. Smart man. He backed the right horse. There's money to be made in that direction."

Kristin refilled everyone's cup. "Donnie mentioned something the other day that got me thinking. Ida, do you remember hearing about a proposal to build a bypass around town? Maybe ten or twelve years ago?''

Ida seemed to concentrate. "Yes, I do," she said, nodding. "They were going to make the highway loop around the edge of town. I was all for the plan until they said they'd have to tear down the bordello to do it, and I told them they could go jump in a lake.''

Jonathan looked intrigued. "You aren't thinking that's what Tyler has in mind now, are you, Kris? If the idea didn't fly a decade ago, it surely wouldn't be feasible today. The hard costs would be phenomenal.''

"What if you owned most of the land where the new road would go?" she asked.

Andi sat forward. "That intersection at Main and the highway has always been dangerous. I remember Ida telling me that a high-school student was killed at the crosswalk a few years ago. There's always an ongoing debate about whether or not to install a traffic light. But I haven't heard any talk at the chamber of commerce about a bypass.''

As Kristin retrieved the remaining cookies from the oven, a thought struck her. If this bypass was indeed Tyler's plan, he must have started laying the groundwork for it long before he knew about Zach. Would it matter to him that by tearing down the old bordello, he would destroy his son's heritage?

"So, Kris, when's the wedding?" Andi asked, changing the subject.

Kristin's grip on the pan tightened, and she

yelped when the heat soaked through to her thumb. She underhanded the pan to the counter and spun around. "Donnie and I are meeting with the boys today. There's still a lot to work out."

"Like what? You love him, don't you?"

Kristin's face turned as hot as the oven mitt. "We're…friends."

Her sister didn't look convinced. "You've been in love with him since you were kids. Don't tell me you wouldn't have been on the next flight home if Zach had been Donnie's."

Kristin yanked open a drawer to find a spatula. Tears made her grope blindly until her fingers closed around a plastic handle. Instead of a spatula, she pulled out a potato ricer. She stared at it blankly, then let go of both the cookie sheet and the useless utensil and slowly melted to the floor.

Andi was at her side a second later. "I'm sorry, sis. I shouldn't have said that."

Kristin hadn't cried in Andi's arms for too long to remember. Usually, Jenny was Kristin's source of comfort, but Jenny wasn't here.

"It's gonna be okay, Kris."

"I did love him, Andi. So much I thought I'd die when he broke up with me. Tyler was a shoulder to cry on and when he kissed me, I told myself, why not? I'll never love anybody the way I loved Donnie and he's not interested in me, so why the heck not?"

"I know, honey. I know. Often our worst mistakes don't feel like mistakes at the time. We do what feels right, then pay for it later."

The honesty in her tone got through to Kristin. They looked at each, and Kris felt a deep love for her sister.

"Well, if that's the way it works, then I definitely *should* marry Donnie. Since it feels like a mistake, maybe everything will turn out okay." She was striving for lightness, but the tremble in her voice betrayed her.

Ida Jane rose—with a little help from Jonathan. "If there's going to be a wedding, I need a new dress. Which one of you is taking me shopping?"

She didn't wait for an answer but shuffled toward the hallway. Her cane had become her faithful companion; its rubber tip made a squeaky sound against the wood floor.

Jonathan refilled his cup, grabbed a handful of cookies then followed her. "Thanks for the cookies, Kris. By the way, I just want you to know that I owe Donnie more than I can ever repay. He stuck with my case when that worthless sheriff, Magnus Brown, was content to let me rot in jail for a crime I didn't commit. So I plan to do my best to see that Donnie wins this election." He looked at his wife and grinned. "I'd marry him myself if I thought it would help."

Andi tossed a dish towel at him. "Go away."

Once the kitchen was clean and the cookies were bagged, Kris started to leave, but Andi stopped her. "Can we talk a minute?"

Kris checked out the window to make sure Zach was still occupied, then she walked to the table and sat down across from her sister.

Andi nibbled the edge of her cookie for a minute, then said, "You know, Jen and I just want what's best for you. And Donnie." She looked at Kris. "You *do* love him, don't you?"

"I don't know," Kris answered truthfully. "He told me he still loves me. That he never stopped loving me."

Andi brightened. "That's good. Isn't it?"

"I don't know." *How can he love me? He doesn't even know me.*

"You don't believe him?"

"I don't know."

Andi let out a familiar snarl. "If you say that again, I'm going to hit you."

Kris stood up suddenly. "That's just it, Andi, I don't know anything. I never did. I thought I loved Donnie and he loved me, but look what happened."

"That was a long time ago, Kris."

"But I'm still me, Andi. I make mistakes. I can't balance my checkbook. I lose track of time and I'm always late. My eleven-year-old son is smarter than me. I'm...dumb."

Andi shot to her feet and grabbed Kristin by the shoulders. "No, you're not. Don't say that."

Kris couldn't meet her eyes. "I've always known it. Everyone's known it. Remember when Ida took me for special testing?"

Andi dropped her hands and stepped back. "That

didn't prove anything. You learn differently. You passed all your classes.''

''With help. Jenny wrote half my papers. You tutored me in math.'' Kristin paced to the sink and looked into the backyard where her son was playing tug-of-war with Harley. ''Ask anyone, Andi, and they'll tell you. Kristin Sullivan is sweet, but not too bright. It's one of the reasons I didn't want to come back.''

She turned around. ''When I lived in other places, it took a while for people to catch on. I'm pretty good at faking it.''

Andi looked close to tears. ''Oh, God, is that true? You really think you're not smart? Is that why you were willing to marry Donnie when it was just a temporary arrangement, but now you're not?''

Kris sighed. She felt overwhelmed and so far out of her league she wanted to run away. But she knew that wasn't going to work this time. ''I could be his housekeeper and care for his child; I'm a good mother, Andi. But Donnie deserves so much more than…me.''

Andi took in a deep breath and slowly marched toward Kristin. Kris knew that look. She swallowed as her sister began to speak. ''Let's get something straight. I'm no Rhodes scholar, but I know this much. You and Donnie have loved each other since you were kids. You've both made mistakes. So what? You're human. Get over it.''

Kris bit down on her inner cheek to keep from smiling.

"This town is facing some big changes. That bypass you mentioned is just the tip of the iceburg. People are moving out of the valley and Gold Creek is right in their path. We need enlightened leadership. Magnus Brown is old-school. He's entrenched power. He won't give up easily, and Donnie doesn't stand a chance unless he has all his ducks in a row."

Kris shifted uneasily. She'd heard some of this last night, but hadn't been paying attention. "I know it won't be easy, Andi, but you're dreaming if you think I'll be any help to him. My reputation..."

Andi cut her off. "You're a Sullivan triplet, Kristin. The town loves you. And you love Donnie. I know you do."

"We haven't even kissed, Andi." Kris ducked her head to hide her embarrassment. "The other night, he wouldn't even let me give him a massage."

Her sister chortled. "Good Lord, the man is slipping. So, go seduce him. See if the spark is still there. You definitely don't want to marry a man with no sparks."

Kristin had always admired her sister's ability to cut to the chase, but she couldn't picture herself seducing Donnie to see if they were still compatible in bed. "His house? My house? Children present?"

Andi heaved a weighty sigh. "Where is Rosemarie when we need her?"

The two looked at each other and broke into

laughter. They fell into a hug, laughing, and suddenly Kristin felt a glimmer of hope.

DONNIE HAD JUST FINISHED putting new strings on his old guitar when a wraith dressed like the Grim Reaper on a scooter appeared in the driveway.

"Hi, Donnie, how's it going?" Bethany Murdock hailed, pushing her silver Razor up to his workbench in the garage.

"Not bad. How are you?" She'd been absent from the office the last two days that he'd worked.

"My annual bout of strep throat. My folks want me to have my tonsils out, but I kinda like 'em." She made a comical face. "Gets me out of school."

Donnie snickered. "Interesting strategy. What's up?" Although she didn't live far from him, she'd never stopped by before today.

"The engagement, of course."

Donnie's stomach tightened. "Pardon?" He tried to remain cool.

Her eyes opened wide. "You haven't heard? Cory's getting married."

The way she said it—with just a hint of a sigh—told him she still had a crush on the handsome young officer. He hoped her misplaced affection would blow over.

"I'd gathered things were getting serious with his girlfriend. Have they set a date?"

Beth nodded, her lips compressed in a frown. "June. I overheard him talking to Ed and Margie. He said she already has the whole thing planned."

Donnie bit down on the smile that wanted to form. He walked over to her and gave her a light hug with one arm. "He wasn't good enough for you, Beth. Besides, in another year you'll be at college and you'll find someone who wants a June wedding, too."

She made a snuffling sound and looked toward his house. "Is your son home?" she asked.

Donnie turned and saw the unmistakable sway of blinds being closed. "Yes. Lucas was with his mom for a few days visiting his grandmother in Redding. He's a little antisocial this morning." *Every morning.*

She nodded at the guitar in his hands. "Do you play?"

"I used to. In high school."

"Cool. I'm on the Homecoming Committee, and we're doing an old-fashioned Battle of the Bands this year."

Donnie smiled. "Suddenly I feel much older than I did before you got here."

"Sorry. Gotta go. See you at work."

Work. Student interns like Bethany added so much to the department. If Donnie was sheriff, he'd expand the program, not bully the kids like Magnus did. The sheriff was extremely short-tempered with clerks.

"I'm off the rest of this week, you know," he told her. "Then I go on nights." *Unless Magnus fires me.*

She frowned. "Oh, yeah, I forgot. But I'll see

you when you come to the engagement party, right?''

The words made his stomach turn over completely. Weddings were about happy parties, congratulations, rings and vows. Very different from what he had offered Kris.

''Donnie? You're going to be there, right?''

He pushed the thought away and smiled. ''Sorry. What party? I'm out of the loop.''

''Cory's bringing *her* to the office Friday afternoon for cake and punch. I wasn't going to go, but Margie asked me to help.''

And you want to see her. He understood. ''Well, I might just have to drop by to check *her* out.''

Bethany whipped her scooter around so it faced the other direction then put one foot on the running board. ''I'd better get home. I have a ton of makeup work. That's the bad part about being home sick.'' Looking back over her shoulder, she called out, '''Bye. See you Friday.''

Donnie walked into the garage. A song he liked—''What's Love Got to Do With It?'' by Tina Turner—was playing on the radio. He turned up the volume, then picked up the old guitar and strummed a few chords.

''Where'd you get that?'' a voice asked.

Donnie pivoted. Lucas was standing in the doorway. ''Good morning and happy birthday, son.'' Donnie would have taken the boy into his arms and hugged him if not for the wary, defensive set of his shoulders.

"It's my guitar. I found it in the shed. Didn't you use it for a while before you decided you prefer the bass?"

Lucas nodded.

"My friend Bethany Murdock was just here. She's a junior. Do you know her?"

"Her sister's in sixth."

"She mentioned Homecoming. Something about a battle of the bands."

An unmistakable gleam of interest suddenly appeared in his son's eyes. Lucas had started talking about forming a band ever since he'd picked up his first guitar.

"Maybe you could check around. See if anybody wants to jam. The gig's still a few weeks away."

"Won't happen."

"How come?"

"Jorry broke his wrist. He played lead."

"I might know somebody," Donnie said. He fingered a C-chord and ran his plastic pick over the strings.

"Who?" Lucas asked suspiciously.

"I'd rather not say until I talk to him first. He might not be interested."

Fortunately the sound of a car in the driveway saved Donnie from further interrogation. "That must be Kris and Zach." He started to motion Lucas forward, when he discovered his son had disappeared.

He set down the guitar. With a silent prayer, he went to greet his guests.

"Hi," he called, wiping his hands on his jeans. He'd gone for casual—T-shirt, faded work-around-the-house jeans and ratty tennis shoes. Kristin was just the opposite: a hunter-green skirt of some soft fabric that came to her mid-shins, an undershirt of the same color with a bright, gauzy overblouse that looked as if she'd fallen into a pile of autumn leaves. Her feet were in flat slippers that gave her a delicate look.

"Thanks for coming, Zach." To Kris, he said, "You look very pretty this morning."

Her cheeks colored. "Thanks." She quickly thrust a plastic-wrapped plate at him.

Donnie fought a grin. He'd never seen her so nervous. If her son hadn't been at her side, he'd have hugged her. "Mmm...cookies. What kind? Not that I'm choosy."

"Chocolate chip. Zach's favorite. I made them for Lucas. Today's his birthday, right?"

Donnie had started to pry up a section of plastic covering aside, but stopped. "That was thoughtful of you."

A mischievous grin appeared on her lips, and she produced a single cookie from behind her back. "I thought you should test one—to make sure he'll like them."

He was touched. He polished off the cookie in three bites and handed the plate back to her. "Delicious. He'll love them."

He turned slightly to usher her ahead of him. "Let's go inside. You can give them to him."

Zach followed a few feet behind. He was a good-looking kid—nose ring aside. His hair was long and, like Lucas's, had been partitioned with some kind of stiffening agent.

At the front entry, Maureen's gold- and rust-colored chrysanthemums provided a cheerful welcome. "You might not recognize the place, Kris. Sandy and I did a lot of remodeling after we moved in." The door was painted the same as the trim—a deep bluish-gray. He had to jiggle the latch to get it to open. "We don't use this door a lot," he explained, wiping his feet on a sisal welcome mat.

"Most people come through the garage, and there's a separate entrance to Mom's apartment. She never used it, but we thought it was a good idea for resale purposes," he said, holding open the door for his guests.

Kristin entered first, looking around as she passed a few inches from him. This time he inhaled. Damn. Same perfume, and just as intoxicating as he remembered.

Zach followed a step or two behind. He moved in a shuffling gait, head down and hands stuffed in the pockets of his baggy jeans. Lucas wore the same style pants, low on his hips, frayed at the heels.

"This is the living room, Zach," he said. "Your mother used to come over a lot when we were kids." The south-facing windows gave the room a warm, cheerful feel. Maureen's decorating touches—a basket of dried flowers, candles and

magazines—were homey. "We added a family
room off the kitchen when we built Mom's apartment. Bedrooms and bathrooms are that way."

He started toward the family room.

"This is okay," Zach said. "Bigger than our last
place." He looked at Donnie. "Where did you say
the bathroom was?"

"Second door on the right," Donnie replied,
pointing down the hall.

As she watched the boy walk away, Kris's shoulders slumped.

"What's wrong?" Donnie asked in a low voice.

"It just hit me that if we get married, I'll be
living in this huge house with two boys. What if I
can't handle it?"

"You'll be fine, Kris. The house is obviously
well lived in, so you don't have to worry about
keeping it pristine. Plus," he added with a grin,
"I'll be here to help."

Kristin shook her head, which made her pretty,
loose curls dance. "Where is Lucas?"

"In his room." Donnie walked to a door adorned
with a very large stop sign. He rapped hard enough
to be heard over the discordant sounds coming from
inside.

A few seconds later the door opened and the
pulsing beat of hip-hop music poured out. Donnie
was used to the volume, but Kristin took a step
backward.

Donnie motioned toward the stereo on the bookshelf. "Down," he mouthed. Lucas complied—slowly.

Donnie marshaled his patience. Lucas could push his buttons faster than a belligerent drunk, but Donnie was getting better at ignoring the attitude. He motioned Kristin to join him.

"Lucas, this is Kristin Sullivan. Kris—" he put his hand at the small of her back and urged her to step forward "—my son, Lucas."

The two shook hands. "Happy birthday, Lucas," Kristin said, handing him the plate of cookies.

Donnie prayed his son's manners would kick in.

Lucas mumbled a barely audible, "Thanks." And reached for the plate.

If it hadn't been Lucas's birthday, Donnie might have taken the calorie-laden goodies from his son's hand. But he didn't.

"Son, we'd like you to join us in the kitchen so we can talk. Okay?"

A thick hunk of black hair moved slightly, apparently signifying compliance.

Donnie followed Kristin out of the room. They didn't say anything, but he could sense her nervousness. They found Zach standing at the bay window, which afforded a panoramic view of the town's namesake, Gold Creek.

Kris joined him. "Pretty, isn't it? I always liked this room." She pointed to something outside. "Look. There's a rabbit. Sarge would love it here, wouldn't he?"

Zach didn't respond, but Donnie had a feeling that's exactly what the boy was thinking.

"You should have brought Sarge with you," he said.

Zach flashed his mother a telling look. She grimaced. "You were right. I was wrong. I'm sorry," she said with a frown.

The boy shrugged and moved away. Donnie motioned for them to follow him. "I made coffee. And there are soft drinks. Let's sit at the table."

They were seated when Lucas joined them. He took the chair farthest from everyone and barely made eye contact when Donnie introduced him to Zach.

An awkward silence fell over the table. Donnie took the lead. He had the most explaining to do.

"Lucas, while you were gone I did a lot of thinking about what's important to me. You're number one." He ignored his son's skeptical sound. "I only agreed to let you move to L.A. because that's what you wanted. I know you were looking forward to it, and I'm really sorry it didn't happen. For *your* sake."

Lucas shrugged.

"Your plan to go live in L.A. made me take a hard look at my life. I didn't like what I saw. I was miserable at work and grumpy at home. I don't know how you and Grandma put up with me."

That brought a small reaction. Donnie went on. "I used to love going to work. I felt as though I was doing some good, but when Sheriff Brown took office things changed. I didn't like my job—or my-self—very much. That's why I applied to the Air Marshals. I needed a change.''

He paused for a breath. "Luckily for me, your mom decided to go to Africa, and I got a second chance to do what I should have done four years ago—run for sheriff. If I win, I'll be able to help Gold Creek, instead of leaving it.''

Kristin's smile felt like an A-plus grade.

"So why marry my mom? I thought you needed a housekeeper to take care of your kid,'' Zach asked.

Lucas bristled. "I don't need no baby-sitter.''

Donnie leaned forward to make eye contact with Zach. "I fell in love with your mother when I was not much older than you.''

Zach's elaborate shrug said "So?''

"If I do this—run for office—it's going to mean nine weeks of intense campaigning. I can't do it alone, Zach. It wouldn't be fair to Lucas. I need your mother.''

"Hire her. We could use the money.''

The boy was bright. "Then she'd be working here and you'd be alone. That wouldn't look good to the courts.''

When Zach didn't say anything else, Donnie added, "I know this seems sudden. But I love your mother, Zach. I think we'd be good for each other. All four of us.''

Kristin spoke first. She addressed Lucas directly.

"Lucas, how do you feel about your dad and me getting married?"

Donnie held his breath as he waited for his son's reply. Lucas looked at his father, then shifted his gaze to the other side of the table. "Why do you care what I think? You're going to do whatever you want. Adults always do."

"I'm sure it seems that way, but in this case, I want to know how you feel. Your dad will be busy with the election. That means you and Zach and I will be here together. I'm not expecting us to be one big happy family, but we'll need to get along."

Lucas didn't so much as blink.

Donnie saw Kristin's lips tighten as though she might be fighting back tears. "Zach, you've had more time to think about this. What are your feelings?" he asked.

"I think the whole thing sucks. Your kid is right, though. You two are going to do what you want regardless of how we feel, so why don't you just cut the bullshit?"

"Zach," Kristin said sharply.

He jumped to his feet. "Forget it. I'm outta here."

"Zach, please," his mother said. "Running away never solved anything. Aren't I proof of that?"

To Donnie's surprise, the question stopped Zach in his tracks. "Aren't you even going to try to work something out with my dad?"

Donnie braced for her answer.

"There's nothing to work out—except where

you're concerned. Besides, like I told you, Tyler and I were never meant to be together. I'm sorry, but I can't change that, sweetheart.''

His face contorted in anger. ''Can't? Or won't?'' He walked toward the foyer then paused in the doorway. ''Live here if you want. I'm going to my dad's.''

CHAPTER EIGHT

KRISTIN COULDN'T FEEL her heart beating. She figured her body was on automatic pilot because she was still breathing, but her brain had turned off. It was the only way to stand the pain of losing her son.

"He doesn't mean it," Donnie said, taking her arm when she started to race after Zach. "Let him cool down. We all say things we don't mean when we're upset, right, son?"

"I guess," Lucas said with a careless shrug.

"But this isn't like Zach," Kristin said, trying to pry Donnie's fingers loose.

A part of her needed to find Zach and apologize, but a part of her craved Donnie's rock-solid assurance that her world wasn't going to end.

Donnie squeezed her hand. "He'll come around, Kris. He just needs to blow off a little steam."

"I don't think so. He's never been this angry." *Maybe he's right not to forgive me this time.*

"Lucas, please get Kristin a glass of water and bring it outside. She needs some fresh air." Donnie put an arm around her shoulders and led her through the house to the patio. "I want you to wait here while I go look for Zach. Will you do that?"

Kristin squinted against the bright sunlight. He guided her to a two-person redwood glider tucked in a nook created by a grouping of shoulder-high photinia bushes. The sun had warmed the padded cushion, and she sank into it.

Donnie left but returned a minute later with a chenille throw. "When I find him, I'll give him a chance to vent. On me. I'm as much to blame for this situation as you are."

Kristin knew that wasn't true. True to form, she'd blown it again.

Donnie squatted in front of her and took her chin between his thumb and index finger. "Kristin, look at me."

She pushed his hand away. She saw the compassion—the understanding—in his eyes. He was offering to share the burden she'd carried for so long alone, but she couldn't accept. "I'm sorry, Donnie. This isn't going to work. I can't marry you. Not if Zach—"

He leaned forward and pressed a kiss to her forehead. "I'll be back as soon as I can. Let Lucas know if you need anything."

He left her then. Kristin pulled her knees to her chest and rocked back and forth. The glider provided a comforting jiggle and she closed her eyes to think.

What a mess. How had life gotten so complicated? She needed to take Zach and go back to

Jenny's little house. She'd focus on building up her business and trying to bring some joy back in her son's life. And she'd pray that Tyler wouldn't make the upcoming custody battle too awful.

Yes, a part of her wanted to marry Donnie—even if it was for the wrong reasons. But she couldn't risk alienating her son.

And what about Lucas? she wondered. Zach had reacted so fast, they hadn't even heard from Donnie's son.

Her first impression of the boy had reminded Kristin of herself at age ten. He seemed so alone. Despite two sisters, Ida Jane and a town full of pseudogodparents, Kristin had often felt isolated.

She'd gone through all the motions—pep squad, volleyball, French club, but she'd never quite fit in.

"Would you be...like...my stepmom?" a voice asked from the doorway of the patio.

Kristin looked up, startled. She hadn't heard the sliding door open. Lucas advanced slowly, carrying a glass of water. She furtively wiped away the tear trails on her cheeks and said, "Don't worry, honey. I don't think your dad and I are getting married. I can't force this on Zach—not after all he's been through."

He didn't say anything. His eyes—so like Donnie's—looked troubled. Stopping an arm's length away, he handed her the glass.

"Thanks," she said and took a sip. She smiled at him. "I had hoped we might be friends," she said. "Stepmother has such an ugly ring to it." Her attempted humor fell woefully short of the mark.

He dropped his chin, letting his hair cover his forehead and eyes. He reminded her of her old sheepdog, Daisy. The likeness almost made her smile.

"It's stupid to get married because your kid needs a baby-sitter."

Her stomach flip-flopped. "You don't want it either, huh?" It was hard to keep the tears back, but she tried. She was the adult here.

"Well…I'd hate a nanny more. Nannies are for babies. Why can't my grandma come back? She's cool, and we get along pretty good."

"Your grandmother and I bumped into each other at the bank before she left. You're right. Maureen *is* cool and she looks great."

"She works out. The doctor said she has high cholesterol."

The length of this conversation amazed her. Was he curious or lonely? Kris was afraid to move lest she scare him away. "How's her sister doing? Maureen went to help your dad's aunt, right?"

Lucas ventured a step closer. He pretended to be engrossed in peeling chipped paint off the upright post that supported the overhang. "Okay, I guess. Grandma likes to help people. Last year, she volunteered in the library at school."

"I used to work in Zach's classroom. I loved it."

"My mom baked cookies—in, like, first and second grade, but…she doesn't cook much anymore. Mostly we eat out.''

Kristin wondered if that had contributed to his weight gain. No doubt he would slim down as he grew taller, but poor eating habits might make it hard to keep off the pounds.

''My dad said you massage people.''

''That's right. Have you ever had a massage?''

''Heck no,'' he said, turning away. She caught a glimpse of his telltale blush.

Something she'd seen in the Gold Creek Chamber of Commerce information brochure came back to her. ''Doesn't your school have a career day?'' His slight shrug might have been a yes. ''Do you think your classmates would be interested in learning about massage therapy? I could bring my bench and give a bunch of five-minute massages.''

He abandoned his task and walked a little closer. ''The kind where you sit up instead of lying down? I saw a guy doing that at the fair last year. Can you make any money?''

''A dollar a minute for a chair massage.''

He looked impressed. ''Sixty bucks an hour. Not bad.''

His grin was so Donnie-like, Kris felt the tears return. She would have liked to get to know this child better.

''Where's my dad?''

''He went to find Zach.''

''Will your son change his mind?''

Her bottom lip started to tremble. *What a cry-baby!* "I doubt it. Once his mind is made up..."

"Sounds like my mother."

Kris hadn't expected such candor. "My sister, too."

Lucas took another step toward her. "My mom's going to Africa."

Kris could see in his eyes how much Sandy's broken promise had hurt her son. "I know. Did you want to go?"

He took a deep breath. "Maybe. I'm not sure. Her husband doesn't like me...uh...kids."

A telling amendment, she thought.

"He was married before and has two daughters somewhere. He doesn't have time for them, either. He's too busy."

Kristin sighed and snuggled down in the glider. The afternoon sun was starting to dip toward the west and a chilly breeze had blown in. "It's sad when families get shortchanged by careers."

"What kind of things do you and Zach do?"

His question surprised her, but she answered honestly. "He helps me run my business. I'm terrible about remembering appointments. He learned how to balance my checkbook when he was eight because I was so bad at it. The bank once called me four times in two weeks."

His eyebrows shot up. "Really? My dad would shoot you."

Kris made a face. "That was a couple of years ago. I'm better now—thanks to Zach and my computer. But that's business. For fun, we go skating sometimes. And we both like to fish. He has to put the worms on my hook. I don't like that part.''

Lucas laughed. It was a nice sound, and Kristin was pleased with herself—until she looked up and saw Donnie, Zach and Sarge standing at the rear gate. She hadn't heard them approach.

She leaped to her feet, still clutching the throw. She raced to her son. She ignored the stay-back look he gave her and wrapped her arms around him. ''I love you, Zach. I can share you, but please don't make me give you up entirely. I couldn't take that.''

He stayed rigid for a few seconds then dropped the dog's leash and hugged her back. ''I'll stay with you, Mom. I probably couldn't take Sarge if I went to my father's place. He lives in a high-rise apartment in Seattle.''

''Really?'' she squeaked, her throat too tight to speak.

''He's planning to move to Gold Creek permanently, but it might take a few months.'' Zach looked to his left to where Kristin sensed Donnie was standing. ''And, uh, Donnie said he has a guitar for me.''

Kris looked over her son's shoulder. Donnie smiled a bit sheepishly.

''I haven't played since Conundrum broke up,'' Donnie said. ''But Lucas plays. Maybe you guys can jam.''

Lucas looked skeptical, but Kristin saw a flicker of interest in his eyes.

"Zach, does this mean you're willing to stay here if I marry Donnie?"

"Yeah, I guess," he said. "Whatever."

"What about you, Lucas?" she asked the boy who was now on one knee petting Sarge. "I know you're not wild about this idea, either."

Lucas shrugged, then looked up at Zach. "Cool dog."

"Thanks. I think he'd like it here."

Lucas pointed toward a good-size doghouse that was painted the same color as the Grimaldo home. "Me 'n Dad built that for Sheba. She died last year. She was a Border collie. If she wanted you to go somewhere, she'd nip at your heels, like she was herding you."

Zach knelt, too. Kristin's heart almost broke at the kindness in his smile. "Sarge used to belong to a miner who died. He likes to chase rabbits, but he never catches 'em."

"Cool," Lucas said. "Rabbits are okay."

Kristin felt Donnie looking at her, and she couldn't stop herself from looking up. His smile was tentative but hopeful. She wondered if they were thinking the same thing: if this truce held, she might actually end up as Mrs. Donnie Grimaldo.

But that wasn't going to happen until she took her sister's advice and tested the spark. She looked at Donnie and said, "Could we take a walk?"

He looked surprised. "Sure. I'll show you the creek." To the boys, who were still petting Sarge, he said, "Lucas, why don't you show Zach the game you got for your birthday. Kris and I are going to be at the creek. Talking.

"Zach, as soon as we get back, I'll show you that guitar. We'll see if it's up to your standards."

Zach didn't say anything, but he looked pleased. And he followed Lucas into the house without hesitation.

"That was nice. About the guitar," Kris said.

He shrugged as he directed her to a path leading away from the yard. "An icebreaker, not a bribe. I swear."

"Those kinds of fine distinctions are sounding pretty political. Are you practicing?"

He walked at her side. They moved slowly since her shoes weren't designed for rocks and loose pebbles. The oaks that lined the upper flood plain of the creek cut the breeze so Kristin could enjoy the brisk temperature without shivering.

"I seriously doubt that I have a prayer in this election, but like Sam said last night, it will be good experience. I'll know what to do differently in 2006."

"What will you do if you lose?"

"Collect unemployment." His wink told her he was kidding. "Actually, I haven't thought that far ahead, but I'd like to stay in law enforcement. Or maybe I'll go back to college and finish my degree. I'm just a year short."

He paused. "Does it bother you? The fact that I might lose."

"Andi says you'll win, hands down."

Donnie chuckled. "And we all know better than to argue with Andi."

They walked the rest of the way in silence, but the chatter of the birds—vocal but unseen—filled the air. As they neared the winding ribbon of trees and reeds, Kris heard the trickle of water. "I expected the creek to be dry this late in the season."

"No. Lucas said it's still knee-deep in spots."

"You don't come down here?"

He shook his head. "I try to give him some space. I felt better about it when Sheba was around, but I know Lucas needs to be alone sometimes."

"How come you didn't get another dog?"

"I thought we were all leaving town."

"Are you disappointed?"

He didn't answer until they reached the granite shelf. To one side, a grouping of willows provided shade and a convenient low branch to lean against. They relaxed, side-by-side, and stared at the ripples on the surface of the creek as water bugs scurried about.

Donnie sighed. "Truthfully? Yes. I still want to see the world, but this isn't the right time. And now, I have a new goal, and a new family. I'm pretty excited about all of that."

She turned to face him. "Are you? Really?"

"Of course."

"Then how come you haven't kissed me?"

He looked surprised, then sheepish. "This is going to sound stupid, but I'm intimidated."

"What?" she shouted. The invisible birds shot

like a cloud of locusts from the willow and disappeared over the rise. "Why?"

"Because you left here a girl and came back a woman. A gorgeous, amazing woman of the world. You've been places and seen things and I'm still here. Just the same me."

The words were so close to what she'd told Andi that morning, Kris couldn't speak. So she let her hands do the talking. She touched his face, his jaw, his brow. There was a new crease that hadn't been there at seventeen. His beard was a little coarser, but if she remembered correctly there was a spot—the size of a nickel—under his chin where no hair grew.

Her fingers skimmed his cheek then gently tilted his head back. Still there. She could remember kissing that spot, tasting it.

He put his arms around her. Even through layers of clothes, she could feel his heart thud against her chest. If she turned slightly, she'd find that resting spot she loved so much.

But she wasn't here to rest. She was here to find the spark that had been missing far too long.

She wound the fingers of her left hand through his hair and brought his face closer. With her right hand, she touched his lips. They parted and his tongue flickered playfully, making her smile.

Their gazes met. And held. He lowered his head. Their lips met. Frank. Curious. Friendly.

Kris closed her eyes and let the sensation envelop her.

Oh, my, yes. The spark was definitely there.

DONNIE HAD TRIED every tactic possible during the past four days, including begging, but Kristin flatly refused to attend the Friday-afternoon engagement party of his co-worker Cory Brandell.

"The moment belongs to the young couple," she'd insisted a few minutes earlier on the phone. "They're doing this the right way for the right reason. I don't think we should detract from their celebration with our news."

Her refusal had irked him, even though he understood what she meant. "I wasn't going to blurt out an announcement," he replied. "I just wanted to introduce you to my friends."

"Most of those people know me, Donnie. I'm the infamous triplet—the one who caused a scandal then left town, returning years later with an illegitimate child. Ask anyone and they'll tell you my life story."

She had a point, but he was like a kid with a secret. He couldn't wait to tell somebody. "Kristin Sullivan is going to marry me," he wanted to yell at the top of his lungs in the center of town.

"Hey, Donnie," Margie called as he entered the common room. "Nice flowers," she said, nodding at the bouquet Kristin had insisted he take to the bride-to-be.

"Hi, Margie. Where's the lady of the hour? I want to get rid of these."

"Cory and the future Mrs. Cory are in with Magnus. What have you been up to all week? I'd like to say you look rested, but, frankly, you look like hell.''

He chuckled. ''Tell me what you really think, Margie.''

She gave him one of her looks—one that said the bull stops here.

Donnie used his free hand to pull a square envelope from his jacket pocket. Kristin had maintained that it was too short notice to issue invitations to a wedding that would take place in two days, but Donnie had prevailed. ''Ten invitations. Simple. Private. Your sisters and their husbands, Ida Jane and a few close friends.''

Jenny had solved the dilemma by purchasing a dozen small watercolor prints, on the backs of which she'd written the date and time. ''This way even if they can't come, they'll have something to remember it by,'' she'd explained when she presented them to him. He'd been touched.

Donnie slipped the envelope into Margie's in-tray. ''I have been a little busy. Courting.''

Margie gaped at him. ''What?''

''That's an invitation to my wedding, but you have to keep it to yourself.''

''It's a secret?'' she said in a hushed voice that made every head in the room turn her way.

He tapped her on the shoulder with his bouquet. ''No. But this is Cory's day, and I don't want to steal his thunder.'' *Not true, but he'd behave—for Kristin.*

Margie carefully opened the cream-colored ve-
lum envelope and peeked inside. Her head popped
up, mouth wide. Oh my God, she mouthed then
jumped to her feet and hugged him fiercely. Donnie's quick reflexes saved the flowers.

"What's going on?" Bethany asked, joining
them.

Donnie had an invitation for her, too, but he
would wait until later to give it to her. "She misses
me," he said with his last bit of air.

Beth obviously didn't buy his excuse, but her
attention was diverted when the door to the sheriff's
private office opened and three people walked
out—Magnus Brown, followed by a young couple
holding hands.

"Hey, Donnie," Cory hailed. "Glad you could
make it. Come meet Meghan."

Donnie crossed the room and presented his flowers.

"Wow, these are beautiful," she exclaimed.
"Thank you so much. I can't believe you're all being so nice to me when I'm taking Cory away from
you."

Donnie glanced at his boss, who nodded grimly.
Cory was supposed to fill Donnie's slot when he
left. Donnie wasn't concerned about that since he
wasn't going anywhere, but he'd been counting on
Cory's support during the election.

Magnus cornered Donnie a minute later. "You
know what this means, Grimaldo? It means you re-

think this silly air marshals thing. I'm going to need you. Your town needs you.''

This was not the time or place to announce his change in plans. ''I've already been accepted, Magnus.''

''Well, too bad,'' Magnus snapped. ''Back when you first suggested this cockamamy idea I agreed to let you leave on a trial basis—in case it didn't work out. But now that Brandell's given notice, I'm going to have to hire someone to replace him. If you leave, I'm going to have to fill your slot, too.'' He glared at Donnie. ''I'll need your answer by the end of next week.''

''You'll have it,'' Donnie replied. *But you won't like it.* He watched while Cory and his bride-to-be cut and served the decorated cake from the Sweet Tooth Bakery. A fixture with the high-school crowd in his day, the shop had changed hands last year. The new owners—a Pakistani couple from San Jose—promptly remodeled eliminating the booths and tables to make room for their catering business. They were delivering a wedding cake to the bordello tomorrow afternoon.

He ate several bites without tasting anything as he made his way to Edgar Olson's desk. After nudging aside a thick pile of folders, Donnie rested his hip on one corner. ''So, how's it going?'' he asked, chasing a few crumbs around his plate with his plastic fork.

"Not bad. Heard you've been a busy beaver."

Ed was in his late fifties. He wore cowboy boots with his uniform and sported a silver mustache that he kept meticulously trimmed. "I cleaned out my garage if that's what you mean," Donnie said nonchalantly.

Ed was a friend and had been a mentor to him since Donnie started with the department as a high-school trainee. Donnie knew him to be calm and unflappable, and there was no one he'd trust more in a dangerous situation.

"Yup, that's what I meant," Ed said with a wink. "Cleaned up some loose ends, too, as I heard it."

Loose ends. Is that what this is all about? Donnie knew it wasn't that simple. He handed Ed an invitation. "If Edith's feeling up to it, we'd love to see you both." Ed's wife—a seven-year breast cancer survivor—had learned last July that the disease had returned.

Ed removed the pretty sheet of paper and read the message then tucked it in his pocket. "I'm sure she'd like that, if she's having a good day. You just never know."

"We're keeping it low-key for obvious reasons."

"What obvious reasons?" Ed asked.

Donnie had to think a minute. Despite that one memorable kiss at the creek, he wasn't ready to call this a love match. True, he loved Kristin, but he had yet to hear those words from her lips. "Second marriages…"

Ed frowned. "Kristin hasn't been married before."

Donnie looked at his mangled piece of cake. True. She hadn't. He dumped the cake in the trash. "I meant me. But you know about the circumstances with Tyler Harrison, and Kris…we decided to do this to solidify her position when she goes to court."

Ed rocked back in his chair and crossed his arms. He was a small, wiry man with surprisingly fast reflexes and a keen mind. "So, this is a sort of marriage of convenience?"

Donnie was beginning to hate that phrase. "Sorta."

"You don't love her."

"I didn't say that."

"You do love her."

"I didn't say that, either."

Ed's mustache flickered. "Guess I'll have to make up my own mind since you don't seem to know."

Donnie didn't care for the hint of sarcasm in Ed's tone. "I know what I'm doing and why, I just don't feel it's something I need to talk about."

Ed sat forward, his expression serious. "Guess this means you didn't get in?"

Ed was the only colleague who knew about Donnie's application. He'd been listed as a reference.

"Actually, I did. But I turned it down."

Ed rose and put a hand on Donnie's shoulder. Eye-to-eye, he said, "Well, the FAM program is missing out on a terrific candidate, but I'll sleep a lot easier knowing you're on the job right here in Gold Creek."

The band of tension across Donnie's neck and shoulders loosened just a bit. "Thanks, Ed," he said with a grin. "I appreciate that."

Ed winked. "No problem. I'll see you Sunday."

Donnie watched him walk away. A man of few words. A good man. Donnie would have told him about the election, but Jonathan had asked him to keep mum until after the formal announcement.

"What's up?" a voice asked.

Bethany. "Hey. Just the person I wanted to see. Would you walk me to my car, Miss Murdock? There's something I wanted to talk to you about," he said, leading the way to the employees' entrance.

"Okay," she said with a shrug. "I gotta get back to school, anyway. They only let me out because Margie asked." She dumped her empty cake plate and napkin in a receptacle near the outer door. "Good cake, huh?"

"Yep, good stuff. I'm getting my cake from them, too, when I get married." He waited for her reaction.

She laughed. "Oh, yeah? When's that—the next millennium?"

He paused beside the Forerunner. "Sunday, actually. Two o'clock at the old bordello. You're invited."

Her mouth dropped open so far he could see particles of cake. "No way," she exclaimed. "Are you serious?"

He handed her the last of his invitations. "Very small. Very simple. I was hoping you'd come so Lucas and Zach aren't the only young people there."

"Zach?" She clawed open the envelope. "Zach Sullivan? That new seventh-grader my sister has a crush on?"

Donnie wasn't surprised to learn Zach was a heartthrob. "That would be the one. His mother is my fiancée."

Beth gave him a knowing look. "The pretty blonde who was here that day to get fingerprinted, right?"

He nodded. "Remember, I told you we were old friends. Actually, we were high-school sweethearts." He held up his keys. "Need a ride?"

She didn't hesitate. She trotted around the car.

As they turned on Main Street, she said, "Maybe marriage is contagious. First, Cory. Now, you."

Donnie smiled. "A real epidemic."

"No, I'm serious. You might want to get checked

out by the doctor before Sunday. What if you caught a bug?''

"Knock it off, Murdock. Kris and I are getting married because we want to. We should have done this years ago, but the timing was wrong.''

"And now it's right?''

He pulled to a stop in front of the high school then said, "I guess I'll see you at the wedding.'' She hopped out, waving her invitation. "See you Sunday.''

Sunday. Two days away. Talk about a rush job. The only thing missing is the shotgun.

ZACH PICKED HIS WAY across a deep spot in the creek using providentially placed rocks. He figured he wasn't the first kid to use this particular shortcut to the Highland Estates. That was the name of the development where Donnie Grimaldo's house was.

His aunt Andi had told him a little bit of the history of Gold Creek while he'd raked the backyard of the old bordello, which was being spruced up for his mother's wedding.

In a way, he couldn't believe his mother was going through with it. Andi had insisted that this was a love match.

"Kris has loved Donnie since they were kids,'' Andi had told him not twenty minutes earlier. "Donnie didn't live here then, but he used to visit his grandparents quite often. Maureen's parents were among the first to build in the Highland Estates subdivision. Then after Donnie's father was killed in an accident, his mother moved here to be closer to her folks.''

Zach wasn't sure why he wanted to check out the Grimaldo house again—this time on his own. He'd used walking Sarge as an excuse to get away from the wedding preparations.

Sarge splashed contentedly at his side until they found a break in the thick clusters of cattails lining the banks on the subdivision side of the creek. Zach followed the dog up the embankment then paused to get his bearings.

There it is. He spotted the house with blue-gray trim on a knoll a couple of hundred yards away. He'd only taken two steps when Sarge's hackles went up. A low growl put Zach on the alert. He grabbed the dog's collar and snapped on the leash he carried in his pocket. His mother had warned him that people could order the old dog put to death if he bit someone.

''Take it easy, boy,'' Zach whispered as they advanced toward a stand of six-foot-tall reeds.

When he was about twenty feet from the spot where he'd heard the noise, Sarge's muzzle lifted and his big black nose sniffed. Zach took a deep breath. His jaw dropped. He knew that distinctive smell. Pot.

A rustling noise told him whoever was in the bushes was about to leave. Zach pulled Sarge behind a car-size boulder. Whispering in the dog's ear, Zach waited until a person appeared. Lucas.

Donnie's kid ambled slowly toward the house without looking back.

Zach sank back against the sun-warmed hunk of granite and sighed. Sarge cocked his head questioningly. "Damn. I'm going to be living with a frigging pothead."

CHAPTER NINE

"WHAT THE HELL is going on here?"

The angry voice slashed through the serenity of Kristin's basement massage studio as welcome as a clap of thunder at a picnic.

Kristin and Lillian Carswell both jumped. They were sitting side by side on the love seat looking at the photo album Lillian had brought along for her regular Saturday-morning appointment. Kris had spent twenty minutes she couldn't spare admiring the woman's newest grandchild.

"I'm sorry. You're...?"

"Sandra Baker."

The name didn't ring a bell. The face seemed familiar, but the artfully blond hair and too-perfect figure in designer wool slacks and silk blouse didn't look local.

"Sandy *Grimaldo* Baker."

Kris inhaled sharply. "Oh. I thought you were on your way to Africa," she said inanely. Lucas had mentioned that his mother was scheduled to leave today.

"They've pushed back production two weeks, so I flew up to see Lucas and take him home with me for a few days. Imagine my surprise when I walked in and found this." She held up one of Jenny's invitations.

Impulsively, Kris snatched the envelope from her as if it were a discount coupon. "You've found it. Thank you. I was looking all over for this. It belongs to Lillian. You remember Lillian Carswell, don't you, Sandy? She was head librarian for as long as I can remember."

Lillian stood up looking puzzled but intrigued.

"I wasn't done with that," Sandy said imperiously.

Kristin handed Lillian the vellum square and ushered her toward the door. "Donnie Grimaldo and I are getting married tomorrow, Lillian. If you're free after church, we'd love for you to join us."

"That nice young deputy? You're marrying him? Well, isn't that smart of you. I always told my girls, 'Marry with your head, your heart will follow.'" She patted Kristin's arm and leaned close to whisper, "Don't let this one give you any guff. She's a slut."

Kristin nearly swallowed her tongue, but Lillian merely winked and walked out.

"I can't believe that old bag is still alive," Sandy said, sitting down. "She would never let us get away with returning books late."

"Lillian is a dynamo. I wish I had half her energy and even a quarter of her knowledge." Kris closed the door.

She'd known this day would come, but she'd

thought she'd have an ocean and several continents between them when it did. She walked to the love seat and sat down.

"I'm sorry this came as such a shock to you, Sandy. Donnie has been trying for days to reach you. He said he left a number of messages on your service."

Sandy's chin rose defensively. "Boyd and I went to Mammoth. The stress of this move has made things...well, anyway. I'm here now, and I want to know what's going on with you and my ex-husband."

Kristin took a deep breath. Sandy was going to be a part of their lives. They could be friendly or things could be miserable for all involved. "Donnie and I are getting married. That's really all there is to say."

"Kind of sudden, isn't it? A week ago Donnie was moaning about his dream job slipping through his fingers. Now he's getting married. To you of all people."

Her taunt hurt, but given their high-school history, Kristin wouldn't have expected anything less. But Kristin was no longer an insecure young girl. She was an adult. A parent. And this woman was Lucas's mother.

She took a deep breath and let it out. "Our reasons for getting married are really no one else's business. But as Lucas's mother—"

"That's right. *I'm* Lucas's mother," Sandy interrupted her. "And as his mother I have every right to know who's going to be living in the same house with him. And why.''

Kris was prepared to lie but changed her mind. If any of this conversation got back to Lucas, she wanted it to be the truth. ''I've loved Donnie since I was a little girl, and he rescued me from some big dog that was trying to hump my leg. I was so embarrassed I thought I'd die, but he was sweet and kind and made me laugh.''

The memory came out of the blue. She hadn't thought about the incident in years. ''We're adults now. We haven't seen each other for a decade. But our feelings are still there. We're just trying to do the best we can and not hurt too many people in the process.''

Sandy's foot stopped bouncing. She tilted her head and studied Kristin. ''I can respect that. I wasn't totally in love with Boyd when I married him. He can be an arrogant SOB, but I couldn't live without him now.''

Kristin swallowed a sizable lump in her throat. ''I'm happy for you, Sandy. Truly. I was hoping we could get along for our sons' sakes. I'll be happy to act as your voice and hands in your absence.''

Sandy didn't answer right away. Then she slipped off the chair and held out her hand. ''While I'm not wild about the idea of Lucas having a stepmother, I always knew it might happen. The fact that you have a son could make it easier.'' A tiny frown puckered her forehead. ''I think Lucas gets lonely sometimes. And then he eats.''

They shook hands. "Lucas will stay with me tonight. I'll change our tickets to a later flight tomorrow because I'm sure he'd like to be at the wedding."

Kristin was tempted to ask if she'd cleared her plans with Lucas's father but decided that was Donnie's battle. Once Sandy was gone, Kris locked the door and lit a stick of incense. Clary sage—for patience and insight. She was going to need both if she was going to do a good job in her new role.

"LET ME PUT those leftovers in the car," Donnie said, taking the white disposable box from Kristin's hand. She'd barely eaten half her dinner—herb and cheese ravioli. Nerves, he assumed. He'd ordered lasagna and had consumed every bite, but he couldn't recall tasting it. "Do you have time for a walk?"

"Sure. It beats sitting home going crazy," she said with a small laugh.

"Are you nervous?"

"Who me?" she asked, bracing her hands on the ornamental hitching rail in front of the Golden Corral restaurant. "Jenny and Andi are handling the reception. You've taken care of the ceremony. All I have to do is show up tomorrow."

Tomorrow. Our wedding day.

He unlocked the car door and placed the box on the seat. He'd heard echoes of the rumors that were racing through town—something about why he and Kris were getting married in such a hurry.

He slammed the door with more force than necessary. Kristin gave him a questioning look.

"Have you seen the changes the Kiwanis Club made to the park? Old-fashioned streetlights and cobblestone paths. The Garden Club planted hedges and did some landscaping."

"I was home for Josh's funeral. We held the memorial there, remember?"

"Oh, right. I forgot. That was a tough time."

"I still can't believe he's gone."

Josh O'Neal had become Donnie's best friend after Josh and Jenny moved back to town. His death had shaken Donnie. "Josh was full of colorful travel stories. My life felt black and white compared to his."

She glanced sideways. "Trust me, Donnie. Travel is great if you have money, but moving from one crummy apartment to another because you can save ten bucks a month in rent isn't fun."

They walked along the raised sidewalk that distinguished the original part of town as an historical, gold rush–era community. Just four blocks long, the wide central street was a mixture of building materials ranging from quarried stone to narrow wooden siding.

She stopped in front of the hobbit-like entry of the Book Nook. A light was on inside, but a small sign in the shape of a clock was hanging on the door. The little hand pointed to the eight. "I wanted to buy Ida Jane some new crossword-puzzle books," Kristin said. "They're good stimulation for her mind."

She consulted her watch but had to twist her arm to read it.

Upside down.

Grinning, he turned her wrist over and carefully pried open the tiny latch. "Put this on by yourself, huh?"

His teasing—and the last vestiges of sunlight— lent a pink tinge to her smooth cheeks. "I was in a hurry. My client wanted an extra half hour on his neck."

Out of nowhere, an image of Tyler Harrison on her table with only a sheet to cover him flashed before Donnie. The unpleasant bite of jealousy disturbed him. "Is business picking up?" he asked, snapping the metal clasp.

She lowered her arm and shook her hand to position the watch closer to her wrist. The birdlike bones in her tiny wrists and ankles had always fascinated him. "I left flyers at all the motels in town. My last client works with the crew contracted to trim trees near power poles. A branch fell on his shoulder."

"Bad for him. Good for you," Donnie said, continuing down the street. "We can stop here on our way back, okay?"

Half a block later they were in front of Patrick's TrueValue. She tapped at a display of lightbulbs. "Remind me to pick up an exterior flood for the shop. It's getting dark earlier."

Donnie made a mental note to take care of the chore.

She resumed walking. She was dressed in a beguiling peasant skirt that came to her ankles and a loose, short-sleeve top the color of a Carmel sunset. Over one arm, she carried a knitted shawl.

"Was it just me?" she asked. "Or did it feel as if the whole town was watching us at dinner? They all know, don't they?"

"Of course." He'd realized there was no way to avoid a public appearance at some point, so he'd asked her to join him for dinner on the eve of their wedding. Lucas was with Sandy, and Zach and Tyler had spent the day in Yosemite. This was his and Kristin's first time alone in a week—*alone* being a relative term. "This is Gold Creek. And you're one of the Sullivan triplets. A wedding is big news."

She snorted skeptically. "I could understand it when we were orphaned babies, but this kind of attention is getting old. Jenny told me there's already a plan in the works for the whole town to celebrate our thirtieth birthday next February."

As they crossed the street, a horn honked. Donnie looked to his right and spotted Pascal Fournier in his cherry-red 1957 T-bird. A popular high-school teacher, the man waved with such enthusiasm, he nearly jumped the curb. The golden retriever in the passenger seat barked.

"I think it's safe to say Pascal's heard about us," Donnie said, rushing Kris to the relative safety of the sidewalk.

She waved and smiled. "I hope he's still teaching when Zach gets to high school," she said as they watched the car roar across the intersection. "He was one of the few teachers who made me learn."

"I liked him as well," Donnie said, taking her elbow to guide her across Main Street to the steps leading to the park. Fremont Park, named for John C. Fremont, adventurer and early landowner in the area, was situated on a knoll overlooking the town.

Her skin was soft and warm, and he wanted to go on touching her. But the concrete steps were only wide enough for single file. Kristin took the lead, which suited Donnie fine. If he couldn't touch her, he'd settle for watching her as she climbed upward.

"Whew," she said at the first landing. "I'd forgotten what a workout this is. I remember when that horrible P.E. teacher made us run up these steps once a week."

"What are you complaining about? Coach made us do it daily at the end of football practice."

She pivoted. "It paid off. The team won the conference title."

Donnie stopped. He had to tilt his chin to look up at her. The pinkish-gray of twilight gave her a magical, fairy princess quality. It was all he could do to keep from kissing her.

His intention must have been plain to see because she quickly turned and sprinted up the second flight. He hurried after her. Fortunately, he'd been working out extra hard the past six months in preparation for the FAM physical, so he had no trouble keeping up. And the strained muscle in his back seemed to have cleared up completely.

"Kristin," he said, reaching for her arm. "Slow down. We need to talk."

She didn't stop until she reached the top, then she bent at the waist, laughing between gasps. "Dizzy." She shook her curls. "Too old." She placed one hand on her flat belly and drew in a deep breath. "Remind me not to do that again anytime soon."

Her tone was bright and full of humor. Suddenly, he knew with absolute conviction, he'd made the right decision. He wanted to be here with her—to remind her not to run up the steps, or do anything else that might hurt her.

Kristin—oblivious to Donnie's thoughts—strolled toward the replica of a miner's cabin in the center of the park. Picnic tables were clustered inside the log shell in preparation for the rain and snow that would arrive in a few months.

"That log cabin always makes me think of winter. Remember the ski trips to Badger Pass and the time you guys crashed our all-girl retreat. We were staying at Mindy..." Her lips puckered in a thoughtful pout. "Oh, what was her name?"

She looked too damn adorable to resist, so he quit trying.

"Who cares?" he asked, drawing her to him.

She bounced against his chest, completely unprepared for his move, but a second later, melted against him.

"I didn't want to do this in a public place," he said, lightly outlining her mouth with his finger. "But at least our sons aren't likely to show up."

He pressed his lips to hers, cutting off her protest. At first he kissed her as chastely as a child might kiss a relative. That restraint lasted all of a millisecond. Her lips parted, and she sighed ever so slightly, a puff of warm air that stirred something in his soul.

He opened his mouth and tasted her. He let instinct carry him. And memory. They'd kissed like this before, when they'd first discovered love. Their blood had raced with overheated passion anytime they were in the same room together. When life was about possibilities, not responsibilities.

Responsibilities. A responsible man didn't maul his fiancée in public. He pulled back, keeping his hands on her upper arms. With breathing space between them—and crisp autumn air—he could think again. "That was not good."

Her forehead puckered. "It wasn't?"

"No. It felt good, but it wasn't smart. We're not sixteen. We don't need to neck in public. We have homes. As of tomorrow, *a* home. And two kids."

She nodded. But her lips were tender and soft, and they showed the effect of his kiss. He pulled her close again and gently brushed his lips across hers by way of apology. "That got a little crazy. Who knew we could still ignite that kind of fire?"

"Sparks," she said with a satisfied sigh. She smiled as he applied butterfly kisses to her cheekbones, her eyes and her nose. "I've heard the body remembers long after the brain forgets."

In the distance, there was the sound of a car door opening and closing, but Donnie ignored it now that they had their emotions under control. This was friendly playful kissing. Nothing to get worked up about.

"Mom?"

Unless you were Zach.

Kris pulled away and tried to step out of his reach, but Donnie caught her hand and refused to let go. "Zach," she exclaimed. "What are you doing here? I thought you and your dad were going to the mountains."

"Been there, done that," another voice said.

A man joined them. Tyler Harrison. He'd apparently been walking toward them but Donnie had missed his approach since he was torn between his concern for Kristin and dealing with Zach's scowl.

"Zach wanted to take Sarge for a run," Tyler added. "I suggested the park."

It was almost dark, and Donnie couldn't see the man clearly. The shadows suggested that he was gaunt but still formidable. The kind of person who came prepared for a fight and never gave an inch. The same way he'd been in high school.

Only now, Donnie had a better understanding of cause and effect. "Tyler Harrison's father was known as the town crook. Try carrying that load when you're a kid, and see how *you* turn out,'' Donnie's anger management counselor had suggested.

Kris's hand clutched Donnie's. He felt her shiver of apprehension, but to his surprise she faced Tyler and said, ''Did Zach tell you that Donnie and I are getting married tomorrow?''

''Zach mentioned it. Yes.'' His tone seemed tinged with sarcasm. ''I assumed it was a desperate ploy to thwart my custody suit.''

Donnie didn't care for the man's attitude, but he couldn't blame him. Not only did Tyler and Kris have issues, but the hard feelings between Donnie and Tyler had never been resolved. Even now, nearly a dozen years later, Donnie could recall the words that had brought them to blows.

Kristin had remained in the car that night, getting dressed. Donnie and Ty were well out of earshot when they'd fought. Even barefoot and in his skivvies, Tyler had challenged Donnie. He'd called him a bootlicking fascist. That, Donnie could have taken, but when Ty bragged about how easy it had been to seduce Kristin, Donnie had lost it. He might have killed the man if his friends hadn't intervened.

Kristin glanced at him with concern—no doubt also recalling the last time the three of them met. Donnie was determined to keep things civil. He wasn't a jealous kid with an ego problem anymore. He was an officer of the law. And a father. His main concern at the moment was Zach.

''Zach, how about we take Sarge to the dog run?

Your mother and Tyler could probably use a minute or two.''

The boy hesitated, but Kristin gave him a nod. He turned around, dog at his heels. Donnie doubted that Zach wanted to talk to him, but he followed, anyway.

When they reached the opposite side of the park where wild grasses remained unmowed and wild-flowers blossomed each spring, Sarge took off. Donnie looked at Zach and said, ''What you saw was a friendly kiss, Zach, nothing more.''

Thank goodness the boy hadn't shown up five minutes earlier. ''Does it bother you to see us kiss?''

''Nah. She's had dates before. She's very pretty.''

''Yes, she is.'' Donnie looked at the boy thought-fully. ''You know, it used to bother me when my mom began dating after my dad died. But then I realized she needed to be more than a mom some-times.''

Sarge suddenly materialized at Donnie's side. He smelled like tarweed—a pungent, low-growing brush that was starting to bloom. ''Do you think you'll have time to give him a bath in the morn-ing?'' Donnie asked. ''That is, if the wedding is still on.''

It was darker in this part of the park, and while Donnie couldn't swear to it, he thought he saw Zach smile. ''It's what my mom wants. Are you still going to teach me new chords?''

Donnie smiled. "Sure."

"My dad told me he's going to move here next month."

The thought made Donnie uneasy, but he could see that Zach was happy about it. "Good. I bet he's eager to spend time with you and get to know you better."

"I guess."

Donnie hoped Ty's motivation was to be near his son and not to build a shopping mall with a bypass around the town. There were aspects of Gold Creek that needed changing, but thoughtless commercial development wasn't one of them. Donnie had his own plans for Gold Creek—and they didn't involve a bulldozer.

"ARE WE GOING to keep things civil?" Kristin asked Tyler.

"I will if you will, but if Zach and I hadn't shown up when we did, you would have been lying down," he said. Although the words were snide, his tone was something else. Bittersweet? Resigned?

And he was right. There'd been a moment when she'd been on the verge of losing control. "Then it's a good thing you showed up. You know how much I hate being the focus of gossip."

Her wry tone must have connected because he smiled. Briefly. Then his look turned serious.

"I have an investigator checking into your past."

Kris wondered what he'd find. She'd been very

careful about dating when Zach was growing up. She seldom let a man close enough to become a friend to Zach and no man spent the night if Zach was home.

"You can hire a dozen," she said, faking a confidence she didn't feel. "They'll confirm that I've always tried my best to be a good mother."

He reclined against the plank picnic table, crossing one ankle over the other. She felt a shiver pass through her.

"What if I find a couple of guys who are willing to testify that you gave them *more* than a massage? What will that say about your fitness to be a parent?"

Kristin's stomach flip-flopped. "I've never been anything but professional with my clients. Massage is about healing, Tyler. Anyone who's ever been a client of mine knows that."

His light chuckle had an ominous ring to it. "I didn't say they were clients of yours. But for the right price, you can find somebody who will say whatever you tell them to say."

Suddenly, her fear eased. If he really planned to do this, she thought, he probably wouldn't tell her about it ahead of time. Curious, she asked, "Zach said you might be moving to Gold Creek?" She looked over her shoulder to see where Donnie and Zach were. "I heard you got married."

"And divorced."

"Was she the woman your mother told Ida Jane about? The socialite from back East?"

His left eyebrow arched in question—just the way Zach's did. "I have no idea what you're talking about."

"When I first moved back to the States with my cousins, I called Ida Jane and asked her to talk to your mother. To get your address or phone number. I was going to tell you about your son."

He looked skeptical. "When was this?"

She told him the date. She could picture it clearly.

"Ida told me that according to Gloria, you were doing great. You were in college and engaged to a woman with a pedigree a mile long." She looked at her hands. "She said you were happy."

He didn't say anything.

"I told myself I was doing you a favor. That I'd already screwed up your life, so by not contacting you I was doing the right thing."

"Bullsh—"

She touched his arm. "I knew it was wrong. Even then. But I was afraid, Tyler. If you married some rich, influential woman, you'd be the perfect family. You'd be able to take Zach away from me. I was struggling to keep food on the table, but—" She looked him in the eye. "Nobody could have loved Zach more than I did. Not even you."

He broke contact with her by standing. "For what it's worth, my ex was no socialite. She's a lawyer who tried to sue me. We were married only two years. And after I left Gold Creek, I didn't contact Mother—or anyone else from this town—for six years.''

Kristin looked up in surprise. "But your mother wrote all sorts of stuff about you in her column. Your business success. Your travels. Ida sent me the clippings.''

He made an off-hand motion. "We create the fantasy we need to get by. Gloria needed to pretend that she had the perfect son. You let yourself believe that I wouldn't *care* that you kept our son a secret.''

"That was wrong, Tyler. But you don't know what I was going through at the time. I'd let down my family, my town. Still, you have every right to be bitter, but—''

He cut her off. "Bitter? The word doesn't come close to describing how I feel.'' He stared at her, eyes narrowed. "You can marry the pope, but it won't help.''

He laughed at his inadvertent joke. The sound was as unnerving as the whine of a dentist's drill.

Her heart beat frantically as she watched him walk to his Mercedes. Zach and Sarge met him there; Donnie kept walking without saying a word to Tyler. His pace increased the closer he came to Kristin.

"The bastard,'' he hissed when he saw her face. "What did he say?''

Kris shook her head. "Nothing I didn't deserve.''

Donnie took her hand and led her toward the steps. "Let's go. We have a big day tomorrow.''

Tomorrow. *My wedding day.* Suddenly, the enormity of what she was about to do hit her.

She looked at the man who would be her husband within twenty-four hours. "If I'm getting married tomorrow, Donnie, I need to know the truth."

"What truth?"

"About why we're doing this. At the moment, I feel as if my whole life has been built on lies. It has to stop here. I can't go into this marriage just to help you win an election or to protect myself from the courts. If you love me, prove it. Make love to me. Lucas is spending the night with Sandy. We could go to your place."

When Donnie opened his mouth, she braced to hear the word no, but suddenly he smiled and said, "Well...if you insist."

CHAPTER TEN

HE'D LEFT the exterior porch light on and was pleased by the homey glow it gave the place, but instead of taking Kristin through the front door as he would a guest, Donnie made a conscious choice to pull into the garage.

"I'd better remember to give you the opener," he said, pressing the plastic remote on his visor. "Mom left hers."

Kristin hadn't said much since her request to go home with him; Donnie wondered if she was having second thoughts.

"What did Maureen say when you told her about the wedding?"

Kris's voice was soft and a little tentative, but he gave her credit for trying to maintain a cool front. "She said it broke her heart not to be here, but she wished us good luck and much happiness.

"What does Ida Jane think about our plan?" Donnie asked. For a man who'd been offered his favorite sexual fantasy on a plate, he sure was having a difficult time bringing himself to act on it. "Your sisters are pitching in to help, but does your aunt think we're crazy?"

He turned off the engine and let his hand fall to the back of the seat so he could touch her hair. One curl wrapped around his finger as if she'd lassoed him.

"She's very excited. She thinks we should have done it a long time ago."

She moved back slightly. "Why do you ask? Are you having second thoughts?"

"Not about marrying you." He rubbed his forehead. "I just regret that you're being shortchanged by my agenda. Maybe we should wait till after the election. I probably won't win the dang thing anyway."

"Donnie, what's really going on here?"

"I resigned today, Kris. And I guess the reality is hitting me now."

She unsnapped her seat belt and shifted sideways to face him. "We ate dinner together, took a walk, made out, and *now* you mention, 'Oh, by the way, I quit my job today'? Why didn't you say something earlier?"

"I didn't want you to feel obligated."

Her eyes went big and she blinked several times then broke out laughing. "Donavon Grimaldo, you're too much. You take the word *gentleman* to new extremes."

He couldn't decide if that was meant as a compliment or not, but when she reached out and cupped his jaw, she said, "Let's go inside. Ty is bringing Zach home around midnight, so we don't have much time."

Donnie leaned into her touch. "Do you want me to carry you across the threshold?" he said, nipping her fingers playfully.

For the briefest moment, he thought she might cry, but then a smile lit up her face and she said, "Sure, if your back is up to the task."

KRISTIN EXITED the car and stood for a moment, looking around. Donnie's garage was neater and cleaner than her house.

"Coming?" he asked, joining her.

There's still time to back out. They weren't touching, but she could feel him. Big, strong, reliable—everything she wasn't. And a longing so intense it erased her fears and made her reach out to put her arms around him.

He might have settled for a friendly hug, but Kristin rose to her tiptoes and plastered her front to his—her bosom to his chest, bellies touching. His surprised gasp turned to a smile of pleasure, and he dipped his head to kiss her.

Nobody had ever kissed her like Donnie Grimaldo. When she sighed with pleasure, he moved against her and she could feel his desire. He linked his hands at her waist then rocked back enough to look into her eyes "I do not have a bad back. Mind if I prove it to you?"

Kris nodded; she didn't trust her vocal cords. He bent and hooked his left arm beneath her knees then straightened. The look in his eyes made her feel desirable and sexy. "I always thought this was a silly ritual, but now I can see its attraction."

His eyes sparkled with laughter. She reached out to open the door. He hefted her up a little more snugly then walked through sideways. The door closed behind them.

Donnie didn't bother with lights. He headed straight toward his bedroom.

Feeling oddly emboldened, Kristin asked, "I don't suppose you'd consider fulfilling one other fantasy of mine, would you?"

He stopped in the middle of the hallway. "What is it?"

A blush heated her cheeks. It was silly, so teen-age girlish, but she couldn't pass up the chance. "Sing to me."

"I haven't sung in years."

"Well, I haven't made love in years, so we're even," she said, then immediately wished she hadn't.

He started walking again.

"When you left for Ireland, I was obsessed by the image of you making love to dozens of sexy foreign men."

Kris chuckled. "At one time or individually?"

"Singularly, but in quick succession." His tone was light, but she knew he was serious.

"Well, there was this guy. A cute young English lad who was sitting next to me on the plane to Lon-don. He seemed pretty interested until I threw up in a bag and accidentally got a little on him. He didn't say another word the whole trip."

He rubbed his chin against the top of her head. "Poor Kris."

They'd reached his room. The door was open and all the curtains were as well. A silvery light filled the room. The bed was huge, and a moonlit rectangle of gray highlighted a two-foot by three-foot section in the center.

"I didn't notice the skylight the other day."

"Sandy's obsession. She wanted one in every room, but I was reluctant to put more money into the house. Thank goodness our contractor agreed that the roofline of the house wouldn't accommodate any others economically."

"It's cool. Aren't you tempted to stay awake all night following the stars?"

"Not lately. Maybe it will be different having you here."

She knew what he meant, but that kind of domestic bliss was almost too scary to think about.

She wiggled for him to let her down.

Once she was standing, he closed and locked the door. "I don't expect Lucas to come home, but I didn't expect Zach and Tyler to show up at the park, either," he said, dropping his keys on the dresser just inside the door.

Kristin moved away. "Wasn't that unbelievable? You don't think Ty's private investigator is following me, do you?"

Donnie put his hand at the small of her back and

ushered her forward. "I didn't know Harrison had hired a P.I."

"He said he needed to look into my past."

"Well, rest easy. I'm sure you don't have anything to hide. And the last time I checked with Ed, there hadn't been any strangers asking questions about you."

"Did you find out whether or not your co-workers are coming to the wedding?"

Her obvious stall apparently didn't fool Donnie, who caught the loose end of her shawl and reeled her to him, inch by inch. "Forget about tomorrow. Tonight we make up for lost time."

His arms were warm and comforting, but his kiss was demanding. He wanted her, and it felt good.

Kristin looped her arms around his neck and kissed him back. Memories of their first kiss—so many years ago—flooded her senses.

"I feel like I've come home," she said, more to herself than Donnie.

He pulled back slightly, his hands resting on her hips. His thumbs idly brushed the side of her belly. "I know what you mean."

"This feels so natural," she said, smiling. "It's as if our first kiss when we were kids was imprinted for life."

Donnie took a deep breath and looked toward the ceiling. "I guess this is confession time."

Her heart stalled at his serious tone.

"You weren't the first girl I ever kissed."

"You told me I was the first. When I was fourteen. You lied?'' Kristin dropped her hands to his chest and pushed him away. He backed up a step, but even in the dim light she could see his grin.

''Who was the little witch?'' Kris said, hands on her hips.

''Cathy Beaumont. We were six. She said kissing meant that we were married. Unfortunately, she didn't tell me this until after we kissed, then I started to cry because I thought that meant I'd have to live at her house. My mother was a much better cook than Mrs. Beaumont.''

His smile was so Donnie—the Donnie she'd loved for as long as she could remember. Her heart expanded within her chest. She stepped close enough to reach the buttons on his shirt. ''Cathy moved away when we were in fifth or sixth grade, right?'' she asked.

Donnie went still, but he said softly, ''I think so.''

''Good. I'd hate to have to hurt her at this late date.'' She undid the buttons quickly. ''You know, invite her in for a free, hot-stone therapy then accidentally drop a rock on her.''

Donnie cocked his head. ''You'd do that for me?''

''For me. I'm the jealous type.''

She separated the two halves of his shirt and gazed upon his bare chest. Very different from her memory. Broader, more muscular. A thick thatch of chest hair filled in the space between his small ruddy nipples. ''This is new,'' she said, running her fingers through the soft, silky mat. "I like what you've done with your chest."

His chuckle rumbled beneath her fingers. "Thank you. They call it age."

"And free weights," she added. He worked at staying fit; she'd known that the minute she'd seen him in uniform.

Thinking about him at the gym made a tingle pass through her body, and the fire that had been banked ignited. If he was as good as she remembered... "Can we make love?"

Donnie shrugged off his shirt and started to undo his belt. "If you insist," he said with a rueful grin. "On one condition."

Kris's gaze was glued to his waistline. "What?"

"You strip for me. The way you did that afternoon at the bordello."

Kris's face turned hot, and she swallowed noisily. She'd hoped he'd forgotten about that. "Uh...I don't know. I'm not seventeen, and it might not be the same without a bottle of cheap wine first."

With one quick jerk, he pulled the belt free of its loops. His jeans were loose and they inched down on his hips. She could see the line of his underwear. *Red briefs?*

Donnie seemed to read her mind, because he grinned and unzipped his pants. *Yep, red.*

"Nice undies," she said. Her voice sounded strangled. She could hardly wait to see him without his jeans, but he didn't give her the chance. He kicked off his shoes and bent over to remove his socks then strolled to the bed, where he fluffed up two already fluffy shams and made a backrest for himself against the headboard.

He flopped onto his back and crossed his legs at the ankles. "Do you need music?" he asked. Amusement—and something else—made his tone husky. "I could hum."

The *something* gave her the courage to step toward the bed. "You could sing."

Their gazes met—just the bed separating them.

Donnie cleared his throat and sang, *"'When years have passed and we look back on what we learned and knew, we'll fondly say this was the place where our spirits grew. Gold Creek High, Gold Creek High...'"*

She ripped off her blouse and threw it at him.

Laughing, he caught it in midair. "Sorry. I'm a little nervous, okay? That's all that came to mind."

Arms crossed at her chest, she shivered. Not from the coolness of the air but from the desire she saw in his eyes.

He took a deep breath and started again. Soft and low, a tune she hadn't heard in ages but recognized immediately. Her favorite Beatles song, "If I Fell In Love With You."

She lowered her arms and closed her eyes, swaying to the melody. Her long, peasant skirt caressed her bare legs like a scarf when she moved. She gathered a handful of material and lifted it to expose one leg then stepped onto the bed.

Soft, yet firm enough to let her move without

losing her balance, the mattress provided a comfortable platform. She looked up at the starlit night framed by the skylight and lifted her arms as she twirled in small circles of her own. His song faltered momentarily, but he picked it up again, humming in places when he couldn't remember the words. Feeling a bit dizzy, she stopped and faced him.

Their gazes held as she worked the waistband over her hips and let the skirt fall to her feet.

She glanced down to be sure she'd worn matching underwear. A skimpy pink bra that Andi had outgrown and white bikini panties with rose-colored butterflies.

He made a sputtering sound. "Hmm...hmm...hmm."

Kristin turned from him, and looking over her shoulder, unhooked her bra. She'd never felt more exposed, or more sensual. Donnie's unzipped jeans were showing the impact of her striptease. With a provocative laugh, she tossed the bra his way. It landed right where she wanted it to—across his zipper.

Donnie looked down and laughed. "Hell, yes, I'm turned on. Damn, girl, you've got moves."

He sat up and extended a hand to beckon her closer.

This meant turning around and moving into the spotlight cast by the moon. Would he see the spidery lines left by her pregnancy? Or the veins in her breasts? Evidence that she'd borne another man's child even though she had always been in love with Donnie.

"You are so beautiful," he said, his voice still deepened as if in song, but the words were slow and purposeful. "It's as if you just stepped out of my memory."

She moved closer, unable to stay back. "I'm not the same person I was, Donnie."

"Neither am I, but this is who we are. And you're amazing. Come here." He patted a spot beside him.

She dropped to her knees and leaned down to kiss him. She watched the lazy, sensual way his eyes closed, and felt a yearning so great, she almost cried out.

Perhaps she did because Donnie answered by wrapping his arms around her bare back and pulling her to him. Her nipples—erect and sensitized— brushed against the hair on his chest. "Oh, Donnie, I need this so badly, but I'm not on the pill. I never could take it because it made me sick, remember? Tell me you have protection."

He stretched to reach the bedside table. From a drawer he withdrew a shiny packet.

"Thank God," she murmured. She closed her eyes and kissed him—giving in to sensations that took her to a place where nothing mattered except loving and being loved. Now and forever.

DONNIE AWAKENED with a start. He hadn't meant to fall asleep. In fact, he'd promised Kristin he wouldn't, but making love two times in quick succession qualified as miraculous in his book, and he'd needed a few minutes to recover. And rejoice.

"Wonderful," she'd whispered against his chest before closing her eyes, obviously replete.

Wonderful was too mild an adjective in his opinion. They'd bonded, swapping souls in the process. He'd known where she was at every second of their joining. When she'd climaxed, he'd been right there, too.

He turned his chin and squinted at the digital clock. Eleven thirty-seven. He let out a small sigh of relief. He didn't want to face an irate Tyler and Zach a second time.

"Kris, honey," he whispered, nuzzling her hair. The wispy curls teased his nose.

"Too early," she complained like a sleepy child.

Too late. "I know, sweetheart, but Zach will be home alone if we don't leave soon."

She lifted her head, blinking. It only took a couple of seconds for her to get her bearings. Donnie knew the minute reality hit her—where she was and what they'd done.

"Oh," she said, sitting up.

The realization that she was naked arrived a few seconds later—giving Donnie enough time to memorize the image of her perfect breasts bathed in moonlight. She clutched the sheet to her chin. "What time is it?"

"Time to take you home."

She leaned across him for a better look at the clock then gave a small gasp. "We have to hurry."

So much for sentimentality, he thought, watching her gather her clothes. She dashed into the bathroom. The door closed with a bang. Donnie felt a pang of regret. He wished they were an old married couple who felt comfortable dressing and undressing in each other's presence.

Sighing, he rose and pulled on his shorts and jeans. He'd just stooped to pick up his shirt, when she flew out of the bathroom. "Quick. I don't want them to see me like this."

Them? "Like what?" he said moodily.

She froze. "Like this." She touched her lips and ran her hand down the front of her blouse. "Like I've just experienced the best sex of my life."

That eased some of his crankiness until she ruined his mood by adding, "Maybe I should jog home."

"Like hell." He buttoned his shirt without looking to see if the ends lined up. He wedged his bare foot into a shoe. "No date of mine walks home."

"Not walk. Run. It's almost midnight."

"Yeah, but you're not Cinderella," he said, hopping on one foot when the tongue of the shoe blocked his effort. "Relax. I'll get you home in time."

She pointed at his shoeless foot and started to laugh. "Maybe *you're* Cinderella, and the Forerunner was a pumpkin in another life."

He finally got both shoes on and grabbed her hand. "Let's go."

The car was cold, and he could see a glistening of frost on the roof as they backed out of the garage. Autumn was officially here. Soon people would be heading off to visit family and friends for the Thanksgiving and Christmas holidays. More travel. And Donnie wouldn't be a part of it. But the idea of leaving Gold Creek—and Kristin—no longer appealed to him the way it had.

"Would you still marry me even if I wasn't running for office?" he asked. She was sitting upright, stiff and on edge.

"You have to run."

Since there was so little traffic, he looked at her long enough to see that she was as serious as she sounded. "Why? I could still get my old job back."

"No, Donnie," she said emphatically. "You know you want this opportunity."

"But what we have between us is great, Kris. The craziness of a campaign could—"

She interrupted him. "I came home to make amends for what I've done in the past and to show people that I've grown up. I'm not afraid to do this, so don't even think about not running. You take on Magnus, and I'll handle things on the home front. We do it the way we planned or we don't do it. I'll take my chances with Tyler's lawyers and you can hire a housekeeper."

He slowed to round the corner near her house.

"But what about tonight? What did tonight mean to you?"

"We needed tonight to bring our relationship full circle. We parted with such anger between us that we never really healed. Now, we're fixed. And now we can get on with our lives."

It wasn't the declaration of love he was looking for.

They drove in silence until he pulled into her driveway. Thankfully, there was no Mercedes waiting. She turned slightly and looked at him. Tears glistened in her eyes, but her chin lifted with resolve. "I'll see you at the wedding." She opened the car door and dashed away before he could even kiss her good-night. At *the* wedding. "At *our* wedding, you meant to say," he muttered. "*Our* wedding."

KRIS PEEKED from behind the curtain to watch the Forerunner back out and drive away. Tears clouded her vision and her throat burned.

Donnie was a good man, and he loved her— maybe even as much as she loved him, but Kristin knew what happened to people who lost sight of their dreams. He'd given up his chance to see the world. He deserved a chance to protect a corner of it. Gold Creek needed him as much as he needed this opportunity. Kris had ruined his plans once. She refused to take responsibility for that again.

Kristin closed the door of her bathroom and turned on the light. Her hair was a disaster. Her lips and eyes puffy, although not for the same reason. She splashed cold water on her face then dried it with a towel.

She sighed and said aloud, "Maybe when I'm eighty-four, people will point at me and say, 'There goes Kristin Sullivan. One of the Sullivan sisters. Created quite a stir in her day, but then she settled down and did pretty good for herself.'"

At the moment, she couldn't imagine how that might happen, but hopefully, she'd regain some optimism by morning.

The sound of a key in the door made her hurry through her ablutions. She stripped off her clothes and put on her faded chenille robe. With a deep breath, she reached for the knob and prepared to face her son.

She stepped into the hallway just as Zach and Sarge came toward her. "Hi, honey, how was your evening?"

He sighed wearily. "We watched a DVD at his mother's. *Blade Runner*. It was okay."

There was so much more she wanted to say. She ached to hug him, but she didn't dare. "You're probably pretty tired, huh? It's been a busy week, and Aunt Jen is coming over at eight to help us pack. We don't have to get everything moved right away, but Sam is going to have some carpentry work done here once we're out."

She flicked off the light and started for her room.

"Mom?"

She turned around. "Yes?"

"Is it true you and Donnie fell in love when you were about my age?"

She nodded. "His grandparents lived here, and I'd see him when he came to visit. I thought he was the cutest boy alive."

"So you're marrying him for real tomorrow? Not just to keep my dad from winning custody of me?"

Kristin sighed. The last thing Kris wanted was to have her son go through life with a mangled perception of love. But she couldn't lie. And despite what she and Donnie had shared tonight, she didn't completely trust her feelings. Love had let her down before. Badly.

"People get married for all kinds of reasons. Donnie and I care about each other a great deal. We're trying to do something good for all of us. You and Lucas. And even Gold Creek. Donnie will make a wonderful sheriff."

He shook his head and reached down to touch Sarge's head. "Well, if you ask me, love sucks."

He walked away before she could correct him, but she had to admit he had a point. Tomorrow she was marrying the love of her life, but she still didn't know if she was doing it for the right reasons. What could be more pathetic than that?

CHAPTER ELEVEN

ZACH HAD ONLY ATTENDED two weddings in his life. His mother's cousin's when he was a baby, and last spring when his friend Ryan's older sister got married. That turned out to be a mega party at the country club and Ryan got to invite four friends so he wouldn't be bored.

Zach hadn't found it boring, although he'd never have confessed that to his friends. He'd liked watching Ryan's family. Especially when Ryan's sister danced with her younger brother.

Zach wasn't sure what to make of his mother's wedding. For something that was supposed to be quiet and small, the preparation seemed to hum with a peculiar energy. By the time Zach and his mother had arrived at the old bordello an hour earlier, balloons, streamers, tables and chairs had been set up in the backyard.

Zach was glad they'd decided to leave Sarge at home—one tail wag and the pretty decorations would have been history.

"What if it rains?" he asked Andi's husband. Jonathan had enlisted Zach's help to set up folding chairs in front of the lattice arch that led to what his mother called the "rose garden." It was mostly weeds as far as Zach could tell.

Jonathan was an okay guy, and probably the smartest person Zach had ever met—except, maybe, his father. Zach wasn't quite sure what he thought about Tyler.

"No chance. Barometer's holding. Front's to the north," Jonathan replied. He straightened up and looked around. Only a few chairs remained in the stack that had been donated by the Garden Club. "I think I can handle this, Zach, but Jenny's never going to finish that arch with the twins' help."

Zach didn't like to admit it, but he got a kick out of the twins. They were so cute. It was hard not to laugh at Tucker's antics, and Lara had the sweetest giggle.

"Gotcha," he said, picking up Lara, who was trying to climb the ladder behind her mother.

The little girl let out a shrill cry—until she saw who was holding her, then she burst into excited chatter. Jenny looked down and smiled. "Hi, Zach. Thanks, honey boy. You're a peach."

Her smile made him feel good inside.

She was looping artificial greenery across the top of the weathered redwood trellis. The dark leaves were sprinkled with tiny white flowers. "Need some help?"

"Hand me another strand from the florist's box?"

Zach put Lara down. She promptly set off after her brother, who was trying to tackle Harley, Andi's puppy. Zach picked up the plastic wreath. It was pretty and the finished effect was nice, but he still didn't understand why they were going to this bother.

"Why all this decoration stuff? You know the wedding isn't like...real, you know."

Jenny's dress fluttered in the light breeze. It was sort of old-fashioned looking with long sleeves and lace under her throat. "Of course it's for real," she said, stepping down. When they were eye-to-eye, she said, "Zach, this wedding is the smartest thing your mother has done since she had you."

He didn't know how to respond to that. Even though Jenny seemed to think otherwise, Zach knew why Donnie and his mom were getting married. Partly to look after Donnie's kid and his house while Donnie ran for sheriff and partly so Zach's dad wouldn't take him away. But the question he really wanted to ask was why didn't any man fall in love with his mother like in the movies? Even his dad wasn't interested.

On the drive home last night, when it was dark and the music was low, Zach had asked his father whether there was any chance he and Kristin might get back together if she didn't marry Donnie.

"Zach, it's not a matter of us getting *back* together. We never were together except long enough to make you." Then he made a sort of strangled laugh, like he couldn't quite believe it happened. "That's how special you are, you know. A tiny window of opportunity opened in this vast bleakness, and two unhappy people found a way to bring a little joy to each other. And you were the result.''

Zach had never heard anyone except a teacher talk so philosophically, and he hadn't known what to say. Eventually, his father turned up the music on the CD player, as if he felt uncomfortable.

''Thanks, sweetie,'' Jenny said when they were done decorating the arch. ''Tucker, Lara, let's go find your daddy so Mommy can help Auntie Kristin get beautiful.'' She pushed the ladder into Zach's hands and smiled. ''Will you put this away for me? Your mother has always preferred the natural look, but that won't do for today.''

Zach smiled. The way Jenny said it wasn't a put-down. Both of his aunts seemed to care about his mother, and Zach liked that. It almost made the move to Gold Creek worthwhile.

As he carried the ladder to the shed behind the empty garage, he pictured his exchange with his mother last night. Zach had been shocked by her appearance. Her face was bright pink, as if she'd scrubbed it in an effort to keep him from seeing how miserable she was, but the redness in her eyes and the way her bottom lip trembled told him she'd been crying.

After talking to her, he'd made up his mind never to fall in love. It just wasn't worth the pain.

''I know what you're thinking,'' a voice said as Zach rounded the corner by the gate.

He nearly jumped out of his skin. How could someone as old and rickety as Ida Jane sneak up on him? "Huh?" he said, playing dumb. It worked with most adults.

She just gave him a knowing look and motioned him closer. He liked Ida, even if she sometimes made him uncomfortable. She was soft, and her smell reminded him of a basket of potpourri his mother used to have. It had gotten spilled during one of their moves.

The thought made his throat feel as if he'd swallowed a bunch of razor blades. And something suspiciously like tears formed in his eyes. He would have bolted, but Ida latched on to his hand and wouldn't let go. Who knew old ladies were so strong?

"Let's sit down. Out of the way. Before someone runs us over."

Her cane made a crunching noise on the pebbled path. She held on tight with her free hand. He helped her sit down on the curved redwood bench. "Your mama taught you such nice manners," she said. "I'm so proud of her. I wonder why she doesn't know that."

She sounded puzzled, and Zach sat down, thinking he might be able to tell Ida why his mother was the way she was. But before he could speak, she said, "Your mother was so tiny when she was born we almost lost her. The nurses kept a round-the-clock watch. I sat by her little isolette and prayed like I never prayed before—or since, I'm ashamed to say."

She closed her eyes a moment, then said, "Growing up, she was always behind the other two girls, but Kristin never gave up.'' Ida smiled as if she was seeing the little girls playing in front of her. ''She was sweet and pretty and people made allowances for her—teachers, coaches. Nobody wanted to see her fail. At anything.''

Zach wasn't sure he understood the point of the story.

''Most times that kind of pampering spoils a person. It makes them smug or cocky, but with your mother it was just the opposite. She didn't believe she could do anything on her own. Without help. And she never really had to—until she went away.''

Zach decided to ask the question that had been bothering him for weeks. ''What would have happened if she hadn't gotten knocked up...I mean—''

Ida's cackle made him look around nervously. This wasn't a conversation he wanted to share. ''Who knows? But if you ask me, getting pregnant was the best thing she could have done. It got her out of the nest, and even though I would have helped her if I'd known about you, your mother felt she had to raise you alone. To prove something to herself.''

She looked at him and nodded as if something just made sense to her. ''She might never have done that if you hadn't come along.''

Surprisingly, Zach felt better than he had all day. All month, in fact. He looked at Ida Jane and smiled. "Do you think this wedding is going to work out?"

She blinked several times. "Wedding?" she said, suddenly looking around in confusion. "But Jenny and Josh already got married. Didn't they?"

Zach had heard his mother and her sisters talk about Ida getting old and forgetting stuff. There was a name for it, but he couldn't remember what they said to do when she dipped out. He looked around for help, but nobody was near. With his heart in his throat, he squeezed her hand and said, "Kristin and Donnie are getting married today."

He felt the tension leave her—as if someone had let the air out of a balloon. She smiled, her eyes a bit watery. "Oh, good. They've loved each other forever."

Zach wanted to believe her, but how could he trust anything she said? She was a sweet lady but she was so old.

"TEN INVITATIONS," Kristin cried, batting Jenny's hand away. The tip of her finger connected with the hot curling iron, and she yelped. "That's all we gave out. How did ten invitations multiply into that—" she pointed to the activity in the backyard "—that Cecil B. DeMille production?"

She popped her smarting finger into her mouth and continued to stare at the crowd that seemed to grow each time she blinked.

Jenny grabbed a hunk of hair and twisted it up

to Kristin's scalp. Kris sighed. "Why are you doing this to me? I have more curls than Harpo Marx."

"I'm taming the beast. Sit down and let me work," Jenny ordered, using the curling rod as leverage to get Kris back to the stool in front of Ida Jane's vanity.

Kris slumped in a pout. "This is crazy. How did word get out so fast?"

In the mirror, she saw her sisters look at each other. "Well, I did tell a couple of people to come," Jenny admitted. "Old friends who I knew would be hurt if we left them out."

Andi nodded. "Me, too. And Ida called a few."

"You let Ida near a phone?" Kris wailed.

Jenny took a deep breath and grabbed Kristin by the shoulders. "Face it, Kris. You're a Sullivan triplet. Of course people want to see you get married."

Kris's stomach felt as if someone had scoured it with bleach. She appealed to Andi for help. Andi was the pragmatic one; she'd find a way to salvage the situation before it got out of hand.

Andi reached into the pocket of her loose-fitting aubergine silk suit and produced a delicate lace hankie, which she used to dab her eyes. Sniffling, she said, "It's going to be perfect. The sun is shining and it's warm and the flowers are so you...oh, it's perfect."

Kris would have shaken her head, but Jenny was mauling another section of hair. Her already turbulent emotions gathered at the base of her skull, causing the steady pain to throb.

"Girls, I need a moment alone," she said. "Please."

Jenny administered a cloud of hair spray before leaving. Kris didn't even glance in the mirror. She rose and walked to the window again. The parking lot was almost full. She dug her fingers at the source of her pain and rolled her shoulders to try to ease the tension.

Suddenly, a hand brushed her fingers away and two thumbs applied a solid, warm pressure to the spot. "Are you okay?" Donnie asked softly, his breath close to her ear. "Headache? Or cold feet?"

She closed her eyes, unable to stop the sensations of pleasure that enveloped her like a hug. The pain in her head disappeared as the smell of him—a woodsy cologne and fresh air—filled her senses. Her hands dropped to her sides. "Both. But I'm doing better now," she mumbled.

His sigh caressed her shoulder where the scooped neckline of her dress revealed bare, white skin. "Good. It's turning into a circus out there. I came to warn you."

"Is Gloria here?" She tensed, but he splayed his hands against her shoulders and massaged until she relaxed.

"No. Both Gloria and her son have shown commendable restraint, whereas my ex took one look at the size of the party and decided to stay."

His cheerful teasing made her step away and turn

to face him. He quickly averted his eyes. "Technically, you're a bride and I'm a groom."

She took his face in her hands and made him look at her. "This is getting way out of hand, Donnie."

His eyes narrowed just a fraction, then he smiled. A Donnie smile. "It's Gold Creek, Kris. What did you expect?" He looked at her tenderly. "Are you still okay with Sam announcing my candidacy today? The campaign consultant he hired thinks it's a great idea." He lowered his head and pressed a soft sweet kiss to her lips. "If you don't like it, tell me and I'll cancel the plan."

After one last quick glance out the window, she sighed. "No, it is a great opportunity." She looked at him. "Do we have enough food?"

Again, he smiled. "Everyone brought food. And tables. And chairs. And coolers full of beer."

She had to grin, too. "Looks like we've got ourselves a party."

He offered her his elbow. "Shall we go?"

For the first time, Kris looked at him, from head to toe. She inhaled sharply. "Oh my gosh, Donnie, you look gorgeous."

He was dressed in a western-style tuxedo with a skinny black tie, pearl buttons and black cowboy boots. His hair looked as though Jenny might have gotten hold of him, too. The waves were right out of a fashion magazine.

He threw back his head and laughed. "Well, thank you. I didn't want to be completely overshadowed by my bride, but I don't think I was successful. All eyes will be on you.''

His look made Kris regret the trouble she'd given Jenny over this dress—a tea-length ivory lace gown with seeded pearls across the bodice. ''It's too fancy,'' she'd argued when Jenny had demanded they buy it. ''It's too much money.''

Jenny had insisted on paying for it. And Jonathan and Andi had offered to cover the cost of the reception. ''We want you to be as happy as we are,'' Andi had said with a gushiness that was so *not* Andi.

''Oops, I made you cry,'' Donnie said, pulling her to Ida's bed—a Queen Anne platform with a lace coverlet. ''Let me get you a tissue.''

He presented her with a whole box then waited while she dabbed her nose and eyes. Jenny had insisted on makeup today, too. ''At the risk of more waterworks, I need to tell you something,'' Donnie said, pulling up the dressing-table stool so they were sitting eye-to-eye.

She swallowed noisily. ''Is this about last night?''

He nodded.

''Are you sorry we did it?''

His head moved from side to side, never taking his eyes off her. ''Then what?''

He took a breath. ''I love you, Kris. Always have. Probably always will, but you were right last night.''

Kristin bit her lip, tasting lipstick.

"I couldn't admit the truth to myself until this morning," he continued. "I love this town and I don't want to see it destroyed by greed and corruption. I can't wait four years. Even if it means I wind up broke and unemployed, I have to try now. Are you absolutely certain you want to go down that road with me?"

His smile was so real and honest she wanted to kiss him, but she knew better than to start something that might lead to more than they intended.

She sat up straight and took a deep breath. "I'm through traveling, Donnie, but I think Andi's right. Given the choice between business as usual and a fresh, honest voice in government, people will pick you. You're going to win and I'm going to be the sheriff's wife. How cool is that?"

He rose and held out his hand. "Pretty cool."

She studied his face—the face she'd loved since childhood. In his eyes was a gratifying look—full of hunger and desire. She smiled and tapped his nose and said, "Sorry, Charlie, we have business to take care of today."

She slipped off the bed and smoothed the wrinkles from her dress.

"We've still got some time before the ceremony," he said, his voice deep and sexy.

She shook her head, then ran her tongue across her bottom lip for good measure and walked away.

Stifling a giggle, she bumped into her sisters in the hall. "Are you ready? People are getting antsy," Jenny said.

"Yeah, the beer's getting warm," Andi added with a wink. "Where's the groom?"

Kris looked over one shoulder. "Oh, he'll be along in a minute. Last-minute jitters."

Her sisters looked at her, then each other. But they had no time to say anything because a second later the groom-to-be walked out of Ida's bedroom.

Jenny swooped down on him. "Places, everyone. It's show time."

DONNIE EMPLOYED what he called his game face as he circulated among the many guests and party crashers who milled about the bordello's garden. The smokers were clustered just outside the fence in the parking lot—a sort of wedding tailgate party. So far, an hour and a half after the ceremony, he was still nursing the same glass of sparkling cider. He didn't want a drink—he wanted his wife.

My wife. No matter how many times he said the words, they didn't seem real. He'd been married once and knew what it was to have a person who shared your name, your bank account, your bed. But he couldn't imagine what it would be like to share those things with Kristin.

And no matter how many times he reminded himself of the practical reasons for this marriage, his heart still swelled with pride when he looked at her. So lovely, so bright and full of joy. Her body language spoke to people, he decided, watching the way she bent over to hug Lillian Carswell. And a minute later, she was laughing, head thrown back, when Pascal Fournier plopped her down on his knee and wouldn't let her go. His brother, Waldo— a giant of a man at six-five, three hundred ninety pounds—shook with laugher when Kris bussed Pascal's cheek.

Kris's playful flirting was never a come-on. Men loved her, but so did their wives. And her hidden assets would soon be in his bed, he thought, recalling their night of passion.

"You've got a dreamy look in your eyes," a soft voice said, taking him by surprise a minute later. "Bored to tears or thinking about all those boxes of mine to move?"

Too embarrassed to admit where his fantasies had led him, he lied. "I was thinking that it was too bad your cousins couldn't make the wedding. Then I was thinking about Ireland, which led me to think about Italy. Remember when we planned to hunt down my father's ancestors?"

"I do," she exclaimed. "Wasn't there a Grimaldo who worked for Ghirardelli when he opened his first store in Hornitos?" When he nodded, she added, "Imagine where your family might have been if he'd moved to San Francisco instead of marrying your great-grandmother—a miner's daughter from Scotland."

It left him speechless that she could recall that kind of detail about his life.

"Look," she said, lifting a basket of party favors—clusters of pastel-colored Jordan almonds wrapped in white netting and tied with white ribbon.

Kris reached into the basket and offered him one. Donnie shook his head with a barely suppressed shudder. Pastel almonds reminded him of his first wedding. He'd munched down a couple of handfuls before some undercooked pork got the best of him. He'd been ill for two days. For some reason, he could eat pork again, but the taste of Jordan almonds still haunted him.

"Please," she begged in a hushed tone, "Lillian made them. She must have spent hours putting them together and tying them—and she has really bad arthritis. I spend half of each massage working on her hands." Stepping close to him, she added in a whisper, "Personally, they're too sweet for me, but it was very thoughtful. We need to pass them out to all the guests."

With a secret wink she added, "Or we get to *keep* them."

Donnie put down his glass and took the handle of the basket from her. "Your slightest wish is my command, Mrs. Grimaldo. By the way, in case you didn't hear me earlier, you are amazingly beautiful. Every man in the place is jealous of me."

Her blush made him smile.

After the last of the almonds were distributed, Donnie looked around for his son. Sandy had planned to leave with Lucas after the wedding, but Donnie had put his foot down. "He's in school, Sandy. He can't afford to miss any more days. I've already heard from one of his teachers that he's falling behind. He might even need a tutor.''

She'd argued, but finally agreed to postpone her flight to L.A. another day so she could spend it with their son. She was going to take Lucas to her cabin as soon as the wedding reception ended.

Lucas was sitting near the serving table, and by the number of empty cola cans in front of him, hadn't moved since he'd been released from duty in the greeting line. Donnie had asked him to serve as his best man. And while Lucas had complied, he obviously hadn't enjoyed the experience.

Zach had walked his mother to the flower-festooned arch with conspicuous pride, his head held high. He wore black trousers and a long-sleeved white shirt. His skinny tie had *Star Trek* images on it. Almost as tall as his mother, he looked older than his years. Donnie had overheard a number of comments about what a handsome boy he was becoming.

Handsome, but prickly. So far, he'd kept to himself, just like Lucas.

Donnie spotted Bethany in a severe black dress. She separated from a group of sheriff's employees and approached him. ''You clean up pretty good for an old man,'' she said, her eyes alight with laughter

''You look nice, too—for being in mourning.''

''Yadda, yadda, I get the same crap from my folks, you know.''

''Sorry,'' he said, glancing to the left when he

saw Kristin join Ida Jane on the park bench. Something Ida said must have made Kris cry because she suddenly put her arms around the older woman's shoulders and stayed there, her back quivering.

Does she need me? The thought made him frown. He would be so busy with the campaign, he might not be around much to help Kris with Ida Jane.

"She's nice," Beth said. "I can see why you love her."

Donnie felt himself blush. He hadn't realized his feelings were quite so obvious. "She's an amazing person. She'll make a good sheriff's wife."

Beth froze. "What do you mean?"

He hadn't meant to blurt it out like that, but there was no sense putting off the inevitable. "Sam's going to announce my candidacy in about five minutes."

"Are you out of your mind? Magnus will kill you."

Donnie took her arm and moved her to a less congested area. "I'm going to give it my best shot, Beth," he said with more confidence than he felt. "You know what it's like in the department. I know I might not make it, but I have to try."

She thought a minute then said, "What happens if you lose? Magnus will never let you work here. Would you move away?"

"Maybe. Or I'll get a job in the Valley and commute. Like every other Californian."

Beth frowned. "My dad used to commute two hours one way to work. He said it was hell. It got so bad he and my mom almost broke up. That's why we moved here. So we could be more of a family. I hardly even knew him when he worked in Santa Clara. He was this moody, unhappy guy who yelled at us on weekends then disappeared.''

Donnie felt an odd twist in his belly. He looked at the table where his son was eating a piece of cake. *Was that his second piece? Or his third?*

Sandy had suggested that Lucas's eating habits were a direct result of Donnie's questionable parenting skills. ''You're never there, and even when you are, you aren't,'' she'd accused. ''He needs to spend time with someone who wants to be with him, Donnie. Not someone who's doing the right thing because it's expected of him.''

Donnie cleared his throat. ''Well, I haven't lost yet.''

Beth grinned. ''That's true. Besides, aren't you the guy who told me you're only a loser if you don't try?''

Donnie gave her a light tap on the shoulder. ''Come on, I want to introduce you to Kristin.''

Beth shook her head. ''Maybe later. She looks busy.''

Donnie turned to find his wife in the crowd. He spotted her amidst a group of older women— friends of Ida Jane's. Beulah Jensen was showing Kristin's ring for the group to see. Donnie was glad he'd gone against Kris's wishes and bought a gold band with four small diamonds.

"Our instant family," he'd told her when he slipped it on her finger.

She'd appeared ready to cry, but then Judge Miller gave him permission to kiss the bride, and Donnie had distracted her from her sadness.

He looked down at his hand. Kris hadn't pressed for a double-ring ceremony. "Save the money for your campaign," she'd said.

Was that it? Or did she not expect the marriage to last?

"You know," Beth said with a sigh, "I really wanted to hate her."

Me, too. At one time. Instead, he said, "Why?"

"Because she's gorgeous. But then I realized she doesn't see herself that way. She's not a show-off. You know, like some of the popular girls, who are only nice to geeks if they think other people are watching."

Donnie touched her shoulder. "You're not a geek."

She made a skeptical sound. "Sure I am. I wear black, I get good grades and my only friends are cops. Are you so old you've forgotten what that means in high school?"

No, he knew. "High school is a brief, but sometimes painful, ritual we subject our children to so they won't blame everything that goes wrong in their lives on their parents."

She laughed and said, "I'll tell that to my folks."

She started to leave but Donnie stopped her. "Wait. Would you do me a favor?"

"Maybe."

"Drag those two—" he nodded toward Zach and Lucas "—together and get them talking. Maybe if you mention music."

She looked less than enthused but agreed to try. "Thanks, kiddo. You're a pal."

Donnie didn't get a chance to see if she was successful because his new brothers-in-law waylaid him.

Sam clapped a big solid arm around Donnie's shoulders and marched him to a table. "Sit, my friend. Man talk."

Jonathan appeared a moment later with three sweating amber bottles—two beers and a cream soda.

"A toast," he said, dropping down on the bench across from Donnie and Sam. Each clinked his bottle with the others. "To our new brotherhood. Friends, husbands and fathers. May we always be there for each other."

Donnie was surprisingly touched by the sentiment. "Thank you, gentlemen. It's an honor to be in such esteemed company."

The carbonated beverage was refreshing, until Donnie noticed Sam and Jonathan exchange a look. He mentally braced himself. "Is this where you tell me to go easy on her on our honeymoon?"

Jonathan frowned. "Hell no. You're on your own in the bedroom. This is where we get serious about your future—in politics. You haven't forgotten about that, have you?"

"I handed in my notice, Jon. I haven't forgotten."

Sam hunched forward and linked his hands. "It's going to be an uphill battle, Donnie. I won't kid you, but Magnus has to go, and you're the only one who can get Gold Creek back on track."

Jonathan lifted his bottle. "Hey, there's our first sound bite." The two men toasted.

"I couldn't do this without your support—both of you. But I've watched the political game in this county for years, and I know it can get ugly," Donnie said.

Sam nodded. "I agree, but at least you have Kristin in your corner."

Jonathan nodded. "Yeah. Free massages, too."

Donnie looked across the yard where his wife was talking to her sisters. Kris glanced his way, and her spontaneous smile produced a response in his heart he couldn't begin to describe.

A moment later, Sam stood up and stepped to the seat of the picnic table. His piercing whistle made conversation stop. Everyone turned to listen.

"You're in luck, folks. It's two-for-one day. Not only do you get a wedding—" He paused for effect. "You get to meet the future sheriff of Gold Creek, Donnie Grimaldo."

CHAPTER TWELVE

IN THE TWO WEEKS since his mother's wedding, Zach had settled in better than he'd expected. It helped that he'd found his spot. For as long as he could remember, his mother had promoted this idea. "And where in this amazingly tiny apartment will we find a spot that is all Zach's?" she would say moments after opening the door to their newest home.

His privacy zone, they had called it when he got older. The places had varied from an empty cupboard with the door removed to a tepee made from a bedsheet.

This time, Zach had chosen a protected area adjacent to Sarge's doghouse. The evergreen shrubs shielded him from the breeze, and the location gave him a clear view of the patio. What made it perfect was that no one could sneak up on him. Zach was damn tired of surprises.

"Here, boy," Zach said, dropping to his butt on Sarge's old mat. He kicked out his legs and settled back against the small but sturdy structure. Sarge, who seemed to love his new home, joined him with a slobbery sigh.

Today was Wednesday. For the first time since he'd moved to California, the weather felt like it might be changing. Zach was sick of summer.

He was waiting for Lucas's friends to arrive. Since the teachers were having something called an in-service day, classes had been released early. His mother had picked up both boys so they could prepare for their first practice.

Zach's gut was in knots and his palms felt sweaty. He told himself it was no big deal, but what if he sucked as bad as he thought he did?

Donnie was the one who'd pushed Lucas to set up this meeting. Zach had protested that he wasn't good enough, but his mother had pleaded with him to at least talk to Lucas's friends.

Talk. Talk he could handle. It was the playing that had him so nervous he could barely sit still. Although Zach had taken guitar lessons off and on for a couple of years—depending on when his mom could afford it—he knew he had a lot to learn.

And while the guitar Donnie had given him was a step-up from the one he had been using, the instrument was different enough that Zach was having trouble getting used to it. Donnie's promise of lessons had taken a back seat to his campaign, but he had squeezed in half an hour with Zach on Monday night.

Instead of rushing off to his next meeting, he'd taken time to sit down and show Zach some chords, which Zach had diligently practiced every spare minute since.

Donnie had called him a "natural."

"You've got a gift, Zach," he'd said.

He knew Donnie's praise was bull, but it still felt good to hear.

Sarge lifted his head, turning toward a noise that Zach had missed. Rising to his knees, Zach spotted Lucas slip out the back door of the garage and disappear in the direction of the creek.

"Stupid kid," Zach muttered, stroking the dog's head. "Talk about screwed up."

Sarge blew out a sigh that made his jowls flap.

It baffled Zach that someone as savvy as Donnie could totally miss the fact that his son was doing drugs. Zach had had his suspicions confirmed that afternoon by the creek. But he hadn't realized how bad things were until he and Lucas rode their bikes home from school together on Monday.

Both Donnie and Zach's mom were away from the house. Zach had gone to his room to do his homework. A few minutes later, Lucas had appeared in the doorway. "Where's the cop?"

"Your dad?"

Lucas had sloughed off his backpack on the stack of boxes that Zach was still going through. The top caved in slightly, and Zach had given him a dirty look, hoping he'd take the hint and leave.

"Nah, I meant your mom. I know where my dad is. Putting up Grimaldo For Sheriff signs."

Before Zach could answer, Lucas had unzipped a side compartment in his backpack and removed something small enough to fit in the palm of his hand. "Want some of this?"

Zach had been six the first time he'd been offered drugs. A fifth-grade boy had tried to get first-grade students to buy little blue pills that he said would make them smarter. "No. And you'd better get that out of the house. My mom's last appointment was at four. She'll be here any minute and she's not as busy as your dad is. If she thinks you're messing around with pot, she'll be all over your ass about it."

"Yeah, right," Lucas had said, obviously unimpressed by the threat. He'd grabbed the backpack and left, exiting the house through the patio door.

Suddenly, a light appeared in the low-roofed building sitting about thirty feet behind the garage. The music shed.

Zach looked at his watch. *He's home early.*

Through the two windows, Zach could see Donnie moving around. The shed wasn't huge—about the size of his and Lucas's bedrooms put together. The little building would make an excellent studio. Acoustically, it beat the garage all to heck.

Once Donnie was done, there would be soundproofing in the walls, special electrical plugs and a heating panel so they could practice during the winter. Donnie claimed it was his gift to the music world, but Zach had a hunch it was more about making sure his new wife's car wouldn't have to sit outside in the cold.

Zach approved. He was still mad at his mother

on many levels, but he was willing to concede that Donnie was a good guy. So far, he'd been pretty cool.

That didn't mean Zach was happy with him. It pissed him off that Donnie was on the run all the time, leaving Zach's mom with this big house and two kids—especially a stoner like Lucas. Zach knew that was their bargain, but as far as he was concerned, his mother was getting gypped.

Not that she was complaining, but she looked like hell. The bags under her eyes told him she wasn't sleeping at night. Which didn't make sense. She should be exhausted. In addition to moving, she'd cleaned Jenny's old place and given a bunch of massages.

He'd overheard her telling Andi that being married to Donnie was like an all-clear signal to people that it was okay to come to her for massages.

He hated that about this stupid town. People knew too much about your life; they all had opinions and you couldn't make a move without somebody reporting it to your mother or your aunt or your grandmother.

Yesterday Gloria had called and asked him to stop by the newspaper office after school. She'd been busy with an interview so Zach had read copies of the *San Francisco Chronicle* and hung out with Jonathan until she was done. Which wasn't so bad, really.

Then she'd taken him to dinner. She told him Tyler was back in Seattle for a few days, but that

Zach could call her anytime and she would gladly pick him up. For the first time she'd seemed kinda lonely.

The only awkward moment was on the way home when she put down guitar playing. "The time you spend playing music could better be used to prepare for college. You could go to Harvard, or any Ivy League school," she'd told him. "Your father can afford it, you know."

Zach wasn't sure what his plans would be in five years. At the moment, he wanted to play music, write songs, survive high school and, maybe, get a girlfriend.

There was one who interested him. She was older than him and a little weird, but he liked her. And her younger sister was pretty cute, too.

Curious about how much progress Donnie had made since the last time he checked, Zach got up and started toward the building. Before he reached the edge of the yard, a horn sounded in the driveway. A second later, Lucas stumbled from the bushes at the far side of the yard.

He froze when he spotted Zach, but hurried off a second afterward. "Are you coming, Goody Two-shoes?" Lucas sneered. "They're here."

Zach petted Sarge again. "Stupid stoner," he muttered. "This'll probably suck big time."

By the time he reached the garage, there were lots of people—mostly strangers. Donnie was talking to the parents who'd driven their son—the keyboardist, Zach guessed—to practice.

The drummer, a tall, rangy-looking guy with orange hair and a mouthful of metal, introduced himself. "Hey, I'm Kyle. We have P.E. together."

That was all they had time for because Kyle's older brother, a high-school student, and his two pals were in a hurry. They unloaded the drums in the far corner of the garage then got back in the truck and took off.

Mike, the keyboard player, was tall and skinny, with some serious acne that his dreadlocks helped cover. He provided not only the keyboard but a second amplifier and two microphones, as well.

It seemed to take forever to set up. Zach stood on the perimeter feeling nervous and out of it. The others chatted about mutual friends and teachers that he didn't know.

He was about ready to split when Kyle said, "Hey, Sullivan, can you play?"

"I guess."

Lucas closed the garage door and plugged his Fender into the amp.

He nodded to Mike, who counted, "One, two, three..."

Zach jumped in without a clue to what they were supposed to be playing. It didn't seem to matter. Nobody else seemed to have a clear musical direction, either.

After about half an hour, the exterior door opened and Donnie walked in. He was dressed in paint coveralls and his hair was speckled with something white. "How's it going?"

Before anyone could answer, Zach's mother appeared. "Hi, boys. I hate to bother you when history is in the making," she said, causing them to smile with her exaggerated wink, "but I'm worried what all those high-octane sound waves are doing to your ears. So, please, indulge me. I'm a mom."

She gave each boy a set of musician's earplugs—the kind that screened out bad decibels.

"And, you can't be creative geniuses without proper nutrition." She produced a plate of brownies.

By the time the other boys left, Zach actually felt as if they might be able to form a band. *If Lucas gets his act together.*

"WHAT IS WRONG with my brain?" Kristin muttered, picking up each individual spice jar on the shelf to examine the label. Tomorrow was her three-week wedding anniversary, but she still didn't know where anything was in Donnie's house. "Basil. Cumin. Allspice," she called out the names. "What *is* allspice? Maybe, since it's *all*-spice, I could use it instead of oregano."

"I wouldn't if I were you," a deep voice said.

Kris swung around in surprise. "Donnie, you're early."

He dropped his keys on the counter and headed her way. "My slave driver brother-in-law gave me the rest of the weekend off to work on my speech for Monday. What a guy!"

Kris set the allspice back on the shelf and moved

out of his way. She was barefoot, dressed in black leggings and a Crater Lake sweatshirt that hung on her like a shapeless grocery sack. She knew her ponytail was ratty and mostly out of its scrunchy. She'd planned to start dinner then take a nice relaxing bath, but she was running late. A client—the fourth of the day—had shown up unexpectedly an hour earlier, begging for a massage.

Donnie didn't seem to notice her messy appearance. He plucked a green-topped glass jar out of the mess and said, "Here. It got squeezed behind the cinnamon."

When he handed the container to her, their fingers touched and Kris felt the impact deep within. "My fault," she admitted. "I came home between massages and baked an apple pie. I must have put the cinnamon back in the wrong place."

"It's your kitchen now, Kris. Put things wherever you want."

He looked as if he might say more, but just then the exterior door opened and Zach walked in. As usual, his eyes revealed none of his inner thoughts.

He was carrying his guitar and a plastic binder. *His songs,* she thought. No matter what else came of this marriage, Donnie had given her son a wonderful gift—music.

"I could use your help setting the table," she told him. "I set out the red-and-white checked tablecloth."

Donnie rested one elbow against the counter and

shuffled through the day's mail. "Where's Lucas?" Donnie asked.

Kris sprinkled a few shakes of the herb into her bubbling pot of spaghetti sauce. "I don't know. Zach, do you know where he is?"

"Nope."

Monosyllabic-grunt-boy had returned. Kris would have been pulling out her hair except that Donnie constantly assured her that Zach was "a neat kid."

"Maybe he's in the music shed," Kris suggested, holding the stirring spoon to her lips to sample the sauce.

With the liquid too hot to touch, she blew on the spoon. When Donnie didn't answer, she glanced his way. The look in his eyes was every bit as heated as the mixture on the spoon.

Zach made a sound of pure disgust, and she hastily dropped the spoon back in the pot. "What did you say?"

His upper lip curled back in a sneer. "Nothin'."

Before she could respond, the phone rang. Nobody moved to answer it. After the third ring, Kristin pounced on it. "Sullivan residence...I...I mean...hello."

"It's Sandy. Put Donnie on."

The snappish tone made Kristin hold out the receiver. "It's definitely for you."

Donnie walked around the counter to sit down on a stool. He took the portable unit from her hand then turned his back to them. Kris could hear every word he spoke, but she made a concerted effort not to listen. "So, Zach," she said, "how's the new song coming?"

"Okay," he mumbled.

Normally, she wouldn't let his prickly tone put her off, but Donnie's fierce "Don't even think it" distracted her.

Zach gave her a knowing look and walked into the dining room, leaving her with Donnie. And Sandy.

"For the last time, Sandy, let it go," Donnie said. Kris heard exhaustion and frustration in his tone. "We can't plan for Christmas until I know whether or not I have the job."

Impulsively, Kris poured him a glass of juice. Since his back was to her and she didn't want to walk around the island, she leaned across the counter, practically lying on her belly and tapped his shoulder.

When he turned to look, his eyes widened and his gaze dropped. Kris glanced down and discovered the bow neck of her sweatshirt was stretched about as low as it could go. She scooted backward, almost knocking over the glass. Donnie rescued it and mouthed "Thank you" as Sandy's voice droned in the background. Kris wasn't sure if he was grateful for the drink or the peepshow, but for some reason, she didn't care. It was enough to see him smile.

Dinner went surprisingly well, she thought an hour later. After hanging up the phone, Donnie left to shower and change. Kris had a cup of tea to steady her nerves.

Lucas showed up just in time to eat, claiming to have been in his room studying. Kris decided his guilty look meant he'd probably been playing video games.

When they were finally gathered together at the table, she decided it was the perfect moment to share her good news. "I got a pleasant surprise from my attorney today. Ty's decided not to fight me for custody. I guess he realized he couldn't win," she said, unable to disguise her glee. "He's suggested a very fair and flexible arrangement."

She looked at Zach and told him, "He's even willing to pay for your college, Zach. Isn't that great?"

There'd been a few lines about why Tyler felt it was important that Zach stay in Gold Creek for his entire high-school experience and what Ty would do if Kristin pulled up stakes, but overall his offer was remarkably generous. It included child support, which would go straight into Zach's savings.

"And he's moving here."

"When?" Donnie asked.

"I don't know. I didn't ask. But I think this means we don't have to go to court. We won." She toasted Donnie with her water.

"I don't get it," Lucas said. "Nothing's changed, right? So how does that mean you won?"

Kris had noticed a listlessness in Lucas the past

few days, but she'd marked it down to worry. Who could blame him for being tense and distracted?

"This is what I wanted," she told him. "I'll be Zach's primary-care provider—like your dad is for you—but Zach will have the option of staying as much as he likes at his dad's. That would be difficult if Tyler lived somewhere far away, like Seattle."

"Or South Africa," Lucas said, his mouth full of pasta.

Since nobody seemed as happy as she was, some of Kristin's high spirits fled. Donnie took a second helping of ravioli. Lucas ate with his head down, barely taking the time to swallow. Zach kept his eyes on his plate, too, but at least his posture was better.

"So, guys," she said, changing the subject, "how was homecoming? Were the bands any good last night?"

"They were okay," Zach said.

"They sucked," Lucas mumbled. "Even we're better than them."

Zach snorted. "Like hell we are. We stink."

Lucas bristled. "Speak for yourself."

Zach's face turned red, but before he could explode, Donnie said, "I should have a little time next week to help you work on your finger positions, Zach, but you're doing fine. Which is a good thing because I can't teach you much more. My musical talent has been reduced to singing a little ditty now and then."

He looked at Kris when he said that and she felt her face heat up. It was a blatant reminder of the passion they'd shared the night before the wedding.

"Mom."

The word punched into her thoughts. She gulped, and something she hadn't quite finished chewing lodged in her throat. A hunk of bread, she thought, reaching for her water glass.

She opened her mouth to cough, but no air would go up or down. She tried to swallow and even squeezed her throat to help it along, but whatever was blocking the passage only became more securely imbedded. She thumped her fist against her chest, trying not to panic.

"Mom?" Zach's voice went up the way it did when he was a little boy. "Are you okay?"

She tried to nod, but her eyes were watering and she was having trouble focusing.

"Donnie, do something," Zach cried.

Donnie was already on his feet. He rushed around the table and pulled out her chair. He jerked her to her feet. Her fingers tingled and little silver dots danced across her vision.

"Breathe," he ordered. Locking his arms around her belly, he pulled her back into his body so firmly she thought she might break in two.

A tiny bit of air found passage, but the clog was still there. Her arms flapped uselessly; tears streamed from her eyes. She didn't want to die.

"Dammit, Kris, breathe." This time he repositioned his hands and jerked even harder.

Her jaw dropped open and the obstacle popped clean out of her mouth like an automatic ball server she'd seen in action at a tennis club.

Kristin crumpled as oxygen returned to her body. Her head was spinning and it hurt like hell to swallow, but she could breathe.

Donnie held her limp body and lowered his head to the back of her neck and whispered, "Thank God. Oh, thank God."

Embarrassed and so giddy with relief she could have wept, Kris pried his hands apart so she could face him. "You saved my life," she whispered. Her throat burned but she felt obliged to add, "Can you believe I did something that dumb?"

"Yes," Donnie said, his face suddenly contorting in fury. "Yes, dammit, I can. That was stupid. My God, Kristin, you could—"

Zach, who'd gone white with fear, leaped to his feet and pulled Donnie's arm back.

"Leave her alone," Zach cried. "She almost died." Even though he was a hundred pounds lighter, Zach pushed Donnie away. "Don't talk to her like that."

Lucas suddenly sprang out of his chair and was facing Zach before Kristin could blink. "Hey, she's his wife, man. Stay out of it. He can talk to her any way he wants."

Clearly incensed and needing an outlet for his anger, Zach tackled Lucas. Although Lucas was twenty pounds heavier, surprise and self-righteous indignation tipped the scales in Zach's favor. The two went down, taking the tablecloth and several plates with them. Angry cries and the dull thud of fist to flesh blended with the sound of dishes shattering on the hardwood floor.

"Zach. No." Kris's strangled cry seared her already raw throat.

Donnie swore and reached down to wrap Zach, who was on top, in a bear hug. He wrestled him back and out of the way of Lucas's vicious kick.

Lucas tried to sit up, but his right arm buckled. His nose was bleeding, tears of anger and outrage diluting the bright-red stream.

Kris grabbed a water glass and a napkin from the table and dropped to her knees beside him. "I'm so sorry," she said as loudly as possible. Every syllable hurt.

To her surprise, Lucas passively submitted to her ministrations. She dabbed cool water around his nose, which was already swollen and inflamed. "How's your wrist?"

Lucas looked across the room to where Donnie and Zach were talking. Suddenly, he jerked back and pushed her hand away. "I'm okay."

He lumbered to his feet and left the room without a backward glance. Zach disappeared, too. His obvious shame at losing control of his emotions broke her heart. Kris would have thanked him for coming to her defense, but he hadn't given her time.

Later. She'd talk to each of them in private. Zach would rant, and she'd let him. Because he needed to vent his frustration. She didn't know what Lucas would do.

Donnie picked up the plates, put them on the table, then walked to her side. "That was entirely my fault. I'm sorry," he said somberly. "I'll talk to them after they cool down."

She could tell he felt remorseful; there was even a little tremor in his hand as he waited to see if she would accept his apology. "Donnie," she said, moving into the shelter of his arms. "You saved my life."

He pulled her closer to him and kissed her. He raked her teeth and the top of her mouth with his tongue. His lips were cruel, demanding, and he barely gave her time to breathe, but that was okay. She'd breathe later.

Finally, she put both hands on his shoulders and pushed. It took a minute for him to respond. When she had his attention, she said huskily, "Our bedroom is more private. Are you coming?"

THE ALARM THAT RANG had an unfamiliar trill, but Donnie sat up anyway.

Blinking, he looked to his left and spotted his wife curled on her side facing him. The down comforter had slipped to reveal her bare shoulder.

Donnie punched his pillow into a thick wad so he could think. They'd made love three times last night, each better than the one before. The first had been an affirmation of Kris's close call. He could have lost her. Just like that. And the thought had made him crazy. He'd handled things poorly, but she'd forgiven him.

After an hour in the privacy of their bedroom, they'd visited their sons. Kris with Lucas. Donnie with Zach.

Zach seemed to accept Donnie's apology with grudging respect—especially after Donnie told him, "I love your mom, Zach. I don't think I really understood how much until I nearly lost her."

Donnie didn't know how Kris's talk went with Lucas. When he slipped into his son's room, he'd found the boy staring blankly at the ceiling. Donnie had noticed Lucas's general moodiness, but he'd attributed it to all the changes in the kid's life.

He vowed to pay closer attention to his son—as much as the schedule Jonathan and the campaign manager had devised for him would allow.

"'Morning."

He turned his chin. Kristin was staring at him, clear-eyed, a hint of a smile on her lips.

"Hello, beautiful." He squirmed down to face her. "How's your throat?"

She adjusted the quilt and raised up to rest her head in her hand. "Better, thank you."

He glanced at the clock sitting on the black lacquered bedside table. He liked the Oriental influences Kristin had brought in; the look was much less prosaic than his boring oak cabinet. Suddenly a thought hit him: his boring oak cabinet was where his condoms were stored.

I made love to my wife three times last night and

not once did birth control cross my horny little mind.

"Oh my God."

Kristin cocked her head inquisitively, her mop of messy curls bouncing with such provocative charm he almost forgot his sudden panic. "What's wrong?"

"We didn't use birth control."

She sat up, drawing the covers around her. "Guess we were too busy thinking about other things."

Her voice still hadn't returned to normal after the choking episode. They'd tried hot tea with honey at midnight, but the Lauren Bacall tone he found so sexy remained.

"It was my fault," he said, seeing her pensive frown.

The line between her eyes deepened. "It was? You planned to weaken my resistance with the Heimlich maneuver, then seduce me and get me pregnant?"

He smiled because it surprised him that she could joke about something this serious.

She scooted closer and laid her chin on his shoulder. "Don't worry. I'm sure it's okay. This isn't the right time of the month for me to get pregnant."

"But it could happen," he argued.

She moved back. "Donnie. Trust me. I know my body. I didn't when I was eighteen, but I do now."

He wanted to believe her. But the thought of a baby made him jump out of bed. He tugged on his sweats and walked to the window. "We never talked about having more children."

Kristin grabbed her robe from the foot of the bed and pulled it on. She fluffed up the pillows behind her and sat stiffly. "You don't believe me, do you?"

"Accidents happen. Neither Zach nor Lucas—"

He didn't have a chance to complete the thought because she flew out of bed and marched to where he was standing. "Don't even think it. Life happens, Donnie. If a miracle took place last night—and that's what it would take for me to be pregnant—then we'd be blessed. If you're not okay with that, then you're not the man I thought you were."

Donnie ran a hand through his hair. "I didn't mean it that way. I'd love to have more children with you, but you've got to admit this would be pretty lousy timing."

She turned abruptly. She took two steps before pausing to look over her shoulder. "What part of this whole thing would you call *good* timing?"

"Kristin…" He started toward her, but she walked to the bathroom and closed the door.

Donnie listened to the sound of the shower running.

As he made the bed, he realized she was right. He'd overreacted. Again.

He straightened the pillows. *A baby with Kristin.* The thought made him smile as he smoothed the comforter on her side of the bed. Unfortunately, he'd blown it. He'd acted like an idiot, and he had a feeling Kris wasn't going to accept this apology as easily as she had all the others.

CHAPTER THIRTEEN

KRISTIN WATCHED Jenny feed Lara the last of her strained peas. The toddler made a raspberry sound, spraying pureed green mush in all directions.

"Lara," Jenny said, laughing. "This stuff is good for you."

The child smiled angelically while her mother wiped splatter from her chubby cheeks. Jenny looked across the table to where Kris was seated and said, "So, tell me again. Why are you mad at Donnie? You don't want a baby. He doesn't want a baby. There is no baby. But he's still in trouble?"

Kristin had fled to the Rocking M before she and Donnie could finish their conversation. She'd known he wanted to apologize. To kiss and make up, but she'd needed some distance to make sense of what she was feeling. Not just anger, but hurt.

"I don't think he trusts me, Jen." Kristin took a sip of her now-cold coffee, then rose and walked to the sink. From the window, she spotted Zach and Sam talking to a cowboy astride a horse. Sam was holding Tucker, who looked ready to launch himself into the saddle. She couldn't help but smile.

Maybe the real reason she was upset was that she wanted a baby. Donnie's baby.

"Sorry, sis, but you're going to have to walk me through the logic. You've lost me."

Kristin dumped the coffee in the sink, then turned around to face her sister. "The reason Donnie first asked me to marry him was so I could move into his house and take care of his son while he went off to the FAM program, right?"

"And to help you out, too. In case Tyler took you to court," Jenny added. She plucked Lara from the high chair after disposing of her daughter's messy bib. "But he changed his mind about going because it wouldn't have been fair to Lucas."

"So he said," Kris returned. "But what if the real reason was that he didn't think I could be trusted to take care of his son?"

Jenny made an impatient sound. "Oh, Kris, that's ridiculous. Donnie's a good man. He was just trying to do the right thing. For all of you."

"That's what I thought. Until this morning." She took a breath to steady her emotions. "He didn't believe me when I told him I couldn't be pregnant. And he was terrified at the thought of us having a baby. That's when I started to wonder. Maybe he doesn't trust me. About anything."

"I think you're making a mountain out of a molehill." Jenny crossed the room and passed Lara to her. "Here. Entertain this young diva for a few minutes. Maybe you'll think twice about wanting to get pregnant," she added with a wink.

The little girl went willingly into Kristin's arms, and Kris felt emotions percolating deep inside. She'd love to have a little girl of her own. Donnie's daughter.

"Hello, sweetie," she told her niece.

Lara's eyes sparkled. Her fine hair—the part not matted with peas—made wispy curls above her perfect ears. Lara answered with gibberish until she discovered Kristin's necklace. Her eyes went wide with wonder as her tiny fingers investigated the polished stone beads.

Jenny, who'd stepped out of the room, returned a moment later with a folder. "Will you give this to Donnie? He'll need it for the meeting tomorrow."

Kris nodded toward her purse which was sitting on the counter. "What meeting?"

"Didn't he tell you? Tyler has asked to speak at the chamber of commerce. He's bringing along representatives from Cal-Trans and the Army Corps of Engineers. Ty faxed Jonathan an outline of his presentation. Your fax machine isn't hooked up yet, is it?"

Kris felt a flutter of unease pass through her. Why hadn't Donnie mentioned this? "Is the meeting open to the public?"

Jenny looked at her. "Yes. I can't be there because Lara has a doctor's appointment, but Ida Jane told me the Garden Club ladies are sending a contingent."

"How come I'm always the last to know?" Kristin asked. "Donnie should have told—"

Jenny interrupted. "It's not a secret, Kris. Jonathan reported it in the paper. Meridian is planning to hold a series of public hearings, but Tyler wanted to introduce his plan to the chamber first. He'll need the members' backing."

Still feeling slightly disgruntled, Kris had to admit she'd been too busy with work and getting unpacked to open a newspaper. "Did I tell you I've decided to hire Lillian? I need someone to handle my appointment schedule."

Jenny clapped. "Terrific. That means you're busy."

Lara—bored with the necklace and looking a little droopy-eyed—made a whimper and put her arms out for her mother. Kris walked to her sister and gave Lara back.

"I've been swamped ever since people found out I was marrying Donnie. He's got a lot of support in Gold Creek."

Jenny motioned for Kristin to follow her. They didn't speak until they reached the twins' bedroom where Jenny quickly changed Lara's diaper, then sat down with her in the rocking chair. Kristin took the nearby windowseat.

"Donnie *is* popular. He's got a great reputation, but you know this town. People are slow to accept change—even good change. Magnus has pulled the wool over their eyes. They don't see the corruption—or if they do, they think it works to their advantage.''

Kristin knew that, but she refused to believe that anyone would knowingly support a man like Magnus when they could vote for her husband. ''One of the reasons I came here today—besides to cry on your shoulder—was to ask Sam if there was a place for me in the campaign. No one's said anything to me about my role.''

Jenny cradled her little girl and whispered a soft lullaby. Lara's eyes closed and her thumb went into her mouth. Jenny smiled serenely then looked at Kris.

''You're on the list, but Donnie asked Sam to back off until you got settled. The move, the boys, your work. He knows you've got your hands full.''

Kristin wanted to believe that. Until this morning, she would have considered the gesture thoughtful, but now she wondered if it was another example of how little faith he had in her abilities. ''Maybe he's afraid I'll say the wrong thing to the wrong people.''

Jenny shook her head. ''Kristin, don't look for reasons to be unhappy. Donnie loves you. You love him. Don't two pre-teens provide enough discord in your life?''

Kris sighed. Jenny was right. As usual.

''Where is Donnie, by the way? Sam said this might be his last day off till the election. I thought you'd be doing something together.''

Kris frowned. She pictured the hurt look on her husband's face when she'd announced that she was taking Zach to the ranch. "I thought we could all go to church together then have breakfast at the Golden Corral," he'd said.

"Jenny and I have to figure out what's going on with Ida Jane. We think her medication is causing problems," she'd explained. Not a lie, but they could have handled it on the phone. "And Zach hasn't spent any time with the twins since the wedding. I want him to get to know his cousins."

"Donnie was going to work on a couple of speeches," Kris said, whispering. "And he has to hook up the new printer."

They'd converted his mother's room into an office where Donnie and Jonathan could run the campaign without people constantly traipsing through the house. Originally Donnie had planned to rent space at the bordello, but this location made more sense. Unfortunately, it also meant that Kris didn't see Donnie as often as she would have if they were in the same building.

And according to Jenny, she'd be seeing even less of him after today. Kristin started toward the door. "I think I'll go now. Thanks for the pep talk."

Jenny looked startled. "Wait. I'll walk you down. I have to get Tucker for his nap, too."

Kris paused, but she was impatient to go. To see Donnie. And Lucas. If they were going to be family, they needed to start acting like one.

ZACH EYED his stepbrother cautiously. Lately, he couldn't be sure how Lucas would react to the least bit of criticism. Lucas's volatile temper and short fuse had been the reason their so-called band broke up. Zach hadn't found out till after he and his mother got back from the Rocking M that today's practice had been cancelled.

"Since it's just the two of us, how about we try that song your dad gave us?"

Lucas was sitting on Mike's amp, fixing one of the strings on his guitar. Zach had been tempted to tell him that if he didn't play like a madman the strings would last longer, but he kept his opinion to himself.

"What for? We suck. Even your mother can hardly stand to listen to us."

That flat, resigned tone worried Zach. And pissed him off.

"Did you ever think the reason we suck so bad is that we never practice?"

Lucas ignored Zach. He set his guitar against the wall and stepped away. When the guitar tipped to one side and started to fall over, Zach lunged for it and managed to keep it from hitting the floor. Lucas didn't even look backward.

"A-hole, this is a nice bass. Are you trying to bust it?"

Suddenly Lucas spun around and grabbed the Fender out of Zach's hands. Holding the guitar by its long, skinny neck, he swung it over his head as if he intended to smash it over the amp. Zach jumped up and wrestled it out of his hands.

Lucas went ballistic, screaming profanities and hitting Zach in the belly so hard Zach saw flashing dots of silver and black. He stumbled backward; as he went down, his elbow punched through the brown fabric of the speaker.

"Shit, man," he swore, but just as suddenly as it erupted, the fight went out of Lucas. He stood there with a glassy look in his eyes then turned and fled.

Zach let out a shaky breath. His gut hurt, and he could feel a knot growing on his elbow. What was he supposed to do now? Let Lucas go on messing with whatever drugs he was taking or tell somebody? Tell who? His mom?

Zach tried to picture the look on his mother's face if he took this to her. Between her work schedule and worrying about Ida Jane, Kristin was frazzled. Besides, what could she do?

He'd be better off telling Donnie, but he was also busy with other things. And although Tyler was due back in town tomorrow, Zach decided it would be disloyal to discuss Lucas with him.

Zach was no snitch. But he didn't want to see Lucas screw up his life—and everyone else's too.

THE NEXT MORNING Kristin locked the door to her shop then dashed up the bordello steps. She'd rescheduled all her appointments so she could attend the chamber of commerce meeting. But first she needed to check on Ida Jane.

Despite the preventative medication she'd been taking, their dear aunt wasn't doing well. The doctors believed she'd suffered a second stroke.

The most recent episode had left her unable to do much for herself. Since Andi was in the third trimester of her pregnancy, and Kris was swamped at work, the sisters had hired a nurse to attend to Ida's needs, monitor her blood pressure and give her the medications. Still, each triplet tried to spend some time with Ida each day.

"Hi, Auntie," she called cheerfully, entering Ida Jane's large, airy room.

Ida was sitting in a wheelchair, which faced the window. The curtains were open, and Kris noticed a small army of finches vying for space at a bird feeder someone had suspended from a shepherd's hook outside the window. "What a great feeder! Where'd that come from? Andi?"

Ida shook her head.

"Jenny?"

Kris dropped a kiss to the top of the silver head. "Must have been one of the men, then. How sweet! They're both such great guys."

Ida's watery eyes narrowed. "Don," she said with surprising clarity.

Kris's hands tingled. "Donnie put it up for you?"

Ida nodded.

"Really? He didn't mention it."

Ida nodded again. This time tears made crooked paths down her cheeks.

Kris comforted Ida with a hug then wiped her face and helped her blow her nose. ''I'm going to put a chicken into the Crock-Pot before I go to a meeting. Wanna help?''

She wasn't sure if Ida's nod was a confirmation or not, but Kris gripped the handles of the wheelchair and maneuvered the awkward thing through the hall to the kitchen.

''Hey, there you are,'' a voice called, startling Ida Jane. ''I checked your office, but the door was locked. I assume that means you're going to the meeting. Do you want to ride with me?''

Andi was dressed for business in her maternity jumper and matching jacket made of dark blue wool. Her orange blouse added a jaunty touch.

''Sure. Thanks,'' Kristin said. ''I'll be ready in a minute.''

''Whatcha making?''

''Chicken and dumplings.''

''Mmm, one of my favorites.'' She rubbed her protruding belly.

Ida Jane smiled and reached out to pat her tummy. Andi covered Ida's hand, smiling serenely.

The scene moved Kristin. She was afraid to predict how many more moments like this they'd share with their great-aunt.

''So are you ready to challenge Tyler to a duel?'' Andi said.

''Will it come to that?'' Kris asked. She leaned

down to set the temperature, then placed the lid on the pot. She double-checked the clock to make sure she'd allowed adequate cooking time.

"Only if he tries to bulldoze the old bordello."

Ida sat up sharply. "No. You can't let him." Her voice raised in pitch, her hand gripped Andi's. "Suzy, don't let 'em do it."

Kristin hurried across the room and knelt beside the wheelchair. She put her arm around her aunt's shoulders and whispered soothingly, "It's okay, Ida Jane. Nobody is going to do anything bad to the old bordello. It's our home. We love the place. We'll protect it."

Ida let out a long sigh and seemed to collapse like a deflated balloon. Kris checked her pulse, then nodded to Andi. A few moments later, a woman dressed in white shoes, white pants and a brightly patterned uniform top entered the room. "I thought someone had stolen my patient," she said. "Good morning, Miss Ida, time for your bath."

Andi and Kris said their good-byes, then hurried outside to Andi's black Mercedes. "Well, that was scary."

Kristin started to say that it was only going to get worse, but she changed her mind. They needed to focus on the battle at hand. Ida Jane had given them a mission, and Kris planned to carry it out.

THE GOLD CREEK Chamber of Commerce building was a converted gas station. The antique gas pumps out front served as interactive displays to give tourists directions to the county's attractions. At the moment, some two hundred citizens were jammed into what had at one time served as a double-bay garage, and all eyes were on Tyler Harrison. Except Donnie's. He was trying to find his wife. He knew she was here; he'd seen her enter with Andi, who was seated at the raised dais along with the other board members, but Kris had melted into the crowd before he could reach her.

"Please look over the material my staff is distributing," Tyler said, his voice carried by a microphone attached to the lapel of his expensive-looking suit jacket. "I assure you that Meridian has no intention of running roughshod over the town of Gold Creek. You will see that what we're proposing is a safeguard from the kind of unrestricted growth we've seen up and down the Sierras."

Donnie declined a copy. He'd spent half the night studying the brochure. He and Sam had discussed it over breakfast. He probably knew what it said as well as Tyler did, but that didn't make it any more palatable.

Tyler gave the crowd time to review the pamphlet, then he nodded to his assistant who dimmed the lights. Someone pushed a giant, projector-type television into place. Seconds later, an image filled the screen. An aerial view showed a mountain range dissected by tiny streams all feeding into one twisting, turning river. Gold Creek.

"The computer tells us this is what the Gold Creek area looked like B.G.—before gold."

Chuckles rumbled through the crowd; people were obviously charmed by Tyler's relaxed, professional demeanor. When the next image flashed on the screen, Ty pointed out the changes people had made to the landscape. The most obvious was the road. A narrow squiggle line with two or three dozen buildings.

Slides showing the evolution of Gold Creek followed. Village, hamlet, town, bigger town. Sprawl became more noticeable. Tyler pointed out new additions, like the golf course and the airport. When he indicated the housing tract where Donnie's house was located, Tyler looked straight at him.

"Finally," Ty said, "we have Gold Creek, 2002. A nice place to live. No one is disputing that, but it's also a town poised for development. You may think I'm the big bad wolf, but believe me, I'm not the only one knocking on Gold Creek's door. People want to escape from the cities in the valley by moving to the mountains. But when they get here, they'll want jobs, movie theaters, shopping malls, a car wash, fast food restaurants."

"Then let them stay where they are," a voice called.

Tyler smiled. "You can try telling them that, Beulah, but change will still come. As it always has. My plan is designed to protect Gold Creek, not destroy it."

The screen changed. Donnie felt the buzz of energy grow. People pointed. "Look at the road," someone whispered. "That can't be good."

Tyler walked to the screen and pointed out the most obvious difference—a four-lane half circle that surrounded Gold Creek. "This is a proposed bypass. It's been on the books for years, but it lacked the necessary support at all levels—local, state and federal. Now I believe it's the only thing that will save Gold Creek from urban sprawl."

The audience hum went up a notch as people discussed the pros and cons. Tyler gave them a few minutes then cleared his throat. "Not only is safety a key issue, but by shifting the growth centers away from the downtown area, we can protect the historic integrity of—"

A voice broke in. "How is destroying the old bordello—a hundred-year-old building—protecting our history?"

Donnie recognized his wife's voice. She was only a few feet away from Tyler. She positively bristled with anger.

Donnie started toward her, but the crowd was too engrossed by the unfolding drama to let him through.

"Look at the terrain, Kristin. There's nowhere else for the bypass to go."

She rose up on her toes. "I'll tell you where it can go." She shook her finger at him and said, "It can go to hell. That building is a part of Gold Creek history. Maybe not the part some people want to remember, but it's Ida Jane Montgomery's legacy—your son's legacy. And my sisters and I will not let it be torn down."

The murmurs escalated. Donnie could feel the sympathy shift. Apparently so could Tyler, because he walked to the podium that had been set up and tapped on the microphone. The clacking sound reverberated. "Okay. I think we can tell that Kristin Sullivan—excuse me, Grimaldo—is not in favor of the plan." His sardonic tone produced a few chuckles. "The microphone is open for public comment, but first let me offer it to Gold Creek's elected officials."

He motioned for Magnus Brown to come forward. Donnie had to admit the older man carried himself well. He looked like a white-haired Daniel Boone. He kept his speech short and to the point. "Anything that saves lives is all right by me. People are coming. Let's put 'em where we want 'em, not where some goldang developer wants to put 'em."

Donnie and Jonathan exchanged a look. They had proof that Magnus had been taking kickbacks from developers for years.

"Now you know where I stand. Let's hear what my opposition has to say about this plan."

Donnie muttered a silent curse. He'd hoped to talk to his wife before he got called to the podium, but fate had conspired against him. This time the crowd gave him room to move.

He took a deep breath. "I studied this plan carefully last night. I was prepared to hate it. But in all honesty, I think it's the right thing to do."

He heard gasps of disbelief. He knew his wife's was one of them. He regretted more than ever not waking her up last night to discuss this. Or canceling his meeting with Sam's bankers. He only hoped she'd listen to the rest of what he had to say.

"However," he said, raising his voice, "it isn't perfect. As my wife pointed out, it doesn't take into account the value of the past. Rewriting history is a dangerous thing. The bordello—once torn down—cannot be replaced. If we lose it, we lose a part of who we are."

He heard some discreet clapping; he couldn't miss Andi's two thumbs-up.

"I will endorse this plan if provisions are made to *move* the old bordello, not bulldoze it. If Ida Jane and her nieces agree, I think the building would be a terrific addition to the historical center."

He stepped back. As he passed Tyler, the look they exchanged said they understood each other. Donnie predicted negotiations between the historical society, the triplets and Meridian would start immediately. With a few compromises on all sides, Donnie hoped they'd be able to put off doing anything for as long as Ida Jane lived.

Donnie exited as quickly as he could break through the throng. People stopped him every few feet to offer their support and promise him their votes. When he finally reached the parking lot, Kris was gone. He might have gained badly needed votes, but had he lost the one that counted most?

THE STEWING CHICKEN in the Crock-Pot filled the bordello's kitchen with a spicy aroma that made Kris's mouth water as she entered the room.

"Smells good, doesn't it?" she asked Ida Jane.

The small, bookcase-style CD player Andi had installed played a pretty song—nothing Kris recognized, but she immediately liked the singer's voice. She listened as she opened the refrigerator to get out the eggs and milk. She quickly finished mixing the dumplings, then added large gooey globs to the bubbling stew. As soon as her hands were clean, she poured two cups of tea and sat down beside her aunt.

She wondered how to explain to her aunt what had happened today. Would Ida understand the magnitude of Tyler's plan. Or the depth of Donnie's betrayal?

"Ida, I should tell you about the meeting."

Her aunt sipped her tea then said, "Donnie did."

Kris sat up a little straighter. "Did what?"

"Told me."

"He did?" Donnie had come to the bordello and hadn't stopped to see her? True, she'd had back-to-back appointments, but still... "What did he say?"

"I forget. But it was nice."

Tears gathered in Kris's eyes. Before she could say anything else, the kitchen door opened and two young people walked in. Zach and Beth Murdock. Kris hastily wiped her face with the floury apron she'd pulled on. "Hi, guys, dinner won't be ready for an hour, but Beth, you're welcome to stay. I made plenty."

The look that passed between Bethany and Zach made Kris's heart skip a beat. "What's wrong?"

Zach seemed to find the courage he needed from Beth's nod. After a slight pause, he said, "Mom, I need to talk to you. About Lucas."

A skitter of apprehension raced down her spine. "Where is he? Is he okay?"

Zach frowned. "He's been avoiding me ever since he socked me in the gut yesterday. He was swinging his guitar like a crazy person and when I tried to stop him, he punched me."

Kris groaned. "Oh, honey, I'm sorry. Why didn't you tell—"

"Zach's not a tattletale, Mrs. Grimaldo," Beth said. "He didn't plan to tell me about this, but we were talking and he thinks Lucas is into some kind of drugs."

Kris's stomach plunged, and her extremities turned to ice. "No. Please, no. He's only ten." She looked at Ida who had nodded off, then herded the kids to the table a few feet away and sat down across from them. "Talk to me Zach. Why do you think this? What kind of drugs? Marijuana?"

Zach shook his head. "That, too, but from the way he's been acting lately, I'd say more like speed or crank."

"Crank is cheapest," Beth said frankly. "And the most dangerous."

Kris had been meaning to take a parents-of-teens drug awareness course, but she hadn't had time. Now she took a deep breath to assess her options.

Donnie needed to be told, but they had to have more to go on than Zach's assumptions. "I guess the first thing I need to do is talk to Lucas. Do you know where he is?"

Zach shook his head. "He wasn't on the bus, but one of his friends said he was in detention. You could call the school and find out."

Kris was mentally calculating the time in South Africa. Sandy would need to be told, too.

"I will. Although I don't remember signing a detention slip." She looked at her son. "Honey, do me a favor and call your father. See if he can come and get you for a few days. Jonathan said your grandmother is on a cruise, so maybe you two could stay at her house."

"Why?" he exclaimed. "I didn't do anything."

She walked to him and put her arms around him. "I know. You're not being punished, but there's bound to be some fallout, and I just don't want Lucas taking his anger out on you." She squeezed him tightly. "Besides, didn't you tell me Gloria just got a new spa? A couple of days in a fancy house with a Jacuzzi sounds like a vacation."

A reluctant smile teased the corners of his lips. "Oh, all right," he said, motioning Beth to follow. "Can I use the phone in Andi's office to call him?"

Kris nodded. "She and Jonathan are at a doctor's appointment and won't be back until later."

Once the kids were gone, Kris started to set the table. She talked to Ida—who was still snoozing—as she walked back and forth to the counter. "I've been worried about Lucas's moodiness lately, but I told myself no one could blame him for being a little upset. His life has been turned upside down.''

Almost as if on cue, the back door opened and Lucas walked in. His coat was black—naturally—and seemed to shroud him. The boy was just a face under a black ball cap—worn backward. The tips of his ears, visible between lanky strands of hair, were bright red from the cold. Kris wanted to scoop him up and hug him tight, but she'd learned that boys of this age did not appreciate such spontaneous displays of affection.

"Lucas. Thank goodness. Zach said you weren't on the bus. I was afraid something might have happened to you.''

"I was on the bus. I sat in the back.'' His eyes shifted to the right when he spoke. "What's for dinner?'' he asked, turning away from her.

"Chicken and dumplings, but I'd like to talk first.''

He must have sensed her tension because he gave her a long, probing look. "Why?''

Kristin took a deep breath. "Lucas, are you using drugs?''

His face turned the same pasty color as her dumplings, and she saw a look of fear, which was immediately followed by anger. He threw his backpack to the floor. The crash was so loud even Ida Jane startled in her chair.

Kristin put a comforting hand on her aunt's

shoulder. For some reason, Ida's presence bolstered Kristin's resolve. "Lucas—"

He cut her off. "Who told you? Zach, right? So I smoke a little pot once in a while. Big deal." He glanced from side to side like a trapped animal. "Why is everybody picking on me? You're not my mother."

Kris kept her tone level. "No, honey, but I do care about you."

"No, you don't. No one does. I'm leaving."

Kris raced to beat him to the door. "No."

He looked angry enough to go right through her, but a voice from the hallway made him freeze. A man's voice. Jonathan popped his head in. "Hey, what smells so good? I'll trade you a squiggly photo of our baby girl for whatever it is."

Kris looked at him pleadingly, and his grin faded. "What's the problem?"

"Lucas and I need your help," she said. "We need you to find Donnie right away."

CHAPTER FOURTEEN

"LUCAS. KRISTIN. What's going on?"

"Thank God, you're here, Donnie," Kristin said, her voice breaking.

Donnie felt a powerful surge of emotion. He'd spent the afternoon trying to catch up with Kristin, but they'd somehow missed each other at every turn. Donnie suspected she was avoiding him. He wasn't surprised. He expected her to be mad; he hadn't expected his brother-in-law to meet him at the door and drag him into the bordello's kitchen where his wife and son stood braced in some kind of face-off.

He stepped closer, looking for a way to defuse the tension that radiated off his son like heat. "Well, I'm here, now. Let's all take a step back and a deep breath and talk about what's going on."

Kristin's gaze hadn't left Lucas, who looked as though he were prepared to run through her to get outside. Donnie placed a hand on his son's shoulder. "Lucas, can you tell me why you're upset?"

He shrugged off Donnie's hand. "She thinks I'm a drug addict."

Drugs. He knew at that instant he'd missed

something. There had been signs. He hadn't been paying attention. He'd been too busy.

"Lucas, I just want to help." Kristin spoke calmly.

"Then leave me alone. All of you leave me alone."

The cry echoed in the kitchen. Donnie glanced around. Ida Jane was in her wheelchair by the table, watching them. Jonathan and Andi had slipped in quietly and were standing nearby. *Back up.*

"I can't do that, son. None of us can. We all care about you, and we're not going to let something bad happen to someone we love."

"That's right," Jonathan said, moving into Lucas's line of sight. "You're going to be a new cousin in a couple of months. Andi and I are counting on you to help out with baby-sitting and changing diapers and stuff."

Donnie watched his son's face. It changed from mad and hurt to confused and incredulous.

Andi marched across the room to stand at Kris's side. She put an arm around her sister's shoulders and said, "I hate to break it to you, Lucas, but this is what we call family. You're in it up to your eyeballs. Your business is our business. And we take care of our own. Right, Donnie?"

He caught the oblique reference to that morning's issue of the bypass and the old bordello. He figured this was her way of showing her support. He gave her a nod of thanks, then lightly touched his son's shoulder. "We have a lot to talk about. I think Lucas and I need some time alone."

Andi guided her sister away from the door. "The back porch is free," she said. "Or the office."

Kristin shook her head firmly and whispered something in her sister's ear. "The back porch it is."

Donnie nudged Lucas in that general direction. Some of the fight seemed to have left the boy, but Donnie sensed he was still ready to bolt. As much as he wanted to hug his wife, there wasn't time. Lucas needed him.

Once the door closed behind them, Donnie directed his son to the top step where they both sat.

"Can you tell me about it?"

"I'm not a drug addict."

"I know that. But if you've tried drugs, which you know are dangerous and illegal, then we have a problem."

"It was just some pot."

Donnie's stomach clenched. *But you're only ten years old,* he wanted to cry. That was the father in him. As a deputy, he knew that age wasn't much of a factor any more. "I'm sorry to hear that. It means I screwed up."

Lucas turned his head to look at him. "What?"

"I owe you an apology, Lucas," he said, putting his elbows on his knees. "I've been so wrapped up in my own problems—first, my career, then the campaign—I failed to pay attention to what was going on with you."

Lucas's frown turned to a sneer. "Yeah, right. Are you going to arrest me?"

Donnie shook his head. "I'm not a cop anymore, remember? But even if I was, I'd try to handle this through the family, not the courts. You made a mistake, but you're not the only one. So did I."

"Me, too," a voice said from behind them.

Kristin slipped past him and trotted down the steps so she was facing them both. "I don't want to intrude, but I need to tell you something, Lucas. You're a great kid. Talented. Smart. Funny. Kind. You could have made my life hell these past few weeks, but you didn't." Her smile was tremulous, her bottom lip quivered.

"You kept all the things that were bothering you bottled up. I should have known you were hurting."

Lucas didn't say anything, but Donnie could see he was close to tears. "We all made mistakes. We're human. But we're going to get through this. Together. Right?"

She nodded. Just then, a car pulled into the parking lot. Kristin spun about. "Tyler," she said. "I asked Zach to call him."

She turned to face them. "Zach told me what you were doing, Lucas. Not because he wanted to—he's not a tattletale—but because he was worried about you. I wasn't sure if you could forgive him, so I asked his dad to come pick him up."

Donnie saw Tyler step out of the car and start toward the main door of the bordello. Two figures emerged from the shadows of the porch. Donnie thought he recognized Bethany's curly hair in the glow of the carriage lights that bracketed the entrance.

Kristin touched Lucas's cheek. "I'll go tell him good-bye."

Donnie put his arm around Lucas and pulled him close. "We have a lot to talk about, son. Tomorrow I'll call that counselor you used to see. We'll go as a family, all four of us."

Lucas sat stiffly for a minute then all the bluster left him. He started to cry. Donnie held him and comforted him. His own eyes were wet with tears, but he wasn't sad. This was a good thing. A start.

And he had Kristin—and Zach—to thank for it.

In the distance, he could see his wife standing in a small cluster a few feet away from Tyler's car. "Do you want to go home?" he asked his son. "Or go inside?"

When Lucas hesitated, Donnie added, "They're our family now, Lucas. What happens to one person affects everyone. And they really do care about you."

Lucas wiped his face with the sleeve of his jacket. "I was kind of a jerk yesterday. To Zach."

"Maybe we should ask him to stay. We could all talk. And eat."

At his son's nod, Donnie rose. He waited for Lucas to join him, and then they walked across the mostly empty parking lot. The night had grown cold. He could see Kristin, who wasn't wearing a coat, shiver. He hurried toward her.

"Hi, everyone. How come you're all standing around outside? I thought I smelled my wife's chicken and dumplings." He took off his jacket and draped it around Kris's shoulders. "Please tell me my nose didn't lie."

She gave him a quick smile before her gaze dropped to Lucas. "I made plenty for everyone, but if you'd rather go home…"

Lucas coughed then said, "I wanna stay and eat. How 'bout you, Zach?"

Donnie saw her eyes fill with tears, and he pulled her to him. Zach looked from Lucas to Donnie to Tyler. "Umm…yeah, I guess."

Tyler nodded. "No problem. I'll catch you later, son."

Donnie took a breath. "Would you care to join us, Ty?"

Tyler looked at him a moment, then smiled. "Only if you promise not to talk business. Your little publicity stunt this morning probably cost me a bundle."

Donnie kept his answer equally light in tone. "*My* publicity stunt? You called the meeting. I just suggested we save the old bordello and move it to the historical center. It was Andi who suggested making it a museum dedicated to women of the Gold Rush."

Tyler shrugged. "Like I said, moving this old monster and converting it to a museum ain't gonna come cheap. But Zach was just telling me how much he likes the old place, so if it makes my kid happy, then it's worth it.''

Donnie realized one person had been left out of the conversation. Bethany. "Can you join us for dinner, Beth?"

She shook her head. "My dad's picking me up on his way home. He should be here any minute."

Almost before she finished speaking a pair of headlights turned into the parking lot. She gave Zach a nod then spoke to Lucas. "Don't worry about me saying anything, Lucas. I won't—as long as you stay clean. We're going to have a new sheriff in town soon, and he's a pretty good guy—but mega-tough on drugs."

She waved then dashed to the waiting car.

Donnie hugged his wife then let out a deep sigh. "Well, I don't know about the rest of you, but this has been a long day, and I'm starved."

IT WAS NEARLY ELEVEN by the time they got home from the bordello. Both boys went straight to their rooms.

They hadn't planned on staying that long at Ida Jane's, but once Jonathan, Tyler and Donnie started talking—with Andi and Kris chiming in from time to time—time flew. Kris couldn't express how good it had made her feel to watch Lucas and Zach doing their homework at the kitchen table after dinner—just as she and her sisters had done when they were that age.

Donnie turned off the hall light and yawned. "Oh, man, what a day!"

She waited until he'd closed the door of their bedroom before turning to face him. "I owe you an apology, don't I?"

He pulled her into his arms. "You didn't really think I'd sell you out just to win a few votes, did you?"

His tone was stern, but his arms were gentle— comforting and safe.

"I love this town too much to see anything bad happen to it. I admit I was ready to jump ship for a while, but that was before you came back. Before I figured out that I wasn't running away because I hated Gold Creek, I was leaving because I'd lost something I needed to find. You."

"Oh..." She sighed, wrapping her arms around his neck. "I'm so glad I came back. I only wish I could have worked up the courage sooner. I'm such a coward."

He moved back slightly. "Coward? You're the bravest woman I know. You took on Tyler this morning, then faced off with my son tonight. You deserve a medal."

"All I want is you. I love you, Donnie Grimaldo."

She kissed him, letting her lips and tongue reveal the depth of her feelings.

"Is it official now? We survived our first kiss-and-make-up fight?"

She nodded. "It was my fault. I'm a little sensitive—"

He shook his head. "No. I panicked, Kris. I looked at the difficulties, not the benefits. A baby— our baby—would be a precious gift any time. I'm sorry I let you think otherwise."

She hugged him fiercely. "I know how important family is to you. I knew it the minute I saw the bird feeder at Ida Jane's. As busy as you've been lately, you took the time to do something thoughtful for an old woman. That really touched my heart, Donnie."

He looked embarrassed. "I have to confess. It was a bribe."

"A bribe?"

He nodded, a look of mischief on his face. "I went there hoping to beg your forgiveness for being a dufus, but you had that Massage-In-Progress sign on the door, so I went upstairs to visit Ida Jane. She was sitting there looking out the window and I remembered how much she liked birds, so I ran to the store. I figured she might put in a good word for me."

Kris blinked back her tears. "She did."

He bent slightly and picked her up, carrying her to the bed. "You're calling in sick tomorrow," he told her sternly.

"I can't. I have six massages—"

He leaned over, bracing one hand beside her head. "Lillian will have to reschedule. You and I are playing hooky."

"We are?"

He nodded. "We'll go hiking or something. And we're taking the boys with us—so wipe that gleam out of your eye. We need a family day."

She sighed. "Your heart is in the right place, but it isn't going to happen. Didn't I hear Jonathan say something about a meeting you have scheduled with city planners and the highway people?"

He groaned and dove across her to plop down with a sigh. "Maybe it's not too late to cancel."

She turned on her side and raised up on one elbow to look at him. "It's too late. Besides, we can't put off doing something about Lucas's problem. I feel terrible that I didn't pick up on it before this."

He rolled his eyes. "You? What about me? I'm a trained professional."

She drew her finger across his furrowed brow. "As you—and my sister—pointed out, we're human. We make mistakes. When I told Jenny about it tonight on the phone, she said, 'We're parents, not psychics.' She's still beating herself up about missing Lara's ear infection. She thought it was just a cold until Lara spiked a fever and the doctor told Jen this had been developing for at least a week."

Donnie smiled. "Your sisters are great."

"I know. I'm really lucky."

"Speaking of getting lucky…" he added with a playful wink that made her laugh.

"Uh-huh," she teased. "What about it?"

He wrapped his arms around her and rolled them both to the center of the bed. "I'm the luckiest man on the planet, and I'd be happy to demonstrate why if you're interested.''

Kris knew why—because they loved each other, but she wasn't about to pass up the kind of proof he had in mind.

"Prove it.''

IT SNOWED THANKSGIVING morning. A fact that made the history books in Gold Creek and was on the lips of every visitor to the Old Bordello Antique Shop and Coffee Parlor.

Normally, the doors would have been closed on a holiday, but today was special.

This would probably be Ida Jane Montgomery's last Thanksgiving, and she had a town full of old friends who wanted to say goodbye.

Kristin had spent the night at her great-aunt's side on a small cot Donnie had set up for her. Ida's breathing had turned labored just before dawn, and Kristin had called her sisters.

Jenny arrived at seven. Andi only beat her downstairs by a few minutes. With just a few weeks to go before Daisy Jane Newhall was due to arrive, Andi moved with an awkward grace that made her sisters laugh.

Jenny and Kristin had tried to talk Andi out of naming her baby after a dog, but Andi resolutely maintained that Ida herself had suggested it. "Our dog was named after Ida's great-aunt, Daisy. There's something poetic about it, don't you think? Besides, I loved that dog.''

Apparently word went out in a hurry, because not long after Jenny arrived, four Garden Club ladies appeared—laden with food. Andi had unlocked the coffee parlor doors, just in time to greet her helper, Linda McCloskey, who'd started brewing the shop's newest coffee blend, pumpkin-spice.

Donnie brought Lucas and Zach with him. Lucas was doing much better in school and had decided to try out for wrestling. He was a completely different boy from the angry, sullen, unhappy kid he'd been. Although Kristin hadn't been able to spend a great deal of time at home during the past couple of weeks, Donnie reported that the two boys seemed to be getting along pretty well. They were even talking about playing music together again.

Donnie's victory three weeks earlier had been nip and tuck. He credited Jonathan's investigative reporting, which led to a Grand Jury indictment against Magnus for alleged bribery charges, as the deciding factor, but Kristin believed the citizens of Gold Creek chose Donnie for the same reason she did—because they knew a hero when they saw one.

Donnie wouldn't take office until January so he was using the time to help finalize plans for the Old Bordello Historic Center. This past week had been filled with highs and lows for Kristin. She knew Ida Jane's time was near. And although she was heartsore at their impending loss, she knew her great-aunt would have been proud of the way every member of her family had pitched in to help.

Ida was never alone—even if the person at her side was a ten-year-old boy doing his homework.

"How's she doing?"

Kristin straightened as her sisters entered the room. She'd been gently washing Ida's face with a warm cloth. "Pretty good. I think she's rallying a little. Probably from all the activity around here."

Jenny handed Kristin a cup of coffee. The smell brought back memories of a Thanksgiving in the not too distant past—when Ida Jane wore purple, and Josh had been alive. So many changes. Some wonderful. Some sad.

She blinked back her tears and took a sip of the fragrant brew.

Jenny moved to the far side of the bed. Andi sat down near Ida and took her hand.

"We're right here with you, Auntie," Andi said, leaning down to kiss Ida's cheek.

To Kristin's surprise, Ida's eyes opened.

Kris stepped closer. She saw a crystal lucidity in the china-blue eyes that had been lacking for days.

"My girls," she whispered. In her eyes was a look of such love and Serenity that Kristin knew her great-aunt's time was near. "You were a gift I didn't deserve.

"I was a poor excuse for a sister. I didn't get Suzy the help she needed in time to save her, but I loved her daughter as if she were my own."

Her breathing was shallow, and the words came with each exhale. "My sweet Lorena. She left us too soon. But what a treasure she gave me. Three perfect babies.''

Jenny's sob filled the space when Ida took another breath.

Andi lifted Ida's hand to her lips. ''Oh, Ida, you were the best mother any girl could hope for. We love you. You know that, don't you?''

Ida's focus was elsewhere, but her beatific smile seemed content and filled with peace. ''She called me Mama. Before she went to heaven…to be with Suzy. 'Take care of my babies, Mama,' she said. 'Just like you took care of me.'''

The end came an hour or so later. Ida's girls were at her side. Their husbands and children were nearby.

From the front parlor, Kristin could hear Gold Creek's citizens as they shared their memories of the ''grand old gal.''

Donnie joined Kris. She leaned into the comforting warmth of his arms and closed her eyes.

''I can't believe she's gone,'' Donnie said. ''It won't be the same without her.''

''We know what we want written on her headstone,'' Kristin said. ''Ida Jane Montgomery—a remarkable woman, a true pioneer spirit, beloved by all—especially her granddaughters, Jenny, Andi and Kristin.''

Donnie kissed her temple. ''She would be touched.''

They had so much to talk about. His job, her business, their sons, the future. But at the moment, they were content to celebrate the past. "I couldn't have made it through this without you," she told her husband.

"Not true. You're Ida Jane Montgomery's grand-daughter. You can do anything. But I'm awful glad you think you need me. And I'm even more glad you came back to me."

She looked out the window. At the bird feeder. At their sons playing tag in the snow with a wet puppy and a patient hound. It had taken her too long and too many miles to find what had always been in her heart—home.

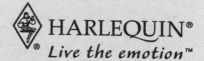

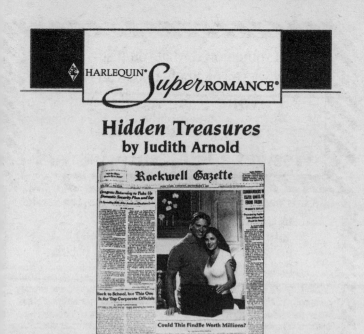
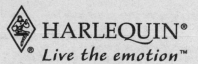

If you enjoyed what you just read,
then we've got an offer you can't resist!

Take 2 bestselling love stories FREE!

Plus get a FREE surprise gift!

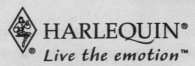